W9-ANM-172

You're About to Become a

Privileged Woman.

INTRODUCING
PAGES & PRIVILEGES™.

It's our way of thanking you for buying
our books at your favorite retail store.

—— *GET ALL THIS FREE* ——
WITH JUST ONE PROOF OF PURCHASE:

$50 VALUE

◆ **Hotel Discounts** up
to 60% at home and
abroad ◆ **Travel Service**
- Guaranteed lowest
published airfares
plus 5% cash back
on tickets ◆ **$25 Travel Voucher**

◆ **Sensuous Petite Parfumerie** collection

◆ **Insider Tips Letter**
with sneak previews
of upcoming books

*You'll get a FREE personal card, too.
It's your passport to all these benefits— and to
even more great gifts & benefits to come!*
There's no club to join. No purchase commitment. No obligation.

Enrollment Form

☐ *Yes!* I WANT TO BE A *Privileged Woman.*

Enclosed is one *PAGES & PRIVILEGES™* Proof of Purchase
from any Harlequin or Silhouette book currently for
sale in stores (Proofs of Purchase are found on
the back pages of books) and the store cash
register receipt. Please enroll me in *PAGES
& PRIVILEGES™*. Send my Welcome
Kit and FREE Gifts -- and activate my
FREE benefits -- immediately.

*More great gifts and benefits to come like these
luxurious Truly Lace and L'Effleur gift baskets.*

▼ DETACH HERF AND MAIL TODAY! ▼

NAME (please print)

ADDRESS   APT. NO

CITY   STATE   ZIP/POSTAL CODE

| PROOF OF PURCHASE |
| SAMPLE ONLY |
| Pages & Privileges™ |

Please allow 6-8 weeks for delivery. Quantities are
limited. We reserve the right to substitute items.
Enroll before October 31, 1995 and receive
one full year of benefits.

NO CLUB!
NO COMMITMENT!
*Just one purchase brings
you great **Free Gifts**
and **Benefits**!*
(More details in back of this book.)

Name of store where this book was purchased_____

Date of purchase_____

Type of store:

    ☐ Bookstore   ☐ Supermarket   ☐ Drugstore

    ☐ Dept. or discount store (e.g. K-Mart or Walmart)

    ☐ Other (specify)_____

Which Harlequin or Silhouette series do you usually read?

_____

Complete and mail with one Proof of Purchase and store receipt to:

U.S.: *PAGES & PRIVILEGES™*, P.O. Box 1960, Danbury, CT 06813-1960

Canada: *PAGES & PRIVILEGES™*, 49-6A The Donway West, P.O. 813,
North York, ON M3C 2E8   **PRINTED IN U.S.A**

She'd been playing with fire when she allowed David Crandall to kiss her.

Not merely permitted, Melanie reflected wryly. Responded enthusiastically was more like it.

Her body still glowed where he'd touched her, and her pulse raced when she recalled his stirring kisses. Without a doubt, David's expertise could have brought her more ecstasy than she'd ever known.

Too bad that was all the seventh Viscount of Castlebury had to offer her: a few nights of bliss and eventually, perhaps, a postcard.

Ah, well. There was no point in dwelling on what almost was…but could never be.

Melanie's mouth curved slightly. It *would* make quite a diary entry, though.

What I did on my summer vacation….

Dear Reader,

Special Edition's lineup for August will definitely make this a memorable summer of romance! Our THAT SPECIAL WOMAN! title for this month is *The Bride Price* by reader favorite Ginna Gray. Wyatt Sommersby has his work cut out for him when he tries to convince the freedom-loving Maggie Muldoon to accept his proposal of marriage.

Concluding the new trilogy MAN, WOMAN AND CHILD this month is *Nobody's Child* by Pat Warren. Don't miss the final installment of this innovative series. Also in August, we have three veteran authors bringing you three wonderful new stories. In *Scarlet Woman* by Barbara Faith, reunited lovers face their past and once again surrender to their passion. *What She Did on Her Summer Vacation* is Tracy Sinclair's story of a young woman on holiday who finds herself an instant nanny to two adorable kids—and the object of a young aristocrat's affections. Ruth Wind's *The Last Chance Ranch* is the emotional story of one woman's second chance at life when she reclaims her child. Finally, August introduces *New York Times* bestseller Ellen Tanner Marsh to Silhouette Special Edition. She brings her popular and unique style to her first story for us, *A Family of Her Own.* This passionate and heartwarming tale is one you won't want to miss.

This summer of love and romance isn't over yet! I hope you enjoy each and every story to come!

Sincerely,

Tara Gavin, Senior Editor

Please address questions and book requests to:
Silhouette Reader Service
U.S.: 3010 Walden Ave., P.O. Box 1325, Buffalo, NY 14269
Canadian: P.O. Box 609, Fort Erie, Ont. L2A 5X3

TRACY SINCLAIR
WHAT SHE DID ON HER SUMMER VACATION

SPECIAL EDITION®

Published by Silhouette Books
America's Publisher of Contemporary Romance

If you purchased this book without a cover you should be aware
that this book is stolen property. It was reported as "unsold and
destroyed" to the publisher, and neither the author nor the
publisher has received any payment for this "stripped book."

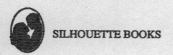

SILHOUETTE BOOKS

ISBN 0-373-09976-2

WHAT SHE DID ON HER SUMMER VACATION

Copyright © 1995 by Tracy Sinclair

All rights reserved. Except for use in any review, the reproduction
or utilization of this work in whole or in part in any form by any
electronic, mechanical or other means, now known or hereafter
invented, including xerography, photocopying and recording, or in
any information storage or retrieval system, is forbidden without
the written permission of the editorial office, Silhouette Books,
300 East 42nd Street, New York, NY 10017 U.S.A.

All characters in this book have no existence outside the imagination of
the author and have no relation whatsoever to anyone bearing the same
name or names. They are not even distantly inspired by any individual
known or unknown to the author, and all incidents are pure invention.

This edition published by arrangement with Harlequin Books S.A.

® and TM are trademarks of Harlequin Books S.A., used under license.
Trademarks indicated with ® are registered in the United States Patent
and Trademark Office, the Canadian Trade Marks Office and in other
countries.

Printed in U.S.A.

Books by Tracy Sinclair

TRACY SINCLAIR

author of more than forty Silhouette novels, also contributes to various magazines and newspapers. An extensive traveler and a dedicated volunteer worker, this California resident has accumulated countless fascinating experiences, settings and acquaintances to draw on in plotting her romances.

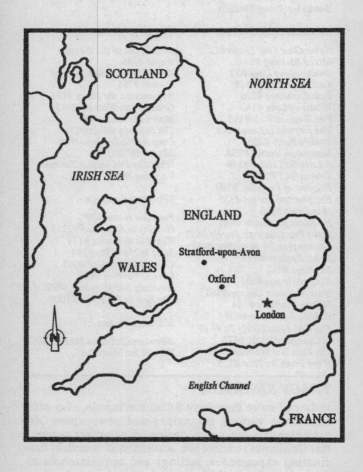

Chapter One

Melanie Warren had been looking forward to her vacation with a great deal of anticipation. She and her best friend planned to fly to London, rent a car and drive around the English countryside, stopping wherever and whenever they felt like it. That had all changed when Delia found out she was pregnant and the doctor advised her not to travel for the first three months.

"I'm really happy for them," Melanie told Sharon, one of the women she worked with. "Delia and Sam have been trying to have a baby ever since they got married. I just wish she'd become pregnant after we got back. It would have been a really great trip." Melanie's voice was wistful. "We had reservations at a castle the first night, but from then on we intended to just wander."

"Maybe you can go next year," Sharon said sympathetically. "Meanwhile, look on the bright side. You can go on a shopping spree with all the money you saved."

"Not really. The airline ticket is one of those excursion rates. It's nonrefundable."

"What a bummer! Before I'd lose that kind of money I'd go by myself."

"The idea occurred to me, but it wouldn't be much fun."

"You don't know that. It might turn out to be very interesting. You'd meet a lot of people you might never have met if you were traveling with someone. I'm sure you won't have any trouble making friends." Sharon looked at her appraisingly.

Melanie's face and alluring figure were outstanding. Light brown hair tipped with gold framed a delicate face dominated by wide green eyes fringed with long lashes. Her features might have been too candy box pretty, except for the generous mouth that gave her face character. She was definitely a woman who wouldn't lack for attention.

Melanie was doubtful about the idea at first, but Sharon was so persuasive that her enthusiasm for the trip rekindled.

The adventure Sharon predicted was rapidly turning into a nightmare as Melanie peered into the darkness, straining to see the narrow road that wound through the English countryside. It was raining so hard the windshield wipers were almost useless. She hadn't seen another car for miles, and there were no houses on either side of the road. At least none with any lights on. It was only nine o'clock, too early for everyone to be in bed, so she had to assume the area was deserted. That meant she was lost. Burford Castle's brochure said it was located near a charming English village and all sorts of other activity.

Melanie forced her tense body to relax. She was only thirty or forty miles from London, not in some uncharted wilderness. Sooner or later she'd find a place to ask for directions.

Her faith was rewarded a short time later by lights glowing faintly on the right-hand side of the road, quite a lot of lights, indicating an inn perhaps. She slowed to a crawl, looking for a driveway or some kind of access lane. The lights glimmered through a barrier of trees.

Suddenly a pair of gates appeared in the wall that had bordered the verge for some distance now. Giant trees obscured half of the weathered sign set in the wall, but Melanie could make out the word *castle* and the letters *bur*. She started to laugh out of sheer relief. Pure dumb luck had guided her here.

A long winding drive ended at a stately English manor house that was everything she'd hoped for. Ivy softened the brick walls, and the huge front doors were impressive. An antique iron knocker was set into the panels, although a doorbell in the jamb was a more recent addition. Melanie chose to use the knocker.

The door was opened almost immediately by a man wearing jeans and a sweatshirt. It was a surprising touch of informality in such an elegant establishment. But any disappointment she might have suffered was quickly compensated for. The man was gorgeous!

He was over six feet tall with an impressive physique. His pullover was stretched across a broad chest that tapered down to slim hips and muscular legs, evident in the tight jeans. He also had the bluest eyes Melanie had ever seen, fringed with thick black lashes that matched his tousled dark hair.

"I was beginning to think you weren't coming," he said. "We were expecting you earlier."

"I'm lucky to have gotten here at all," she answered. "I've never seen rain come down this hard."

"You'll get used to it." A grin showed even white teeth in his virile, tanned face. He held out his hand. "I'm David Crandall."

This wasn't the British reserve Melanie had been warned to expect. Her own hand was enveloped in a strong grip as she said, "It's nice to meet you."

David turned as an older man entered the hall. He was impeccably dressed, in contrast to David, and his face was expressionless. Melanie was delighted. This had to be the butler. The man was straight out of Central Casting, almost too perfect for the part. But even if it was all a show put on for the tourists, this was the kind of gracious living she had come to experience.

"It's all right, Bevins," David said. "I was passing through the hall so I answered the door." He turned back to Melanie. "I expect you'd like to get settled in. Your room is right next to the nursery."

"How nice," she said tepidly. Was that supposed to be a perk? Fortunately she was an early riser.

"The children are already in bed. They wanted to stay up and meet you, but it didn't seem like a good idea, since you were delayed."

"Oh, uh . . . that was good thinking," she answered. This was almost too much hospitality, but she supposed it was part of the package deal. "Children need their sleep," she said brightly. "How old are they?"

David stared at her with a slight frown. "They're nine."

"They're all the same age?" she asked, puzzled.

"There are only two, Ariel and Ashley. They're twins."

"Two little girls, how nice." Melanie wondered if she could ask to be taken to her room without seeming impolite.

His generous mouth thinned to a straight line, giving his strong face an autocratic look. "Ashley is a boy."

"Oh, I'm sorry! In America, a lot of young girls are named Ashley. It's quite trendy right now." Melanie was embarrassed at her blunder, but he didn't have to make such a big deal of it.

David was definitely scowling at her now. "I would think you might at least remember their names."

"How could I when I never heard them before?"

He folded his arms and pinned her with a piercing stare. "What kind of nonsense is this? Who the devil are you?"

"I could ask you the same thing," she flared. "Do your employers know how you greet a guest?"

"If that's the way you prefer to think of yourself, I don't suppose it matters greatly. But you'd better be damn good with those kids," he warned in a steely voice.

As Melanie began to wonder if he might be seriously disturbed, Bevins entered the hall once more.

"Miss Morton just phoned, sir," he said. "She has been unavoidably detained, but she will be here first thing in the morning."

"Then who is this?" David asked as he swung around to look at Melanie. "If you're not the new nanny, who are you?"

"Is *that* who you thought I was? Well, it explains a lot."

"Not to me, it doesn't. What are you doing here?"

Melanie was getting very tired of this arrogant man, gorgeous or not. "I'm sorry I'm not who you were expecting, but that's no excuse for rudeness. My name is Melanie Warren, and I have a reservation. Now if it isn't too much bother, could someone get my bags out of the car and show me to my room?"

He listened to her tirade, uncertain whether to laugh or be annoyed. "Is this some kind of joke? Did one of my so-called friends put you up to it?"

"If you can find anything funny in the situation, I wish you'd share it with me. I'm cold and I'm wet and I've been driving around in circles for hours. Is this the famous Burford Castle welcome I was led to expect?"

As comprehension dawned, David's eyes sparkled with mischievous laughter. "I've dined there on occasion, but I've never stayed overnight. Unless their rooms are a lot better than the food, you're lucky you didn't find the place."

"Now who's playing games?" she asked in annoyance. "Don't tell me I'm in the wrong place. I distinctly saw your sign at the entrance."

"You have lovely eyes." His expression became strictly masculine as he gave her a comprehensive look for the first time. "It would be a shame to hide them, but you really should wear glasses, at least for driving."

"I have twenty-twenty vision," Melanie informed him crisply. "I know what I saw. The sign was partially obscured, but I could read Castle and part of—" She paused as uncertainty took over. There were no other guests around, and he seemed more interested in his children than paying customers.

"I think what you read was Castlebury Manor," David said gently. "Or a portion of it, anyway. I must have the gardener trim those trees."

Her cheeks turned a becoming shade of rose as she recalled her imperiousness. "I'm really sorry. It was so dark out and the rain was coming down in buckets. When I saw your sign . . . I mean, I just naturally assumed . . ."

"It was an understandable mistake," he said soothingly. "Especially for a stranger to these parts."

His good manners didn't lessen her embarrassment. "Well . . . I'll get out of your hair," she mumbled, backing toward the door. "I hope your nanny gets here."

"I can't let you go out in that storm. I'd worry about you." He smiled charmingly. "Come in and have a drink. You must be chilled."

After only a token protest, Melanie let herself be persuaded. Partly because she needed directions, but mostly because David intrigued her and she wanted to know the rest of the story. Could this imposing manor possibly belong to him? He seemed too young. If he had nine-year-old twins, though, either he married young or he was older than he looked. What was his wife like? The questions went on and on.

David led her into a library that had the quiet elegance of old money. A priceless oriental rug looked like an heirloom, and so did the oil paintings that decorated the walls. It didn't have the chaste feeling of a museum, however. The couches and chairs were the finest quality, but everything looked comfortable and homelike.

He indicated a mahogany cabinet that held a silver tray filled with crystal decanters. "What can I fix you to drink?"

Melanie hesitated. "Could I possibly have a cup of coffee instead?"

"Of course." He tugged on a damask bellpull next to the draperies. "Take off your wet things and sit here by the fire." He indicated the couch that faced a huge stone fireplace where several massive logs were blazing. "The evenings can turn chilly in England at the end of summer."

Under her raincoat Melanie was wearing a short beige skirt and a matching sweater. She tugged at the sweater self-consciously as David gazed appreciatively at her slender figure. His wife better keep him on a short leash, Melanie thought cynically. This was a man who had enjoyed many women—and who wasn't through looking yet. Although in all fairness, he was being a perfect gentleman.

"So, what made you decide to stay at Burford Castle?" David came over to sit on the couch next to her, stretching out his long legs and crossing them at the ankle.

"My travel agent told me a lot of the nobility are offering accommodations to a limited number of guests. Staying in a castle sounded a lot more glamorous than a plain old inn."

"If you like drafty rooms and mediocre cooking," he said negligently. "Shelby Burford knows as much about running a hotel as I do about being a ballet dancer."

"You know the Earl of Burford?"

"We went to school together." David slanted a glance at her. "Are you meeting friends there?"

"No, I'm traveling alone. A friend was supposed to come with me, but her plans changed at the last minute. Since all the arrangements had been made, I decided to come by myself."

Bevins came in answer to the bell and David requested coffee. When the butler had left he said, "That sounds rather lonely. Do you have friends here in England?"

"No, but I don't panic at the idea of being alone."

His expression changed subtly as he gazed at her lovely features framed by the long fair hair that curled softly around her shoulders. "I shouldn't think a beautiful woman like you would be alone very often."

Melanie was suddenly very much aware of his lean body, so deceptively relaxed next to her. "Many times it's by choice," she said crisply. "I'm not one of those people who needs somebody to hold her hand."

"It isn't a matter of necessity. Companionship simply makes things more fun."

"I suppose so when a person is married—like you are," she added pointedly.

Her veiled disapproval amused him. "Do I look like a married man?"

"It isn't that easy to tell. Even if a man is wearing a wedding ring, which you're not."

"There's a very good reason for that. I—" he paused as the butler entered carrying a silver tray bearing an antique coffee service. "Thank you, Bevins, that will be all for tonight."

Melanie tensed as David filled a thin, bone china cup instead of letting the butler pour. Was it significant that he dismissed the man for the evening, or was she being a little paranoid? This wasn't Dracula's castle in Transylvania. But the wild storm outside and David's seductive manner were jangling her nerves.

"Cream and sugar?" He was looking at her inquiringly.

"Just black, please."

"Shall I put a shot of brandy in it to warm you up?"

"No thanks, this will be fine." She accepted the cup and took a hasty gulp. "You've been very kind, but as soon as I finish this I really have to get going."

"You'd be very foolish to push on to Burford Castle tonight. It's a good forty miles from here. You must have taken a wrong turn leaving London."

"Oh, no!" She didn't relish the thought of getting lost again, which was bound to happen. "Is there a village near here? I might be better off staying at an inn tonight and continuing on tomorrow in the daylight. Maybe I can phone the castle and tell them I'm delayed, so they don't give away my room."

"No problem. You can stay here tonight. I'll ring up Shelby and tell him what happened."

"I wasn't angling for an invitation. Just point me toward the nearest inn."

"Your sense of direction isn't the greatest." He chuckled. "I'd have visions of you wandering about all night, knocking on strange doors. You're much safer here with me."

She wasn't so sure. "Shouldn't you ask your wife before you invite a stranger into the house?"

"That was a misconception I was about to clear up. I'm not married. So you see, it's perfectly proper."

Melanie couldn't help laughing. "Your logic eludes me. Why is it any more proper for two single strangers to spend the night together?"

"I was offering you your own room." Something kindled in his eyes as he gazed at her. "Unless you have other arrangements in mind—in which case I'd be happy to accommodate you."

"I can see Englishmen are no different than American men." She set her cup down decisively. "Goodbye, Mr. Crandall."

"Don't go. I was only teasing you, for which I apologize. My offer was quite genuine, with no strings attached. You can have the nanny's room. It's all made up and you can push a nice stout chest against the door." He grinned impishly. "I rarely batter down doors in the middle of the night."

Melanie felt a little foolish. "I'm sure you don't have to," she remarked without thinking.

"That's a nice compliment." He laughed. "Then you'll stay?"

"It's an offer I can't refuse." She returned his smile.

"Splendid! Are you tired? Do you want to go to your room, or would you prefer to talk for a while?"

"It's lovely here by the fire, but you don't have to entertain me."

"It's the other way around, believe me! I don't know what to do with myself after the children go to bed."

"Are you a recent widower?" Melanie asked tentatively.

"I've never been married. The twins are my older brother's children. Richard and his wife, Marie, were killed in an automobile accident six months ago." David's handsome face sobered. "It was on a night very much like this. They were coming home from a party when a drunken lorry driver plowed into them."

"I'm so sorry," Melanie murmured. "It must have been a devastating blow."

"Especially for the children. It was the second tragedy to strike within a year. They had recently lost their grandfather, which brought a lot of changes to their lives. When Richard succeeded to the title, he had to move his family here to manage the estate." David sighed. "Now I'm all the poor kids have left."

Melanie was having trouble assimilating the facts. This rugged man in tight jeans and a pullover didn't look like a member of the peerage. At least not her conception of one.

"What title is that?" she asked cautiously.

"My brother became the sixth Viscount of Castlebury after our father died."

"Does that mean you're now the seventh Viscount?"

"Something I never expected or wanted to be." He grimaced. "Richard was the steady one. He was raised to take over, and even *he* had trouble running the estate."

"Is it difficult to get help way out here?"

"That isn't the problem. We have tenant farmers, and some complicated entailments. Everything has to be accounted for, but the bookkeeping system is incomprehensible."

"Ledgers can seem that way at first glance, but they really aren't."

"You've never seen any like these. Father had his own way of doing things and he didn't have the patience or the inclination to explain them. If Richard had trouble figuring out the operation, how the devil am I going to cope?"

"You can hire someone to put in a bookkeeping system."

"I guess I'll have to eventually. Right now my first concern is the children. It didn't help matters that their nanny got sick and had to leave. I'm really worried about them."

"Were they very attached to her?"

"Reasonably so. She'd only worked for the family for about a year, but it was one more person who deserted them. They must feel they can't count on anybody."

"You're here," Melanie said gently.

"Yes, but I don't know anything about being a parent. We had a good relationship without any responsibility on my part. I took them out for treats and brought them home before they got tired and cranky."

She smiled. "Isn't that the ideal time to dump them on the nanny?"

"I only hope this one is patient. The twins have changed a lot lately."

"In what way?"

"They were always great kids, well-adjusted and fun to be with. After their parents died they became very quiet. I realized they were grieving, but it isn't good to keep everything pent up inside. I try to spend time with them. We were always the best of buddies, but they're so remote these days. I can't seem to get back on the old footing."

"They've been through a lot of trauma. I'm sure they'll come out of it," Melanie said, since she didn't know what else to say.

"They already have to some extent, but I'm not sure this next phase is healthier."

"What do you mean?"

"Ariel and Ashley were normal children. They got into trouble, but for the most part, accidentally. Now, it seems they look for mischief. I was so happy to see them coming out of their shells that I hesitated to reprimand them for anything." He ran strong fingers through his thick, dark hair. "I hate to threaten their security by disciplining them, but I don't want them to turn into little monsters, either."

"What kind of stunts are they pulling?"

"Nothing really horrendous, so far. Just worrisome things like disappearing for hours without telling anybody where they're going, and snitching things like biscuits after they've been told they can't have any."

"Maybe they're hungry."

"Scarcely. Biscuits are what you in America call cookies."

"That still doesn't sound so terrible."

"Tell it to Mrs. Crossiter, the housekeeper. Her kitchen is strictly off-limits, and the twins are aware of it. That's how I know they're just being contrary."

"Couldn't you persuade your housekeeper to be more flexible?"

"You've obviously never met the woman. Father hired her right after Mother died. Richard and I were grown and had left home by then. Mrs. C. was in charge of the house and she ruled everybody but Father with an iron hand. She doesn't care much for children to begin with, and she's rapidly losing patience with the twins. I'm afraid she might give notice."

"It seems to me you'd be better off without her. She doesn't sound like a very warm or understanding person."

"She's not ideal for a household with small children," he admitted. "But if Mrs. Crossiter left it would mean another upheaval in the household, something I'm trying without much success to avoid."

"Well, cheer up. Maybe the new nanny will be a real-life Mary Poppins and all your troubles will be over."

"From your lips to God's ears!" he said fervently. "We could use a little luck around here."

"You've had more than your share of *bad* luck," Melanie said gently. "Things are bound to change."

"I'm sorry to be dumping my woes on you this way." He gave her a wry smile. "It isn't like me at all. I'm usually a very upbeat fellow."

"Nobody can keep a stiff upper lip all the time, not even a British Viscount," she teased.

"Poor Melanie." His voice deepened a note. "This isn't how you expected to spend the evening."

That reminded her of where she was supposed to be. "I forgot to call the castle! Do you think it's too late?" She glanced at her watch. Incredibly, it was almost ten-thirty.

"Probably, but don't worry about it. I'll ring there in the morning."

"Are they usually full up? I wouldn't want to lose my reservation."

"That's no problem. Shelby would give up his own room for a paying guest," David said derisively.

"I've read that a lot of titled people have been forced to open their homes because of taxes. It's too bad, even though I'm glad of the opportunity to stay in a castle."

"Don't sing any sad songs for the earl. He doesn't have a cash flow problem, he's in it for the money."

"You sound disapproving."

"I guess I am. I don't think you should put a price on hospitality. Especially when necessity isn't involved."

"What he's doing makes a lot of people happy, though. Me, for instance."

"I can think of more acceptable ways of accomplishing that."

There was no mistaking the sultry look on his face as he gazed at her. Melanie was suddenly conscious of the silent house and the fact that any servants had gone to bed. Not that she was worried about David making a pass. A man with his looks and charm could auction off his nights and make a fortune. Still, she didn't want him to think she was interested in joining the bidders.

Looking ostentatiously at her watch she said, "Well, it's been a long day."

"I guess you want to turn in," he said reluctantly. "I shouldn't have kept you, but it's so long since I've had someone to talk to."

"Don't you have any friends in the neighborhood?"

"This isn't exactly London." He smiled. "The nearest neighbors are a couple of miles away."

"Is that where you lived before, in London?"

"I have a town house there. I'll keep it of course, but I doubt if I'll get up there very often. At least not until I get the twins settled down."

"Perhaps your friends will come to visit you here. You have plenty of room."

His firm mouth curved sardonically. "I'm not counting on it. I'm afraid it's too quiet here for them."

Melanie got the picture. David was a playboy, used to being out every night with a different glamorous woman. It must be especially difficult for someone like that to be suddenly saddled with a home and a ready-made family.

"I don't mean to complain," he said. "The twins will come around and everything will work out."

"I'm sure it will, but it's quite a responsibility. Are you the only person who can take over? How about your sister-in-law's parents?"

"That isn't a viable solution," David answered without elaborating. "Are you hungry, by any chance?" he asked, changing the subject. "I didn't have much dinner and I'm starving."

Melanie hadn't had *any* dinner. She had expected to stop somewhere along the way, but the storm drove food out of her mind. Once he brought up the subject, she became aware of hunger pangs.

"Your housekeeper might not take kindly to being asked to fix a snack at this hour," Melanie said hesitantly.

"Her disapproval would be even more pronounced than usual—and Mrs. Crossiter has elevated censure into an art form." He grinned. "No, I wouldn't subject you to that. I was thinking of making a raid on the kitchen."

"She lets you in her kitchen?"

"This will be our secret. What can I make you to eat?"

"Practically anything. I skipped dinner."

"Why on earth didn't you say something sooner?"

"I didn't want to be any more trouble than I already have been."

"On the contrary, you're like a breath of fresh air. I don't want you to leave. Wait here and I'll be back with whatever I can find."

"I'll come with you. No offense, but I have a feeling you'll have trouble recognizing the refrigerator."

"That's where you're wrong. It's that rectangular box where wine is chilled."

"Very good! Can you also identify the bread box? I want something I can chew before I swallow it."

David had led her down a series of hallways, past a lot of rooms she could only see into dimly. They finally reached the kitchen, a huge room that was slightly forbidding.

It reminded Melanie of an operating room. Everything was white—the walls, the floors, the uncluttered counters. There was no color anywhere, not even bowls of fruit or decorative canisters. She would have found it a depressing place to work, but it fit the image David had drawn of Mrs. Crossiter.

"Let's see what's here." He was peering into the refrigerator. "A joint of ham, homegrown tomatoes and the remains of an apple tart. How does that sound?"

"Divine! I'll get some plates and silverware. Do you know where they're kept?"

"Just open drawers until you find what you need." He carried the food to a square butcher-block table in the middle of the room.

Dishes were stacked in the cupboard with almost military precision. The drawers were equally neat. The spoons and forks were nested and the knives were lined up with the cutting edges all facing the same way.

"I'm afraid to touch anything," Melanie remarked. "Mrs. Crossiter will know if one thing has been moved."

"It will give her something to complain about besides the twins."

"I wouldn't be surprised if every fork and dish had a number and an assigned place. She'd be a credit to the United States Marines."

"Do you think they'd be willing to make a trade?" David grinned. "I could be persuaded to pay them."

Mrs. Crossiter might have been a pain in many ways, but she was a good cook. The ham had been glazed with honey, and the apple tart was meltingly delicious.

David watched with amusement as Melanie polished off everything on her plate. "I don't know how you stay so slim," he remarked.

"Someone took a survey and found out that men like women who are dainty eaters. I guess that's why I'm still single." She laughed.

"There has to be some other explanation." He looked at her with frank male admiration. "Haven't you ever been attracted to anyone?"

"Dozens of times."

"No, I mean to one special man."

"Dozens of times," she repeated, smiling impishly. "That's why when it happens, I know I'll get over it."

"I feel sorry for the men who fall in love with you."

"You're in no position to criticize. I get the impression that there have been a lot of women in your life, but you're still single, too."

"Because I haven't met the one person I want to spend the rest of my life with. Which doesn't mean I'm not looking for her. You, on the other hand, seem to be avoiding any commitment."

Melanie's face sobered. "That's not true. I keep hoping there's somebody out there for me, but I must admit I'm beginning to lose faith."

"What qualifications does your perfect man need to have?"

"I'm not looking for perfection," she protested. "That would be too hard to live up to. I'm not perfect myself."

"You don't have any flaws that show." His gaze traveled from her lovely face to the curves of her breasts, accentuated by the clinging sweater. "And I doubt that I'd find any hidden ones."

Melanie was annoyed at the warmth that spread through her body. Damn, but the man was good! He'd subtly reminded her that he was an exceedingly virile man, without ever once getting out of line.

"We were talking about the qualities people look for in a partner," she said tartly. "I'd list companionship and a sense of humor."

"Those are important certainly, but they're not enough without the touch of magic that makes two people want only each other."

"You're describing sex, which is what men really mean when they talk about love. A man can go from one woman to another and feel the same way about all of them. I'm looking for one who is completely satisfied with me."

"He'd be out of his mind if he wasn't."

His husky voice was seductive, conjuring up erotic images that made Melanie's pulse beat faster. David must be a magnificent lover. Practice makes perfect, she told herself sardonically. How many women had experienced the joy that lean, hard body could bring? Too many. She didn't intend to join their ranks.

"You're very flattering," she said lightly.

"No, I'm being honest. Many men must have told you how desirable you are."

"It's always nice to hear." She stood so abruptly that her chair tipped over and landed on the bare floor with a loud clatter. "Oh dear, I'm not usually this clumsy."

"No problem," David said easily.

Melanie started to gather up the plates. "I'll wash these dishes and put them away so Mrs. Crossiter won't find out we invaded her domain."

It was too late. An older woman in a shapeless bathrobe stuck her head in the kitchen warily. Her gray hair was in curlers and she was carrying a poker.

"Oh, it's you, sir." Her disapproving glance took in both David and Melanie. "I heard a noise in here and I thought it was burglars."

"I'm sorry we disturbed you, Mrs. Crossiter," David said. "Miss Warren dropped by and we were having a late snack."

"That explains it." The woman's displeasure deepened as she took in the dirty dishes and unaccustomed clutter on the counters.

"I was just about to clean up." Melanie knew it was ridiculous, but she felt like a teenager caught making fudge on a hot plate in the dorm.

"That won't be necessary, Miss." The housekeeper's thin lips almost disappeared as she compressed them in a straight line. "That's my job—although it certainly has changed since the old gentleman passed away." The last part was muttered almost under her breath.

The muscles in David's square jaw bunched, but he kept his voice pleasant. "It's late. Why don't you leave the clearing up until morning?"

"I really wouldn't mind doing it," Melanie said.

"You're a guest. Miss Warren is staying overnight," he told the housekeeper.

"I see." In two words, the woman managed to make Melanie's innocent visit sound like an orgy.

His eyes chilled. "She will be staying in the room next to the nursery. The new nanny phoned. She won't be here until tomorrow."

"Don't count on her lasting too long. Those children are imps of Satan."

"They're normal, high-spirited youngsters," David corrected her sharply.

"Tell that to Mr. Thompson. He was up here complaining again today. They sneaked into his barn and took the horses out for a gallop."

"Why didn't you tell me about this sooner? I'll have a talk with them first thing in the morning. The children could have been seriously injured!"

"If you ask me, those younguns could use a touch of the crop themselves." After seeing the ominous look on David's face, Mrs. Crossiter realized she'd gone too far. "Not that I was suggesting such a thing. But it's time somebody took them in hand."

"They're my responsibility and I will be the one to discipline them, if and when I see fit. Is that quite clear?" Without waiting for a response, he said to Melanie, "I'll show you to your room now."

She followed him silently, aware of the anger radiating from his taut body. David might be a playboy in his private life, but he cared deeply about his niece and nephew. She had to respect him for that.

He stopped halfway up the staircase. "I'm sorry to involve you in my household squabbles."

"Don't be. I was the cause of this one."

"Not really. Mrs. Crossiter loves to tattle on the twins. I'm really concerned, though. They've had riding lessons, but they could get hurt riding unsupervised. This time I'll have to discipline them."

"I suppose so, although what they did doesn't sound too horrendous."

He smiled wryly. "You're very lenient. You must like children."

"I've never had much contact with them, but I do think they should be treated like people."

"Adults have to be held to account, too."

"I didn't mean you should let them get away with this latest caper. You can't overlook dangerous behavior. But it's important to find out why they're suddenly doing these things. Maybe they're just trying to see how far they can go before you crack down."

"I'm right on the borderline." David's jaw tightened. "I was on the verge of booting Mrs. Crossiter out of here just now."

"She'd never win any Miss Congeniality awards, but this isn't the time to fire her. You're already one nanny short. How would you manage without a housekeeper?"

"I don't suppose you'd like the job?"

"No thanks, I don't do windows."

As they reached the top of the stairs and started down a long corridor, he said, "I never did ask what kind of work you do."

"You wouldn't be interested. It isn't very glamorous."

He frowned slightly. "I don't know where you got the notion that I'm a superficial person, interested only in the pursuit of pleasure."

"It isn't up to me to judge," she said neutrally. "Why should you work when you don't have to?"

"Where did you get the idea that I don't work?"

"It was a natural assumption," she said uncertainly.

"An erroneous one. I've built a very satisfying career in London, one that I've put on hold until I get things straightened out down here."

"I'm sorry for jumping to conclusions. What do you do?"

"I—" He paused, cocking his head slightly.

"What's wrong?" Melanie asked.

"I thought I heard a sound from the children's room," he answered in a lowered voice. "I must have been mistaken. They've been asleep for hours."

They continued on to a room toward the end of the hall. It was pleasantly furnished with a double bed covered with a floral spread, a desk and good reading lamps. Through a door was a private bathroom.

"I hope you'll be comfortable," David said. "If there's anything you need, don't hesitate to ask."

"I can't think of anything more I could want. It's a lovely room," she said politely.

"I'm sure you're tired, so we'll continue our conversation in the morning."

"I expect to be out of here early."

"That's not very complimentary," he teased. "Although I can't say I blame you. I'm afraid I was a complete bore, dumping my troubles in your lap that way."

"I enjoyed our talk, and you were more than hospitable," she assured him.

"Well, if there's nothing more I can do for you, I'll let you get some sleep. See you in the morning."

Melanie was happily surprised to find her luggage had been brought up from the car. She took out her nightgown, wishing she'd brought something warmer. The short blue chiffon nightie had seemed practical, since it was lightweight and took up so little room in the suitcase, but she'd forgotten that the English didn't keep their houses as warm as Americans are used to.

She brushed her teeth hurriedly, anxious to get into a warm bed. But her discomfort was forgotten when she started to think about David. What a mass of contradictions he was. A handsome charismatic playboy, living in a country manor house with a couple of mischievous kids. Could there be a more unlikely scenario?

She wondered what kind of work he'd given up to come here. Something fascinating, no doubt—like the man himself. Melanie had a feeling she'd think about David often, wondering if duty would triumph over his sybaritic nature. Or would he tire of the responsibility and go back to his old haunts? It was frustrating to think she'd never find out. No other man had ever intrigued her so thoroughly in such a short space of time.

Melanie was lost in thought as she threw back the covers on the bed. Suddenly something leaped out at her with a hoarse croaking sound. She screamed and jumped backward when a huge bullfrog flew through the air toward her.

In her panic to get away, Melanie stumbled against the upright suitcase she'd left next to the bed. It caught her behind the knees and she fell flat on her back as the frog changed course and made for the open window.

The thick carpeting cushioned her fall, but the breath was knocked out of her and she couldn't move. Was she hallucinating, too? For a dazed moment she heard what sounded like muffled giggling.

An instant later, the door flew open. David appeared in the entry wearing only black silk pajama bottoms slung low on his lean hips. Even in her traumatized state, Melanie was struck by the perfection of his torso. Broad shoulders tapered down to a narrow waist and flat stomach. He had the superb body of an athlete at the height of his powers.

"My God, what happened?" he exclaimed.

"I tripped over my suitcase."

Melanie struggled to disentangle her legs and sit up, but David knelt beside her and put an arm under her shoulders.

"Are you hurt?" he asked anxiously. "Shall I send for a doctor?"

"No, I'm fine. The only thing I hurt was my dignity."

Melanie had decided not to tell David about the frog. Once she could think clearly, she realized the twins had put it there as a surprise for the new nanny. It was actually kind of funny, but she was afraid this would be one prank too many. David might lose his temper, and then regret it.

"Let me take a look." He drew her against his chest and probed the back of her head with gentle fingers.

She realized he was only showing concern, but the circumstances were very provocative. The thin layer of chiffon separating their bodies was woefully inadequate. She was tinglingly aware of his hard chest pressing against her breasts, and her cheek nestled in the hollow of his neck. He smelled of lavender soap and his skin felt firm and warm.

Melanie knew the situation was explosive, but perversely, she didn't want it to end.

"I can't feel any bumps." He finished the exploration of her scalp. "You were fortunate."

"Yes, I . . . I guess so."

David's expression changed as he looked at her dazzled eyes and softly parted lips. His fingers curled around the back of her neck, tangling in her long silky hair. Excitement raced through Melanie, fueled by his smoky blue eyes and the promise of his taut, virile body.

For one incomprehensible instant she wanted to clasp her arms around his neck and let him fulfill that promise. Then common sense took over. What was the matter with her? This man was a virtual stranger! As his head dipped slowly toward hers, she scrambled out of his arms and stood.

David didn't try to stop her. He rose more leisurely, regarding her with unmistakable male interest. Melanie's clear skin turned a bright rosy pink as she realized what a provocative picture she must present. The short baby doll nightie only came to the top of her thighs, and the sheer chiffon gave tantalizing glimpses of her breasts. She folded her arms over them to hide the fact that her nipples were tightening embarrassingly. If only she'd taken her robe out of the suitcase!

David was amused at her embarrassment, but he tried not to show it. "It's chilly in here. Why don't you get into bed," he suggested.

"No, I . . . I mean I will when you leave." She hoped he'd take the hint.

David was reminded of his reason for coming. "What happened in here? Why did you scream?"

"Oh . . . I, um, thought I saw somebody trying to climb in the window. It was only the branch of a tree. I'm not usually the nervous type, but I guess the storm made me jumpy."

"That's perfectly understandable. It's as dark as the inside of a pocket tonight."

While he walked over to close the window, Melanie decided to get into bed. It might look rather suggestive, but it was better than standing there nearly nude.

"That should calm your fears." He came back to stand over her. "Is there anything else I can do for you?"

"No, I'll be fine now." She pulled the covers up to her chin.

"Would you like a cup of hot cocoa to help you sleep?"

"That won't be a problem." She faked a huge yawn. "I'll be asleep in five minutes."

"You're very fortunate." He smiled wryly, gazing at her piquant face. "Something tells me I'm going to have a lot of trouble falling asleep tonight."

Melanie stared into the darkness for a long time after he left. She was still shaken by the emotions he'd awakened in her. David wasn't the first handsome man she'd been sexually attracted to. Women weren't naturally immune. But how could she even have considered letting him make love to her?

There was no doubt that it would have been a memorable experience. He'd probably mastered every nuance of lovemaking. That hard body could bring a woman ecstasy. She could almost feel his hands stroking her bare skin, his mouth intensifying the pleasure until she was taut with desire.

Melanie turned over abruptly and buried her hot face in the pillow. Fortunately she'd only suffered a momentary aberration. The seventh Viscount of Castlebury had enough notches on his belt.

Chapter Two

Melanie was self-conscious about meeting David the next morning, but he acted as though nothing had happened between them. Actually nothing had. It was only her overactive imagination that was making her feel guilty.

She was dressed and ready to leave when he knocked on the door. "I wouldn't have wakened you, but I heard you stirring around," he explained.

"Yes, I'm all ready to leave," she said brightly, looking away after a quick glance.

She hadn't been mistaken about David's potent male appeal. He managed to look sexy even in gray wool slacks and a white cabled fisherman's sweater. They emphasized his rugged masculinity.

"You can't start out without breakfast," he protested.

"I'll stop someplace along the way."

"I won't hear of it. That would be shockingly inhospitable. Besides, I'd like you to meet the twins."

It was an experience she couldn't pass up. Melanie was curious about the little devils who'd been responsible for last night's traumatic incident.

They looked more like angels. Whatever else they might be, Ariel and Ashley were beautiful children. They had blue eyes and dark hair like their uncle. Ariel's was caught up in a silky ponytail tied with a polka dot ribbon. They were already seated at the dining room table, whispering together when David and Melanie came into the room. He thought the apprehension they tried to hide was because of yesterday's incident with the horses, but she knew better.

"I'm so glad to meet you," Melanie said after David had introduced her. "Your uncle has told me a lot about you."

"Miss Warren is from America," he said when the twins remained silent.

"Are you going to stay?" Ariel asked tentatively.

"No, I'm leaving right after breakfast," Melanie said.

When the twins looked at each other in dismay, David said, "This isn't the new nanny. Miss Morton was delayed. She'll be here this morning."

"Your uncle is hoping she'll be permanent," Melanie said casually. "I'm sure you want to keep him happy."

David looked puzzled, but before he could comment, a maid entered, wheeling a cart covered with platters of bacon and eggs, bowls of cereal and a basket of scones. She was young and cheerful, the direct opposite of Mrs. Crossiter.

"Good morning, Julia." David greeted the girl with a smile as she served them.

"Good morning, sir. Terrible rain last night, wasn't it? I hear some of the roads were washed out."

"Did you have any trouble getting here this morning?" he asked.

"No, sir. Clara and I started out early, just in case, but the damage is in the other direction."

"Julia and Clara come in by the day," David explained to Melanie. "They live with their families in the village."

"It must take a lot of people to run this place," Melanie observed, glancing out the window at the rolling lawns that stretched as far as she could see. "You need a small army of gardeners to take care of the grounds alone."

"It's a change from my town house in London," David admitted. "I'll show you around after breakfast."

"I really have to push on. As you know, my sense of direction isn't the greatest." She laughed. "I need to allow myself time to get lost."

"I'll draw you a foolproof map. You can spare half an hour," he coaxed.

"Well . . ." She was curiously reluctant to leave.

"We have a pretty little pond with lily pads and bullfrogs," he said, pressing his advantage. "Although I don't suppose the frogs are an inducement."

"I like to hear them croak at night—as long as it's from a distance." Melanie flicked a mischievous glance at the twins who were keeping very silent.

As they avoided her eyes, Julia returned. "Mr. Thompson is here, sir. He wants to talk to you. Shall I tell him to come back after breakfast?"

"No, I'll speak to him." David rose, fixing the twins with a stern gaze. "Don't disappear. I want to talk to both of you when I return."

They looked so miserable that after he left, Melanie said gently, "I know this is a difficult time in your lives, but it's hard on your uncle, too. He's trying to do the best he can for you. It would make things easier all around if you met him halfway."

They looked at her with closed expressions. "Are you going to tell him what happened last night?" Ariel asked.

"There was no harm done, so what's the point? I wouldn't advise you to try the same thing on the new nanny, however." Melanie smiled. "You're already skating on thin ice after the horseback riding incident yesterday."

"We didn't hurt them," Ashley muttered.

"Your uncle is worried that *you* could have gotten hurt."

"We had our first riding lesson when we were five years old," Ariel said indignantly.

"That's very impressive. I'm sure you're both excellent riders, but you shouldn't ride somebody else's horses without asking first. You wouldn't like it if someone took your property without permission, would you?"

"The horses needed exercise," Ashley said. "Mr. Thompson keeps them cooped up in the stable all day."

"That's not good for them," Ariel said earnestly. "They need to run. They'll get sick if they just stand around all the time."

"Mr. Thompson doesn't pay any attention to them," Ashley said. "We talk to them and bring them lumps of sugar and apples and stuff."

So the children weren't just being mischievous, Melanie thought. What they did was still wrong, but their motives were pure. "Maybe your uncle could make arrangements for you to exercise Mr. Thompson's horses—with an adult along," she added. "I gather you don't have your own stables."

"There's one near the pond, but it's been empty for a long time," Ariel said.

"Grandfather didn't want to be bothered with horses. Father was going to buy us each one for Christmas, but—" Ashley shrugged.

Melanie's heart twisted at their efforts to be stoic. "Maybe you'll still get your horses. Christmas is only a few months away."

The twins looked at each other in sudden desolation and Melanie knew they were picturing the holidays without their parents. While she was casting about for something comforting to say, David returned.

"Thompson just told me the road to Chistwick was washed out in last night's storm," he announced. "That's the road you would take to Burford Castle."

"I don't believe it!" Melanie groaned. "I bet I'd have less trouble getting to the South Pole. Is there another road I can take?"

"It involves about a thirty-mile detour. You'd almost be better off going back to London and starting out again."

"I said I wanted to see the countryside, but I meant something other than the highway in and out of London," she said grimly.

"You're welcome to stay here until the road opens up," David offered.

"I wasn't hinting for an invitation," she protested.

"I'm sure you weren't, after your experience last night. But I guarantee you won't be visited by ghosts—or anybody else." He smiled impishly.

Melanie could feel her pulse rate speed up at the memory, but she tried to look as amused as he.

"What did you plan to do when you got to the Castle?" he asked.

"Just go sightseeing around the neighborhood. I wrote down a few places to visit."

"There's just as much to see around here. We have plenty of crumbling Roman walls and haunted castles. Pick your poison."

"They have a super toy museum in Bath," Ashley said unexpectedly. "Ariel and I could show it to you."

Melanie was surprised and pleased by the offer. From what David had said about their remote behavior, the twins were paying her a great compliment.

"If you wouldn't mind dragging around with a tourist, I'd be glad of the company," she answered casually. "It isn't much fun to go to museums alone."

"That's settled then," David said with satisfaction. "Perhaps you'd like to unpack while I have a talk with the children."

"Could I speak to you for a few minutes first—alone," she added.

After a moment's hesitation, David sent the twins out to play. He clearly dreaded having to discipline them and wanted to get it over with.

"I thought I should tell you something before you talked to them," Melanie explained. "They didn't ride Mr. Thompson's horses as a prank. He keeps the poor animals penned up in their stalls all day. The children were simply exercising them. I know they should have asked first," she hurried on when David frowned. "But it isn't like they were being malicious."

"How do you know this?"

"They told me."

He stared at her in surprise. "You must be a sorceress. I've tried without success to establish a rapport with those two, and you have them chattering like a pair of squirrels in five minutes. How did you do it?"

The corners of her mouth twitched. "Let's just say we came to an understanding."

"How? You just met them."

Melanie smiled bewitchingly. "It's all in knowing what not to say." Before he could press her for a better explanation she said, "The twins are waiting for you with a great deal of trepidation. Don't you think you should put them out of their misery?"

"And my own." He groaned. "Their instincts might have been good, but I really have to discipline them."

"I suppose so," she answered neutrally.

"I can tell you don't approve, but what else can I do? I can't let them run wild."

She hesitated. "Do you really want my advice?"

"I'd welcome it."

"Well as long as you asked." Melanie's face lit with animation. "This is a perfect opportunity for the three of you to become close again. Mr. Thompson obviously doesn't care about his horses, and the twins love animals. Their father promised to buy them each a horse for Christmas."

"I didn't know. The children didn't tell me that, either."

"It was just another thing they couldn't talk about."

"I'm glad you told me. I'll make sure they aren't disappointed."

"Christmas is still months away and they need something to take their minds off their troubles right now. Why don't you buy Mr. Thompson's horses and put Ariel and Ashley in charge of caring for them?"

"They're nine-year-old children!"

"I wasn't suggesting they do any of the heavy work, but they're old enough to fill feed buckets and do little chores around the stable. It would give them a sense of responsibility and a new interest in life."

David stared at her with dawning enthusiasm. "It might at that! I can have the old stables renovated and we could all ride together."

"It might solve a lot of your problems."

"I agree." He took both of her hands and held them tightly. "You're a miracle worker. Would you consider moving in permanently?"

Melanie laughed to cover her instant reaction to his touch. "Wait until you see if my solution works."

"I have a feeling it will. If you'll excuse me for a few minutes, I'm going to make two youngsters happier than they've been in a long time."

The twins were bubbling with excitement when they returned to the dining room after the talk with their uncle.

"Uncle David is going to buy Mr. Thompson's horses for us," Ariel told Melanie excitedly.

"They'll be our very own!" Ashley's eyes sparkled.

"But you're only going to ride them when an adult is with you," David reminded them.

"We promise," they chorused.

"Can we go for a ride right now?" Ashley asked.

"I have to work things out with Mr. Thompson first." When their faces fell, David said, "Why don't you show Miss Warren around Bath in the meantime?"

"It's better than hanging around here," Melanie said to console them. "I don't know about you, but time always drags when I'm waiting for something."

"Will you come with us?" Ariel asked her uncle.

David was gratified by the request, but he declined it regretfully. "I'd like nothing better, but I have to be here when the new nanny arrives. Have fun with Miss Warren. I wish *I* could." He gave Melanie a mischievous smile.

Melanie learned a lot about the twins on the drive to Bath. Their talk with David had made them a lot more communicative. They chattered on happily about the new horses and their plans for taking care of them. Melanie had already guessed that was the reason for the children's unexplained disappearances. She decided to do some further sleuthing.

"I'm afraid your uncle and I got in trouble with Mrs. Crossiter last night," she remarked with a tinkling laugh. "We made ourselves a midnight snack and she caught us at it."

Ashley's smile changed to a scowl. "We're not allowed to go into the kitchen."

Ariel nodded sadly. "Nobody is. When Mummy was alive we made gingerbread men, but only on Mrs. Crossiter's day off."

"She won't ever let us have biscuits like Mummy did," Ashley said. "She told Uncle David we took some, and he said he'd speak to us about it."

Melanie began to understand why David's rapport with the twins had deteriorated. They thought he was allied with the repressive housekeeper. Well, that was easily cleared up.

"Grown-ups say things like that to keep the peace. It doesn't mean they agree with the person."

The discussion ended because they'd reached the charming little city of Bath.

The twins reluctantly accompanied Melanie into the famous Roman baths. They were much more interested in the restaurants and shops, especially one that displayed a mouthwatering array of fudge in an irresistible variety of flavors.

"Later," Melanie promised. "I have to see the baths. Do you realize they were built by the Romans almost two thousand years ago?"

The children were unimpressed with the irregular, cave-like depressions carved out of rock that dotted the sloping underground path. The large pool in the atrium, ringed with stately marble columns that reflected in the green water, met with more approval.

"It's like a big swimming pool." Ashley knelt down and dabbled his fingers in the water. "It's warm, too."

"That's because the baths are fed by the only hot springs in England," Melanie said. "My guidebook says you can buy a glass of mineral water in the Pump Room upstairs that's the very rainwater that fell here ten thousand years ago." After a look at their dubious faces she laughed. "I think I'd rather settle for a Sally Lunn. How about you?"

The famous buns that originated in Bath were still served in Sally Lunn's house, supposedly the oldest in town. They were served toasted with butter or clotted cream. Melanie chose the cream.

"This is blissful," she declared. "I just hope it won't spoil your appetite for lunch, although it's still early yet. What would you like to do now? We'll take turns choosing."

Ariel of course chose the doll museum, much to Ashley's disgust, also predictably. In spite of his disdain, he enjoyed himself. While they oohed and aahed over the lovely porcelain dolls, he inspected the wealth of stuffed animals.

Melanie was especially enchanted by the handmade dollhouses, some of them three-story Georgian heirlooms. She and Ariel rhapsodized over the exquisite miniature furnishings in the numerous rooms.

"I always wanted a dollhouse," Melanie said.

"You can play with mine," Ariel offered. "We can have a tea party."

"That would be fun. Shall we invite all your girlfriends to bring their dolls?"

"I don't have any friends," the little girl answered matter-of-factly.

"I can't believe that," Melanie protested.

"We used to live someplace else. I had friends there, but Ashley and I don't know anybody here."

"You will when school starts."

Ariel shook her head. "We go to public school."

Melanie knew that was what the English called their private schools. "Well, you'll see your friends when classes start again," she said consolingly. "That isn't far off."

"We have to go to a different school," Ashley said. "Our old one is too far away."

Melanie's heart ached for these poor displaced youngsters. They'd lost everything that was dear and familiar to them. Now they had to move into another strange environment. It would be a daunting prospect for an adult, let alone a child.

"You'll make new friends," she said awkwardly.

"I guess so." They both looked back at her unemotionally.

"Hey, we're wasting time." Melanie changed the subject with forced cheerfulness. "It's Ashley's turn to choose what we do next."

Their detachment disappeared. "I choose the American Museum," he said.

Melanie was surprised, but when they toured the museum she understood its attraction. Ashley was fascinated by the teepee and the Conestoga wagon used in the great migration west, and Ariel gravitated toward the Hopi kachina dolls. While the children were occupied, Melanie gave her attention to the beautiful Greek Revival mansion housing the exhibits. Her guidebook said Winston Churchill delivered his first political speech here in the late eighteen hundreds when it was Claverton Manor.

After a thorough examination of the museum, Melanie suggested lunch. She was hoping for a quaint English inn with window boxes and typically British dishes like beefsteak-and-kidney pie, but the twins had other ideas. They talked her into a crowded, noisy place featuring hamburgers and chili.

"I didn't have to travel thousands of miles to go through an American museum and eat a hamburger," she said in mock complaint. Actually Melanie was delighted to see the children having such a good time.

"But it's a British hamburger." Ashley grinned.

"We'll have an English tea," Ariel promised.

The afternoon flew by as they went from one attraction to another. They gazed down from the Pulteney Bridge—a smaller version of the Ponte Vecchio in Florence—at the boomerang-shaped Pulteney Weir below. The foaming water of the dam was a striking contrast to the tranquil green lawns and colorful flower beds in the park that surrounded it.

From there they strolled along the Royal Crescent, a collection of thirty Georgian stone houses with Ionic columns, set behind curving iron fences. Then on to Bath Abbey, the site of a ruined Norman cathedral where a bishop was supposedly inspired by a dream to rebuild the church.

By the time Melanie and the twins started home in the late afternoon, even the children were tired. She smiled fondly at them. "You two are good sports. You really made my day."

"There are lots of other places to see," Ashley said. "Can we go with you?"

"If your uncle will let you, although I don't know how long I can stay."

"You just got here last night."

"Yes, but this visit wasn't exactly planned. I don't really know your uncle."

"He's very nice," Ariel assured her. "I'm sure he'd want you to stay. He likes pretty ladies."

"Somehow I got that impression," Melanie answered dryly. "Well, we'll see."

The twins couldn't wait to tell David about their eventful day and to show him the little souvenirs Melanie had bought them.

"It was very kind of you, but you shouldn't have," he protested. "You did enough by giving them a nice day out."

"Wait till you hear about all the things we ate." Melanie grinned. "You might not thank me. Don't expect them to eat any dinner."

"I used to stuff them with sweets and then bring them home." He returned her smile wryly. "Now my chickens have come home to roost. If they're sick in the night, I'm going to call you."

"We're never sick," Ashley said indignantly.

"Except that time after Susan's birthday party," Ariel reminded him.

Melanie laughed. "I hope the new nanny showed up."

"She did," David said. "I'd like you and the children to meet her."

Jean Morton was in her thirties, just a few years older than Melanie, but that was the only similarity between them.

There was nothing wrong with either her face or figure, they were simply nondescript. Jean was the kind of person who would be ignored at even a small gathering.

Her personality was equally colorless. She was pleasant enough to the children, but warmth just wasn't one of her strengths. They returned her greeting politely, but without much interest.

Melanie was the one who was disappointed. She'd hoped for someone more outgoing, although maybe English nannies weren't supposed to be. It was certainly none of her business, but she'd developed a real rapport with the twins after their fun-filled day together.

"Scoot upstairs and take your baths," David told the twins.

When he and Melanie were alone he said, "They certainly seem happier. I only hope it lasts."

"I'm sure it will," she answered. "They're adorable children. I couldn't have asked for better companions today."

"I hope you'll have a similar opinion of me," he said lightly. "Will you have dinner with me? There's a little place in the village that's quite decent."

"Do you think you should leave the children? It's Miss Morton's first night here."

"They need to get acquainted with each other, and you deserve a reward. Although I don't claim to be any prize." He smiled deprecatingly.

Melanie couldn't imagine any woman who would agree. David didn't have a single flaw that she'd discovered so far. Besides being handsome and virile, he had exquisite manners and a sense of humor. He also liked "pretty girls," she reminded herself before she got too carried away.

"Is it a date?" he asked.

"I'm really not hungry," she answered weakly.

"I'll make the reservation for nine o'clock. You will be by then." Without giving her a chance to contest the point he said, "I had your things moved to one of the guest rooms while you were out. I hope you don't mind. Miss Morton should be near the children."

"Of course, I understand."

"Your new room is in the opposite wing. If you'd like to come upstairs I'll show you where it's located."

Melanie followed David up the stairs to a bedroom that was larger and more luxurious than her former one. It had a four-poster bed with a flowered tester, a damask chaise longue and an exquisitely carved escritoire, in addition to various other pieces of furniture.

"This is gorgeous!" she exclaimed.

"I would have put you in here the first night except that the bed wasn't made up. You can imagine the martyr act Mrs. Crossiter would have put on if I'd asked her to take care of it." He smiled wryly. "That might sound cowardly, but I've settled for peace at any price."

"I think you're wise. Don't forget, I saw Mrs. Crossiter in action."

"And she wasn't even warmed up then." He laughed. "Well, if you need anything, just call. My room is right next door." He left before she had time to react.

Because he knew she'd object? Melanie wondered. Although that was nonsense. David wouldn't do anything so crude as to pay an uninvited visit. Still, it didn't do a lot for her peace of mind to picture him in bed just a few feet away.

The country inn they went to that night was just the sort of place she'd hoped to see when she planned this trip to England. A cheerful fire in a big stone fireplace gave the room a cozy atmosphere, and a lot of the diners seemed to know each other. A few nodded to David, but an older woman seated with a large party at the far end of the room gestured for him to come over.

"That's Lady Tyndall, one of my neighbors," he told Melanie. "We'll have to go over and say hello. Sylvia is a good friend, but she doesn't take no for an answer."

He led Melanie over to the table where the older woman and Melanie exchanged equally interested glances. Lady Tyndall was a large woman with a no-nonsense air about her. She was somewhere in her fifties, with short graying hair that she chose not to color. Her skin was relatively unlined and her features were good, but she didn't bother to enhance them. A touch of lipstick was the only evidence of cosmetics.

After the introductions were made she said to David, "How are those wonderful children, and when are you going to bring them over to see me?"

"Soon," he promised. "I've had my hands full lately."

"So I gather." She flicked a glance at Melanie. "Well, I must say you have good taste."

"You mustn't mind my wife," the older man sitting next to Sylvia remarked. "She's determined to be one of those colorful characters the English are famous for."

Melanie smiled. "How can I be offended? She paid me a compliment, even though I'm afraid she's gotten the wrong impression."

"Well, we'll let you get on with your dinner," David said before the older woman could comment further. "I'll be in touch."

"I'm sorry about that," he told Melanie after they were seated at their table and had given the waiter their orders. "Sylvia really means well. She's been wonderful to the twins and me since the accident."

"I didn't take offense, but you'd better set her straight before you have trouble with your real lady friends," Melanie said lightly.

His firm mouth curved in a little smile. "You're sure there are hordes of them?"

"You're a very eligible bachelor. I imagine a lot of women would just love to lead you down the aisle."

"How attractive is a man with a ready-made family?"

"That wouldn't be a drawback for anyone who's met the twins. They're terrific."

David laughed. "I get the feeling they'd be more of an incentive for you than I would."

"I'm not a candidate for the job."

"You have something against marriage?"

"Not at all, but my life is quite satisfying the way it is right now."

"What do you do? I never got around to asking."

"I'm a C.P.A. for a large accounting firm in Los Angeles."

"I'm impressed. You're looking at somebody who can't balance his checkbook."

"I'm sure you have other talents."

"So I've been told," he murmured. "Would you like a demonstration when we get home?"

"No, thank you," she said primly. "I'll take your word for it."

He gazed at her for a long moment. "You obviously think I'm a womanizing wastrel whose sole interest in life is the pursuit of pleasure. What made you jump to that conclusion?"

"I didn't mean to imply any such thing. I think your concern for your niece and nephew is very admirable. In fact, I want to discuss them with you."

"Later. We're talking about us now. What have I done to create such a bad impression? Outside of last night's regrettable incident in your room—which you must admit was completely spontaneous—I've tried to be a perfect gentleman."

Melanie's cheeks warmed and she ducked her head. She was afraid to look at David for fear her vivid imagination would play tricks and she'd picture him half nude and splendidly male. The way he'd been last night.

"A man would need to have ice water in his veins not to react under those circumstances," he said in a velvety voice. "You're a very alluring woman."

She took a deep breath to banish the memory of that incident. "I'd rather not be reminded of my clumsiness."

"Anyone can trip, especially when they're upset." He looked at her speculatively. "Its funny. I never would have figured you for someone who could be easily spooked."

"I'm not, usually. I explained the circumstances." Before he could pursue the subject she said, "This is a lovely restaurant, but it must seem provincial to you after all of the elegant places in London."

"Believe it or not, I don't go out every night to glamorous restaurants and nightclubs."

"You expect me to believe you stay home and watch television?"

"Sometimes, when I get home from work late."

"What kind of work do you do?"

"I'm a free-lance photographer."

"That sounds like fun."

A look of annoyance crossed David's face as he paused while the waiter refilled the wineglasses and removed their soup plates. When they were alone again he said, "It isn't fun, it's a valid job."

"What do you take pictures of?"

"Anything and everything—fashion layouts, portraits, sporting events. Action shots are tricky, but I find posed subjects equally challenging. Anyone can snap a picture and get a likeness, but capturing the real character of a person is another story. I'll show you some of the things I've done if you're interested."

"I'd like very much to see them. I didn't mean to denigrate your work."

"That's all right, you aren't the first," he said wryly. "A lot of my friends think it's a hobby. They don't understand why I can't always come out to play."

"I suppose it's because you don't really have to work."

"Everyone has to work at something meaningful, otherwise life is pointless," he said quietly.

Melanie was beginning to realize there was a great deal more to David than first impressions had led her to believe. "Will you be able to pick up where you left off when you solve all your household and family problems?"

"That's the best part about being a free lance. I can work here if I ever manage any spare time."

"What is there to photograph here?"

"You, for one thing." He stared at her appraisingly. "I'd like to do a study of you. Your bone structure is exquisite. Would you consider posing for me?"

Melanie began to wonder if she'd fallen for a slick line. David wasn't being seductive, but she had a feeling that would come later. Along with the suggestion that she pose nude.

"I've been asked to do a gallery show and your face would provide a smashing contrast," he continued. "Most of my other subjects have weather-beaten faces that show years of experience."

"You're only talking about a head shot?" she asked warily.

He nodded, gazing at her abstractedly. "I usually prefer to shoot in black and white, but it wouldn't capture all those glorious shadings of gold in your hair. Are they natural?"

"Yes, the result of years in the California sun."

"That means you like the outdoors. Are you interested in sports? I don't really know anything about you. We always seem to talk about me."

"You lead a more interesting life. This trip is the most exciting thing that's happened to me all year—and I'm traveling alone. Does that tell you something?" She laughed.

"A beautiful woman like you should lead a very glamorous existence. Don't tell me *you* stay home every night watching the telly."

"No," Melanie admitted. "I date, but nobody special."

"That's too bad," David murmured.

"Why? I have a good job, a lot of friends and the freedom to do anything I want. A woman doesn't have to be married to be happy."

"How about children? You're so good with Ariel and Ashley. Don't you want to have some of your own?"

"It sounds as though you're interviewing for a wife," she answered lightly. "My advice would be to stick to nannies. If they don't work out it's easier to fire them than to get a divorce."

He raised an amused eyebrow. "You're quite right. I would do a lot of things for my niece and nephew, but marrying someone I didn't love isn't one of them."

"You're in an enviable position. Since the twins satisfy your paternal urge, you don't have to get married."

"You are a very cynical lady. How about love as a reason?"

"At the risk of sounding even more cynical, I'm sure you've been in love before—probably many times."

"There's a difference between love and physical attraction. One lasts forever, the other fades."

"Which one?" She laughed. "Plastic surgeons perform miracles nowadays."

He gazed at her with narrowed eyes. "I don't think you're as misanthropic as you pretend to be. Every human being wants love."

"I suppose so." Melanie sighed unconsciously. "Too bad it isn't guaranteed by the Constitution."

"That would take all the fun out of looking for it." He grinned.

It was a perfect description of David's philosophy of life, she thought. He would go from one woman to another like a bee sipping honey, never pausing for long. His only real commitment was to the twins.

The subject was dropped when the waiter arrived with their entrée, and they didn't return to it. During the rest of dinner they discussed local attractions that Melanie should see.

"You won't want to miss Glastonbury Abbey," David said. "King Arthur and Queen Guinevere were supposed to have been buried there."

"Really?" Melanie's green eyes sparkled. "I always thought they were fictional characters."

"Not at all. Legend has it that monks in the twelfth century discovered their grave. Inside were two skeletons, one of a gigantic man and one of a woman with a lock of golden hair that crumbled at the touch."

"I'm glad they were reunited at the end," Melanie said softly. "Was there also a real Camelot?"

"It was supposed to have been at Cadbury Castle not far away. Roads can still be traced between the two sites."

"I wouldn't miss that for anything! You'll have to draw me a map."

"I'll do better than that, I'll take you there."

"That would be lovely, but can you spare the time? I know you have a lot of estate business to take care of."

"It seems that's all I've been doing lately. I deserve a break. We can go tomorrow if you like."

"I'd like that very much." Melanie was surprised at just how greatly the idea appealed to her. "Do you think the children would enjoy it?" she asked hastily.

"I doubt it, but we can ask them." He gave her an amused look. "If you're reluctant to be alone with me."

She tried to look equally amused. David was entirely too good at reading her thoughts. "Why would you think a thing like that?"

"You said they were good company today. I thought perhaps you might find me dull by comparison," he replied smoothly.

"Not at all, unless you insist on eating American junk food. I'll never achieve the English experience if I hang out with those two."

"I'll be happy to supply any experience you like."

"I think you're due for some R and R in London," she commented dryly.

He chuckled. "You can't blame a chap for trying."

The waiter brought the check. After putting down some bills David said, "I'm afraid there isn't much to do here after dinner."

"That's fine with me," Melanie answered. "It's been a long day and I'm tired. Besides, we really should go home. This is the new nanny's first night with the children. You probably want to be sure everything is okay."

"Fortunately they're not babies, but I would like to check on things if you're finished with your coffee."

"I've had more than enough. It was a delicious dinner."

Lord and Lady Tyndall and their party were leaving at the same time. As they met at the door she said to David, "Would you like to come over for an after-dinner drink and a few hands of bridge?"

"I appreciate the invitation, but we want to get home to the children," he replied, taking Melanie's hand.

Sylvia watched speculatively as they walked away. "That sounded very domestic, didn't it?"

"Don't start matchmaking," her husband warned. He turned to a man in their party. "Women feel the same about a bachelor as nature does about a vacuum. Neither can resist trying to alter the situation."

"That's because it's an unnatural state," Sylvia said calmly.

"David looks perfectly happy to me."

"He does, doesn't he?" she mused.

"I don't suppose it would do any good to tell you not to meddle?"

"None at all." Lady Tyndall smiled. "David needs someone to help him raise those adorable children."

"He already has a lady friend. Didn't you mention that he was going with that woman with the peculiar nickname?"

"Bootsie Addersley. That's not the only thing peculiar about her," Sylvia sniffed. "She's most unsuitable for David. This girl looks a lot more possible."

"They might just be casual friends," her husband pointed out. "And if they're not, they'll discover it on their own."

"Cupid can always use a helping hand." She looked thoughtful. "I must drop over there the first chance I get."

Chapter Three

The twins were excited about a day out with David and Melanie when they found out about it at breakfast the next morning. But they weren't thrilled with the idea of visiting an abbey—especially since they'd never heard of Camelot.

"It was a wonderful play with beautiful music," Melanie told them. "They also made a movie out of it. If there's a video store in the village we can rent it."

"You don't have to go with us if you'd rather stay home," David said.

"There's nothing to do here," Ashley complained.

"You can show Miss Morton around the house and grounds."

"Can we ride our horses?"

"They're still at Mr. Thompson's, and I think it's best if you don't go down there for a while. You're not to ride without me, anyway."

"Well, when can we get them?" Ariel asked.

"As soon as the stables are repaired," David answered. "I'll call a contractor before I leave this morning."

The twins exchanged a glance and came to a telepathic agreement. "We'll go with you," Ashley said.

"I really think you'll enjoy it," Melanie told them.

"There's a flea market in the village," Ariel said ingenuously. "Maybe we could stop there first."

"Not today," David said. "It's quite a drive to Cadbury Castle. Besides, they just have a lot of old junk at flea markets."

"We went to some antique shops in Bath," Ariel said. "They had old stuff, too."

"There's a difference between antiques and junk," he said.

"What's the difference?"

"Several hundred pounds." David laughed.

"It's fortunate for the teaching profession that you took up photography," Melanie remarked dryly.

"All right, suppose you explain it to them."

Luckily for her, the twins were single-minded. "It would be lots of fun," Ashley urged. "They have really neat things like lead soldiers and marbles."

"And funny clothes you can wear to play dress-up," Ariel put in. "Can we go, Uncle David, please?"

"Maybe tomorrow," he said.

"The flea market is only open today. It won't be there for another whole week!"

"That's an eternity to a child," Melanie murmured to David.

"But you wanted to go to Camelot," he protested.

"We'll rent the movie."

"Can we go?" Ariel asked eagerly.

"I suppose so," he answered. "I hope you know what a good friend Miss Warren is."

"It's Melanie. We're on a first-name basis," she said. "Well, if everybody's ready, shall we get started?"

"Right-o." David summoned the butler and said, "We're going out for the day, Bevins. Please inform Miss Morton."

"Yes, sir," the man answered impassively.

As the children raced ahead of them, Melanie said, "Does Bevins ever show any emotion?"

"If he does, I've never seen it. Although, I heard him raise his voice once when he was arguing with Mrs. Crossiter. They detest each other." David sighed. "We're not a very cheery household."

Melanie couldn't deny their obvious shortcomings. "Maybe Miss Morton will be an improvement."

"She isn't exactly Miss Warmth, either," he said sardonically. "She should fit in here nicely."

Before Melanie could comment, Ashley leaned out of the car window. "Come on! All the good things will be gone."

The flea market was held in a large open field on the outskirts of town. It was a jumble of little stalls displaying cheap costume jewelry, used clothing, household equipment, discarded toys and much, much more.

The twins gravitated toward the toys while Melanie and David strolled after them. Every few minutes, one or the other of the children would return to tug at their hands, wanting to show them some plaything they couldn't live without. Unless it was rusty or had sharp edges, David usually bought it for them.

"You're a real pushover, you know that?" Melanie said indulgently.

"I suppose you're any different? If *you* weren't such a soft touch we could be in Camelot right now. That was the kind of romantic spot I had in mind." His teasing voice deepened as he brushed a strand of windblown hair off her forehead.

It was an innocent gesture and she knew he was joking, but his fingers felt subtly caressing on her sensitized skin.

Melanie tried to steel herself against the excitement that raced through her.

"How romantic could it be with two nine-year-olds in tow?" she asked a little breathlessly.

As though to remind him, Ariel tugged on his arm. She was holding a tattered black feather boa that had seen better days. "Look, isn't it beautiful?" she asked excitedly. "Can I have it?"

"What on earth would you do with such a thing?" he asked. "It looks like a deceased animal that led a deprived life before it died."

"I like it. And it's only fifty pence," the little girl wheedled.

"They're offering you that much to dispose of it? Hold out for more," he advised.

"Uncle David!" she exclaimed indignantly.

He was torn between a desire to make his niece happy, and repugnance for the ratty object.

Concealing her amusement, Melanie intervened. "It's lovely, but black is a difficult color to wear," she told Ariel. "It can make your skin appear sallow. Why don't you look for a pink one, or maybe a light shade of blue? Those are good colors for you."

"Good show," David said as the little girl accepted Melanie's opinion and hurried off. "But what if she finds one?"

"Then it's your turn to think up an excuse. Try to find one more creative than the truth." She chuckled.

"I find it difficult to lie to women."

"You're doing fine right now."

They were laughing together when an older woman approached them. The camera around her neck and the airline flight bag over her shoulder identified her as a tourist. She was holding a blackened and dented silver pitcher.

"Excuse me, but can I ask you a question?" She charged ahead without waiting for an answer. "Is there any chance this pitcher was stolen? I've heard a lot of the things at flea markets are, and I wouldn't want to get in trouble with customs back in the U.S."

"I'm sure there won't be any problem," David said. "Your pitcher probably came from somebody's attic."

"You think it's a genuine antique?" the woman asked eagerly.

"I've been told I'm not an expert on the subject." He slanted a laughing glance at Melanie.

She knew what the woman wanted to hear. "It could very well be an antique," she said, ignoring David's incredulous stare. "People today don't always appreciate old family heirlooms."

"You're an American!" the woman exclaimed happily. "It's so nice to meet somebody from home. Where are you from?"

"California," Melanie answered.

"I'm from Chicago, but my cousin's boy moved to San Diego with his family. Do you like living in England?" the woman continued without pausing for breath.

"Well, I—"

"I try to make life interesting for her." David's eyes glinted with devilry as he put his arm around Melanie and kissed her cheek.

The woman gazed at them admiringly. "You're certainly a handsome couple, if you don't mind my saying so. It's no wonder your little girl is so pretty."

"We're certainly blessed," he agreed, drawing Melanie even closer. "Our little girl has a twin brother."

"And we'd better check on both of them, dear," Melanie said sweetly. When they had moved away she said, "What on earth got into you? Why did you let that woman believe we're married?"

"You said to be creative." He grinned. "I was practicing."

"You caught on awfully fast."

"It wasn't difficult to pretend we belong together." He gave her a melting smile.

Remembering the feeling of his lithe body cradled against hers, Melanie didn't have any trouble with the idea either. She quickly banished the silly notion.

"Okay, pal, let's go look for our children," she said lightly. "This might be the only chance I'll have to say that."

"You don't mean it. You'd make a wonderful mother."

The twins converged on them from different directions, both wanting to show off some rare find. They settled the matter by dividing up temporarily. David went with Ashley, and Melanie went with Ariel.

It wasn't the kind of day Melanie had ever spent. She doubted if David had either, but they both enjoyed it, as well as the days that followed.

They took the children on sight-seeing expeditions through ancient castles and quaint villages. They had lunch at picturesque inns and attended a cricket match where Melanie cheered as lustily as the others, even though she had only a sketchy understanding of the rules.

After a full day she was perfectly content to spend a quiet evening at home, although David worried about it.

"I wish there was something more exciting to do," he fretted on the second night they stayed in. "This can't be very much fun for you."

"I'm having a wonderful time," she assured him. "You've taken me places I never would have gone by myself."

"The evenings are so dull, though."

"Is that your subtle way of telling me you're bored with me?" she teased.

"What man could ever get bored with you?" he asked in a husky voice. "No, I'm concerned that you'll get restless and leave. You didn't come on vacation to sit around every night doing nothing."

"You and the twins wear me out so during the day that I'm exhausted by the time dinner is over."

They were having coffee in the softly lit library, sitting next to each other on a couch in front of the fireplace. A cheerful little blaze made the atmosphere cozy.

"You're just being polite. Maybe we could drive into the village tomorrow night and see a movie. Although that isn't much in the way of excitement," he said ruefully.

"I really don't need to be entertained. You've done more than enough for me already."

"Not nearly as much as you've done for me. Your presence here is like a ray of sunshine on a very dark day."

"I'm glad if I could help. You've had a really rough time of it," she said gently, covering his hand with hers.

It was an instinctive gesture of sympathy, but David clasped her hand tightly and turned his face to hers. "You've made life fun again, something it hasn't been for a long time."

Melanie's heightened senses were acutely aware of everything about him, the lock of dark hair that fell over his high forehead, the easy grace of his lean body, the overpowering masculinity that reached out to her like a magnet.

"It will be again," she murmured, unable to drag her eyes from his sensuous mouth. "London isn't that far away. You can go back—for a visit, anyway."

"Everything I want is right here." His fingers combed through her long hair, drawing her face closer to his. "You're an enchanting woman."

Melanie tried to laugh, aware of how volatile the situation was. "Your judgment might be a little clouded. I don't have any competition here."

"That's something you don't have to worry about. No sensible man would want anyone else if he could have you."

"David, I don't—"

He wasn't listening. Drawing her into his arms, he lowered his head. "I've wanted to do this for days." His lips moved over hers, gently at first, like a bee savoring honey.

Melanie knew she should call a halt before things got out of hand, but she couldn't force herself to do it. She *wanted* him to kiss her. Ever since David had held her in his arms that first night, she'd wondered what it would be like. Now she knew. It was like the rest of him—perfect!

When he parted her lips for a deeper kiss, conscious thought was suspended for the moment and sensation took over. His mouth was a flame that warmed her, then set her on fire. The suggestiveness of his tongue was heightened by his hard body molded against hers. When she clasped her arms around his neck, David's embrace tightened.

"Beautiful little Melanie," he said huskily. "You're so responsive. I knew you'd be like this."

"I'm not usually," she said breathlessly, striving desperately for control. Everything was happening too fast. She drew away. "This is a mistake."

"You don't really believe that." He gently lowered her onto the cushions and leaned over her. "Can you honestly say you don't want me?"

She couldn't hide her reaction when his hands caressed her body seductively, creating an aching desire.

"Don't fight it, darling," he said softly. "We need each other."

Melanie's passion suddenly died as she realized his need was merely physical. David was a healthy, virile male who'd been without female companionship for too long. She certainly wasn't immune to the powerful sexual attraction between them, but there had to be something more. Melanie faced the fact that she could easily fall in love with David. Unfortunately, all he was looking for was a bed partner.

She wriggled free of him and stood. "I'm sorry, David, but I don't indulge in casual affairs."

He stared at her in surprise—as though this seldom happened, she thought ironically. Then his expression changed and he got up slowly to face her.

"Does that mean the desire is mutual, but you aren't going to satisfy it?" he asked derisively. "You *will* admit to active participation?"

"I find you very attractive," she said curtly. "That should satisfy your male ego."

"You think that's what this is all about?" His face was abruptly austere. "I don't count my worth by the number of women I can bed."

"I didn't say that."

"Then perhaps you'll explain what happened just now. I didn't seduce you, Melanie. You wanted me as much as I wanted you—or else you're a damn good actress. I didn't think you played those kind of games."

"I don't!" How could she explain that some kind of feeling had to be involved, when he obviously didn't have any for her? "Can't we just let it drop?" she pleaded.

"I suppose I'll have to, since you won't tell me the truth. Just once I wish a woman would say what's really on her mind!"

"Be careful what you wish for." She smiled wryly. "You might get it."

"I'd really like to." His annoyance vanished as he reached out and touched her cheek. "I want to know what I did wrong."

His husky voice made Melanie's nerve ends quiver. Before he could work his spell again she said, "It wasn't anything you did. It was just one of those unfortunate incidents."

His eyes focused on her generous mouth. "I can't really regret it," he said softly.

"Good night, David," she answered firmly.

He didn't try to stop her, but she was very conscious of his impassive gaze watching her leave the room.

As she undressed for bed, Melanie realized she'd have to leave Castlebury Manor. David would never suggest it—not in so many words. He was too much of a gentleman. But the situation would be impossible after what had just happened.

It was too bad. They'd developed a rather good relationship during all those excursions with the twins. The sexual attraction between David and herself had always been present, but never troublesome. It had even added a little extra zing to the occasions. Until tonight.

Melanie blamed herself for not realizing she was playing with fire when she allowed David to kiss her. Not merely permitted, she thought wryly. Responded enthusiastically was more like it. Did she think it would stop there? They weren't teenagers, innocently making out. Her body still glowed where he'd touched her, and her pulse raced when she recalled his stirring kisses. David's expertise could have brought her more ecstasy than she'd ever known.

Too bad that was all he had to offer, a few nights of bliss and then bye-bye baby, drop me a postcard. Her mouth curved sardonically. It would make quite a diary entry, though: *What I did on my summer vacation.*

She turned over restlessly. There was no point in dwelling on what almost was and could never be. It was time to make plans. Much as she'd like to leave immediately, that would be a little awkward. They'd promised to take the twins to a village fair tomorrow in a township nearby. David could take them without her, but the children would be disappointed if she didn't go. They wouldn't understand her spur of the moment decision to leave. Melanie could just imagine David's mocking expression as she struggled to explain her reason.

The alternative was to stay one more day. It shouldn't be too uncomfortable, since they had a full day planned and the children would provide a buffer between herself and David. As for the evening, she'd go to her room right after dinner. He wouldn't believe her excuse that she had to pack and get to bed at a reasonable hour in order to start out early in the morning, but he'd accept it.

That settled her problem, but Melanie still couldn't fall asleep. She was all too conscious of David in the room next door, his long body stretched out in bed wearing only pajama bottoms.

Melanie's plan was a good one, except that nature double-crossed her. She awoke in the morning to the sound of rain pattering on the windows.

"Oh, no!" she groaned, burying her head in the pillow.

Their trip to the fair would have to be canceled. That left her free to leave, but she didn't relish braving another rainstorm like the one that had brought her here. What would they do all day cooped up in the house together? Melanie got up and dressed reluctantly.

The twins weren't any happier than she. "Why did it have to rain today?" Ashley asked petulantly, shoving his cereal away.

"I doubt if it was a plot to make you unhappy," David answered dryly. "Good morning. Did you sleep well?" he asked Melanie with a hint of derision.

"Like a log. It's too bad about the rain," she went on quickly.

"We could go to the fair anyway," Ariel suggested. "Maybe it will stop by the time we get there."

David shook his head. "Your optimism is admirable, but I'm afraid this looks like one of those all day rains. Besides, the fairgrounds would be a sea of mud."

"Then what are we going to do?"

"We've been out every day this week. Surely you can amuse yourselves for one afternoon."

"Doing what?" the little girl persisted.

"I don't know." David looked at Melanie for help.

It was the nanny who answered unexpectedly. Usually she said very little. Wiping her mouth daintily with her napkin she said, "This might be a good time to review your schoolwork. Classes start soon."

"It's summer holidays!" Ashley exclaimed indignantly.

"We don't have to learn anything in the summertime," Ariel agreed.

It was not a happy household that morning. For the first time the twins were cranky, and tension between Melanie and David was just under the surface. Even the servants were affected. Mrs. Crossiter seemed sulkier than usual as she banged things about in the kitchen.

"Is something bothering Mrs. Crossiter this morning?" David asked Bevins ironically, since they all knew that was her perpetual state.

"It's her day off and the rain has spoiled her plans." Bevins' face wore the nearest thing to a smile that Melanie had seen there.

"The best of plans don't work out sometimes." David glanced at Melanie. "You just have to accept the fact."

Ashley reclaimed his uncle's attention. "What can we do today?"

"I have an idea." Melanie lowered her voice conspiratorially. "After Mrs. Crossiter leaves, let's bake cookies."

The twins' faces brightened momentarily, then Ashley's expression dimmed. "She'll know we were in her kitchen and she'll be mad at us."

"What does she do when she gets angry?" Melanie asked.

"She tells Uncle David."

"Then there's no problem. He already knows."

The children looked at each other with dawning delight. "We used to bake biscuits with Mum. Can we, Uncle David?" Ariel asked. "Please!"

"Of course you may." He gave Melanie an appreciative look.

"Let's start right now," Ashley said.

"We have to wait till Mrs. Crossiter leaves," Melanie reminded him.

"How soon do you think that will be?" he asked impatiently.

"Not very long. Why don't you go change out of your good clothes? There's no point in getting flour and stuff all over them."

"I'll help you." Jean folded her napkin and rose.

"We don't need help," Ashley exclaimed in outrage. "We're not babies!"

"Nevertheless, your uncle pays me to supervise you," she said firmly.

After they left, Melanie said, "Poor Miss Morton must be worried about her job. She doesn't have much to do. Of course she will have as soon as I leave." Melanie was paving the way for her announcement, but David didn't give her a chance.

"It's really good of you to be so kind to the children," he said quietly. "I'm in your debt."

"Oh, well, I didn't have anything to do today, either."

"I'm sure you could have found something more stimulating. I'm afraid we're spoiling your holiday."

When he put it that way, how could she say she was leaving? David was only feeling grateful, but it would still make her look unappreciative of his generous hospitality.

"You're wrong, I've had a wonderful time, but I do have to think about leaving," she said carefully.

"Because of last night?"

"No, of course not!"

He knew she was lying. "If I've driven you away I'm sorry, but that's the only thing I regret."

She gave up the pretense. "It's time for me to go, David. What happened last night could very well happen again. We're very attracted to each other."

"Is that bad?" He gave her an appealing smile.

"In this case, it is. Don't ask for an explanation," she said as he opened his mouth. "Just take my word for it."

"All right, if you'll promise not to leave."

"It's the only sensible thing to do. Last night was... uncomfortable for both of us."

"That isn't the way I'd describe it," he said wryly.

Melanie's color rose at the memory of the brief, but passionate interlude between them. How could David look just as sexy this morning in jeans and a sweatshirt as he'd looked last night by romantic firelight?

"You've just demonstrated why I can't stay," she said. "You simply won't accept the situation."

"I'll admit I'm not happy about it, but it's your decision to make. If I promise not to refer to the incident again, will you change your mind?"

"I don't understand why you want me to," she said helplessly.

His face sobered. "You've performed miracles with the twins. Since you came, they've turned back into normal, happy children. You can't know how much that means to me."

"I'm glad to have helped, but I can't stay forever. What difference does it make if I leave now or a week from now?"

"Happiness is a habit, just like sorrow. Every day you spend with them is positive reinforcement. I know it's only a temporary solution, but they'll be going off to school soon and that will keep them busy."

"I've been wanting to talk to you about that," Melanie began, when the children came running back into the room.

"We're all ready," Ariel announced.

"But the coast isn't clear yet. Maybe we can play a game until you-know-who leaves." Melanie winked at the children who giggled delightedly. "Do you know how to play Go Fish? All we need is a deck of cards."

The twins each took one of her hands as she started to lead them out of the dining room. Their faces were animated and they both talked at once as they told her about the card games they knew.

"Melanie?" David called to her. "You see what I mean?"

"Yes, I see. You really play dirty," she said plaintively.

"Does Uncle David cheat?" Ashley asked. Both children looked shocked.

"No, of course not. It was just a joke. On me." Melanie muttered the last words under her breath.

The cookie bake ran into a few obstacles. To begin with, Melanie didn't know the first thing about baking cookies.

Ariel looked at her pityingly. "Didn't your mother ever teach you to make biscuits?"

"Actually, no. She said it would be tampering with the free enterprise system. That's why bakeries were in business."

David was lounging against a cabinet, watching the proceedings with amusement. "Your mother sounds like a very politically motivated woman."

"Not really." Melanie grinned. "She just hated to cook."

The twins were looking at her with worried faces. "What are we going to do?" Ariel asked.

"Not to worry. There must be a cookbook around somewhere." Melanie opened drawers until she found one. "Here we are." She ran a finger down the index page. "We lucked out. There are scads of recipes. What's your pleasure, almond crescents, date-filled oatmeal squares, pecan kisses? Here's one that sounds interesting, penuche strips. I wonder what those are."

David smiled. "I suggest you stick to something simple, since this is your maiden voyage into the culinary arts."

"That doesn't mean I have to be unimaginative. As long as I don't know what I'm doing anyway, I might as well go for the gold." She grinned.

"Too bad you don't carry that adventurous spirit to its logical conclusion," he murmured.

"If you're going to harass the cook you'll have to leave," she said sternly.

Ariel pulled at her sleeve. "Could we make gingerbread men?" Her voice was wistful.

Melanie's mock frown vanished. "Whatever you like, honey," she said gently.

The preparation took hours, since they had to search for each ingredient and the proper utensils. Then everything had to be carefully measured, sifted and mixed. The twins helped Melanie with the instructions, feeling very superior that they had experience and she didn't.

They were all very proud when their first efforts came out of the oven, a little lopsided but smelling delicious. David had left to do some office work, but he returned to sample the result.

"Superb," he pronounced after the first bite.

"It should be, after all our work," Melanie said. "I'll never turn up my nose at another fig newton."

"We'll let you make those penuche things next week when Mrs. Crossiter goes off on her free day again," Ashley promised.

Melanie was abruptly brought back to reality. For a little while this afternoon she'd felt like part of the family. But she wasn't.

"I'm afraid this was my one and only performance." She carefully kept her voice light. "I won't be here next week."

"Where will you be?"

"All over. I have a whole list of things to see."

"We'll go with you," Ariel said anxiously. "Anywhere you want."

"That would be lovely, but it just wouldn't work out. The places I plan to visit are miles from here, too far to bring you back at night."

"We can show you some more places around here," Ashley said eagerly. "There are lots of things you haven't seen yet."

"We never went to Camelot like you wanted," Ariel reminded her. "We'll go there with you."

"A most delightful spot, where cares are all forgot," David sang softly. "How can you pass up a visit to Camelot?"

Melanie kept a firm grip on her emotions. "It's better this way. I'm afraid the reality wouldn't live up to my expectations."

He gazed at her steadily. "Is that really the way you want to go through life, never taking a chance?"

Jean entered the kitchen, saving Melanie the necessity of answering. The nanny looked disapprovingly at the twins. "They shouldn't be eating biscuits this close to dinner."

"It's a special occasion," David said. "We're having a going-away party for Miss Warren."

"Please don't go!" Ariel begged. Both twins turned woeful faces to Melanie. "At least stay until Saturday."

"That's almost another week," Melanie said.

"You mustn't argue with an adult," Jean told Ariel. It was obvious the woman wasn't unhappy to see Melanie go.

Ariel ignored her. "The stables will be finished on Saturday and we're getting our horses," she told Melanie. "I want you to see me ride."

"Me, too," Ashley chimed in. "We're real good."

Melanie looked pleadingly at David, but he remained silent. Without his help, she couldn't disappoint the twins. "Well, maybe I can stay another couple of days, but I don't know about a week."

There was general rejoicing, except for Jean. Her rather thin lips were compressed in a straight line. "I suppose I'd better get the children's dinner started."

"I'm not hungry," Ashley said.

Jean turned to David with a triumphant look, although she didn't comment directly. "I'll give them dinner in the nursery tonight."

When that was met by howls of protest from the twins, David said, "We rather enjoy eating as a family."

"Whatever you say, Mr. Crandall," she answered stiffly.

Melanie waited until the nanny had departed before remarking, "I really don't know why you need her. She doesn't have much to do now, and when school starts she'll have even less."

"The children's clothes need seeing to, and somebody has to keep track of their doctor and dental checkups. Things like that," he said vaguely. "And of course they'll be home on holidays."

"It sounds like a very cushy job to me."

"Would you like it? I offer fringe benefits." He grinned.

"I've heard about customs like yours," she joked. "They're called *droit du seigneur*—privilege of the nobleman."

"If you were my employee, it would indeed be a privilege," he murmured.

No private conversation ever lasted long around the twins. "Can we go out to dinner?" Ashley asked.

With a last, mischievous smile at Melanie, David turned to his nephew. "It's too wet out. Mrs. Crossiter left dinner for us in the fridge."

After dinner was over and the children had gone to bed, Melanie and David took their coffee into the library. She was a little wary after last night's fiasco, but he respected her stated wishes. David wasn't above teasing her suggestively when the children were present, but not when he and Melanie were alone.

They talked idly for a while before David said, "I want to thank you for giving the children a wonderful day."

"I enjoyed it, too. The only other thing I ever baked was a potato." She grinned.

"No one would guess. You looked very natural in the kitchen with flour on the tip of your nose and two youngsters getting in your way."

"Just call me June Cleaver." When he looked blank, Melanie explained. "She was the ideal mother on 'Leave It to Beaver,' an old television show about an impossibly perfect family. Obviously I'm not right for the part."

"You gave a good performance today. I didn't know you were acting."

"I wasn't. It's funny, but I never realized having a family could be so satisfying. This visit could ruin my whole life," she said with a quick laugh.

"Or change it for the better. Maybe you'll have second thoughts about reality not living up to your expectations."

Melanie refused to let the charged moment develop into anything more. "It was sweet of the twins to offer to go to Camelot when they don't really want to."

"You made a couple of true friends." David's smile changed to a slight frown. "I wish they weren't so dependent on adults. They don't seem to have any playmates around here."

"That's because they don't know any of the local children."

"They haven't lived here very long. I've enrolled them in a school not far away. I hope that will help."

"They'll still have the same problem during holidays and summer vacation."

"What can I do about it?" David asked helplessly.

"I have a rather radical suggestion. Why not send them to the village school, at least for a year."

"The twins have always gone to public school," he said slowly. "Richard and I did, too."

"These are different circumstances. They've had so many tragic changes in their lives. It seems a shame to send them off to someplace new when they're just getting accustomed to living here and being with you. Of course it would tie *you* down somewhat. I suppose you're counting on returning to London when they go back to school."

"Not permanently, by any means. I can go back and forth once they're settled and the household is running smoothly. It's not myself I'm worried about. I'd want to be sure I was doing the right thing for the children. How do I know they'd be happy at the village school?"

"You don't, but they're not all that high on going to a new public school."

David looked at her sharply. "How do you know that?"

"By talking to them," she said succinctly.

"They told you that?"

"Not in so many words, but their lack of enthusiasm spoke volumes."

"Is that all?" he scoffed. "No child wants to go back to school when summer is over."

"If you say so," Melanie answered neutrally.

"You really think it would be a good idea?" he asked, uncertainty written on his face.

"*I* do, but you're their guardian. Think about it, though," she couldn't help adding. "They'd be in a familiar environment, with the one person who spells security, and they wouldn't be virtual strangers in their own village."

"You make some powerful arguments," David said slowly.

"It's something to mull over, anyway. You don't have to make up your mind this minute."

"I might as well. It won't get any easier." He was silent for a long moment, staring at her with narrowed eyes. "All right, I'll give it a go."

"You can always send them to the other school if it doesn't work out." Melanie was a little apprehensive now that she'd convinced him.

"It will." He grasped her hands and brought them to his lips. "You're my good luck charm."

"Call on me anytime. No problem too big or too small." She smiled.

"I'll bet you could even make sense out of my incomprehensible ledgers."

"Why not? I'm on a roll."

She was only joking, but David took her seriously. "You wouldn't mind taking a look at them?"

"Are you sure you want me to? I mean, a person's finances are rather private."

"I shouldn't have asked. You get paid for that kind of expertise."

"That wasn't what I meant at all," she protested. "After everything you've done for me, it's the least I can do, if that's what you'd like."

"You don't owe me anything."

"Maybe not, but that doesn't mean I can't return a favor. Don't argue," she said as he prepared to. "Go get your books."

David left the room briefly and returned with an armload of leather-bound ledgers. He dumped them on the coffee table, shaking his head ruefully.

"If you can decipher these, I'll be a true believer. They look to me like they're written in Sanskrit."

"Let's see what we have here."

Melanie examined the books, confidently at first, then with growing perplexity. She asked questions, some of which David could answer, most he couldn't.

"Your father had a rather unconventional way of making entries," she said. "A lot of them seem to be duplicates, yet I can't be sure."

"That's what's driving me bonkers. The other accounts are just as inconsistent."

"Well, let's see if we can figure them out. Look at this last entry. Is it rental income, or does it come from investments?"

David put an arm around her shoulders, leaning closer so he could study the figures. Melanie wasn't even conscious of it until she turned her head to ask another question. Their faces were so close that her lips almost grazed his cheek. She held her breath, unable to turn away.

"I'm not sure, but I think it's..." His words trailed off as he, too, became aware of the intimacy of their position.

His arm tightened unconsciously and tiny lights flickered in the depths of his blue eyes. They stared at each other for a seemingly endless moment while Melanie battled the warm tide of desire that threatened to engulf her.

It took every ounce of self-control to break the electric bond between them, but she finally managed to wrench her gaze away from his. She closed the ledger and stacked it on top of the others.

"You were right about your father's bookkeeping system," she said without looking at him. "I thought I could straighten it out in a couple of hours, but this is a full-time job."

"At least I don't feel so stupid if you can't understand it, either."

"It will take a professional several weeks to track down all the inconsistencies and put in a new system for you. I suggest you hire one as soon as possible. You could be losing a great deal of money through sheer negligence."

"Have you ever come across anything this fouled up?"

"This is one of the more mismanaged examples, but estate transfers can be very complicated. Don't worry about it, a good C.P.A. will straighten you out."

David looked at her consideringly. "Will you take the job?"

"You're joking, aren't you?" She stared back at him incredulously. "I live on the other side of the world!"

"I'm not asking you to move here, just to take me on as a client. Don't you ever do a job in another city?"

"Yes, but that's different."

"Why?"

"Well...for one thing, I'm on vacation." That was all she could come up with.

"I suppose I can muddle along for another couple of weeks, or whenever your vacation is over."

"I can't ask for more time off. I'm expected back at the office."

"It won't be time off. You'll be working." David looked at her appealingly. "This isn't for me, it's for the children. It's their inheritance I'm trying to conserve. Everything's been thrown at me at once and I don't know where to turn."

"There are a lot of competent accountants in England," she said weakly.

"I'm sure you're right, but I don't know any. I trust you." When she hesitated, he said persuasively, "You're already here, so it's even simpler than doing somebody's books in another city. Just close your eyes and imagine you're in Chicago."

"Not even close." She laughed.

"All right, pick a city. I'll pay anything you ask. What do you say?"

Melanie refused even to consider the idea originally, but it wasn't actually that outrageous. She did travel in her work, and she *was* here already. The opportunity to spend more time with David and the twins wasn't the incentive, she assured herself. The job itself was. David's books would present quite a challenge.

"Okay, you've just hired yourself an accountant." She smiled. "I'll call my office in the morning. Everyone is going to be terribly jealous, but since I'm bringing in a new client, there won't be any problem with my staying on for as long as the job takes."

"Excellent!" Something flared in his eyes and was masked instantly. "Let's have a drink to celebrate." While he was pouring two snifters of brandy, the doorbell rang.

"It sounds as if you have company," she remarked.

"I hope that's Mrs. Crossiter saying she forgot her key."

"She'd never do anything that human." Melanie grinned.

"Hard to believe, but it has happened." He raised his glass. "Forget about her. Here's to our new relationship. May it be successful."

As they clinked glasses, a female voice drawled from the doorway, "It looks as if I got here just in time. Is this a private celebration, or can anybody join in?"

Bevins appeared behind the woman. "Lady Hermione Addersley," he announced.

Chapter Four

The woman lounging in the doorway was stunning. It was a better word to describe her than beautiful, although she gave that illusion. Her red hair was cleverly cut to soften her rather sharp features, and she exuded the confidence of a beauty. Her excellent figure didn't need any artifice. It was shown off to full advantage in a black turtleneck sweater and a very short gray skirt, a casual outfit, but unmistakably expensive. Her relaxed pose and the smile on her face were deceptive. She was assessing the situation with narrowed eyes.

David had frozen initially. He recovered swiftly. "Bootsie! This is a surprise. What are you doing way out here in the country?"

"Since you won't come to London, we decided to come to you."

"We?" he asked warily.

"Pamela and Dennis Hightower are with me. They're waiting to show Bevins which suitcases to bring in from the car."

"You're staying over?" David asked.

"Well, of course, darling. You don't think we'd motor all this way just to say hello and ta ta?"

"I don't suppose so, although you've done more impulsive things in your day."

She laughed merrily. "We *have* had some rather ripping times together, haven't we? London isn't the same without you, luv. When are you coming home?"

Melanie began to feel increasingly unwelcome. That was what the woman intended, she thought grimly. But David wasn't doing anything to counter the impression. Now that his lady friend was here he didn't need *her*.

"If you'll excuse me, I have something to do," she said evenly.

"Don't go!" His fingers closed around Melanie's wrist, an action that didn't go unnoticed by the other woman. "Forgive my bad manners. I haven't introduced you two." After the introductions had been made, David said, "Melanie is visiting from America."

"How nice." Bootsie looked at her without expression. "Where are you staying?"

"She's our guest—the children's and mine," he said smoothly. "Melanie has been a great help with the twins."

"Where are the little angels?" Bootsie was all eager anticipation when she turned to David. "I brought them some gifts."

"That was sweet of you. The children are asleep now, but you can see them first thing in the morning." His eyes twinkled with mischief. "They get up very early."

"But *I* don't, as you very well know." She slanted a sensuous glance at him.

Melanie got the picture, as she was supposed to. It annoyed her nonetheless. Surely David could do better than this crass woman whose charm must be limited to the bedroom, since it wasn't evident here. Obviously charm was not his first priority.

Fortunately for David, the arrival of another couple saved him from having to reply to Bootsie's suggestive remark.

The Hightowers were an attractive couple who'd been given an extra measure of good looks to make up for their lack of brain power. If they were interested in anything beyond having a good time, it wasn't apparent to Melanie, as she discovered quite soon.

"So this is where they buried you," Dennis Hightower said jokingly to David. "We had a devil of a time finding this place."

"To quote from Melanie's compatriot, Mark Twain, the reports of my death are greatly exaggerated," David said dryly.

"You might as well be," Pamela Hightower declared. "How do you stand all this solitude? Not to mention the lack of decent restaurants and clubs anywhere in the vicinity. It would make me quite strange!"

"How could we tell the difference, my dear?" Her husband laughed.

"I suppose *you* could exist outside of London," she pouted.

"Jolly easily. I'd simply get on a plane for Paris."

"I do hope you won't be too bored here. How long were you planning to stay?" David asked casually.

"Only a couple of days. We're on our way to a house party at the Metcalfs'. It's their last bash of the season before they come back to civilization."

"Why don't you come with us, darling?" Bootsie took David's arm and hugged it to her side. "They'd love to see you. It's been an eternity!"

"I haven't been away that long," he protested. "You make it sound like years."

"It seems like it to me," she answered softly.

"Do come," Pamela urged. "We'll have a smashing time. You know how zany the Metcalfs are."

David was aware of Melanie's sardonic gaze. He also knew the tenaciousness of his friends, so he tried to shelve the subject. "It's certainly something to think about." He pulled on a velvet cord to summon the butler. "Right now, I imagine you want to unpack. We'll need to have two rooms made up," he said to Bevins who had appeared.

"Yes, sir. Mrs. Crossiter hasn't returned yet. Shall I ask Miss Morton to attend to it?"

"I suppose you'll have to."

"Put me in the room next to the Viscount's," Bootsie instructed the man, giving David a suggestive smile.

"Miss Warren is in that room, your ladyship, but we will endeavor to make you comfortable in the rose room at the other end of the hall."

The butler's face was as impassive as ever, but Melanie got the impression that he was enjoying himself. Underneath that stoic exterior was a lively sense of mischief, she suspected.

Bootsie reacted angrily to the news that Melanie had usurped her place, but before she could comment, Pamela said, "I'd better hang up my clothes before they get too terribly wrinkled. I don't suppose you have maids to take care of it for us?" she asked David.

'We have a couple of cleaning women who come in every morning, if you can wait until then," he answered blandly.

"I honestly don't know how you manage!"

"It's amazing what the human spirit can take without cracking," he agreed.

She nodded. "It must be difficult for you."

"Pamela, you goof, don't you know when you're being had?" Her husband chuckled. "Come along, let's go upstairs and unpack. Then we'll see what kind of entertainment we can scare up. Are you coming, Bootsie?"

Eyeing Melanie, she answered, "No, you two go ahead. I'll do it later."

"Can I fix you a drink?" David asked, to cover the awkward little silence that fell.

"A gin and bitters would be divine," Bootsie replied, trailing a playful finger down his cheek. "You know just how I like it, darling."

Lighten up, Melanie wanted to tell her. I know you're having an affair with David and I couldn't care less. So stop trying to impress me.

As he picked up a cut crystal decanter Bootsie said, "I have so much to tell you. You'll never guess who's getting a divorce!"

"You're right, the possibilities are endless," he answered ironically.

"Don't be so cynical," she pouted. "This will shock even *your* socks off. It's the Wellingtons!"

David's eyebrows lifted as her prediction hit home. "I thought theirs was the perfect marriage."

"We all did. That's what makes it so delicious. All this time he's been having an affair with his manicurist. Can you believe it?" Bootsie laughed merrily. "Valerie got even with him, though. Wait till I tell you what she did."

"This can't be very interesting for Melanie," he said, glancing at her uncomfortably. "Perhaps we can postpone the newscast until a later date."

"I'm sure she realizes we have a lot to catch up on. You don't mind, do you?" Bootsie asked Melanie. She continued without waiting for an answer. "On a happier note, Frances and Ian are finally getting married. You simply have to move back to town, David. There will be all sorts of parties."

"I'll be there for the wedding, certainly. When is it going to be?"

"Not until December, but surely you're planning to return before then. What is there to keep you here in this godforsaken place?"

"A slight matter of two children and an estate to run."

"You don't have to isolate yourself here to fulfill your obligations. That's what servants and business managers are for. I just don't understand you, David."

He looked at her impassively. "I suppose that's true."

"Don't get me wrong," she said hastily. "I adore those two precious children, but they need to be with their peers. They'll be happier in boarding school and so will you."

Melanie waited to hear what David would answer, but Dennis called down from the stairs.

"Bootsie, come up here right away. Pamela has a crisis."

A look of annoyance crossed Bootsie's face. "Tell her I'll be up in a few minutes," she called back.

"She'll be having hysterics by then. She needs you now."

"Oh, all right," Bootsie muttered, stalking out the door.

"Pamela probably forgot her favorite lipstick," Melanie remarked acidly when she and David were alone.

"She is a bit of an airhead, but she means well."

"Which is more than I can say for your insensitive girlfriend. She'd make a great matron at the Oliver Twist orphanage. I adore those two precious children," Melanie mimicked in an affected voice. "If you believe that, I have a few choice acres of swampland I'd be willing to sell you."

"Aren't you being a little hard on her?"

"*I'm* judging her intellectually. You obviously use a different standard."

David looked at Melanie's flushed cheeks speculatively. "Bootsie has never been exposed to children," he said smoothly.

"They're not a disease!"

"I only meant that perhaps her maternal instinct might be stirred if she got to know them better."

"When did you have in mind? Between her dressmaker fittings and the endless parties?" Melanie banged down her brandy snifter and stood. "I don't know why I bother. It doesn't matter to me what you do with your life."

"I thought we were talking about her relationship to the children," he said softly.

"Can you honestly see her as a surrogate mother?"

"Maybe not, but you're rushing things just a trifle. Bootsie and I haven't made any commitment to each other."

He might not think so, but if he escaped from that man-eater it would be a miracle. Women like her succeeded through sheer persistence. She would probably blindside him one night while they were making love.

Melanie didn't want to think about that. "What kind of a name is Bootsie for a grown woman, anyway?" she asked crossly.

"I've forgotten the origin, but she's had it since school days."

Dennis joined them, shaking his head. "Well, this one's going to cost me."

"What was the crisis?" David asked.

"A bottle of perfume spilled in her suitcase. Pamela says she'll need a whole new wardrobe."

"Surely her clothes can be cleaned."

"I jolly well hope so. Those dresses cost a bloody arm and a leg."

The two women returned, Pamela looking surprisingly cheerful. "That nanny of yours is a positive angel, David. She thinks she can get the spots out."

"That's good news!" her husband said fervently.

"I'll still have to replace everything," she said, dashing his hopes. "The scent will never come out."

"That was your best perfume," he reminded her.

"Yes, but who wants to go about smelling like Scandalous perfume on every occasion? People will think I bought great quantities at a bargain basement."

"Well, don't worry about it tonight," Bootsie said. "Let's all go down to the pub in the village and drown our sorrows."

"David will have to buy." Dennis grinned. "My wife plans to bankrupt me."

"Not to worry," David answered. "You're my guests one hundred percent. Is everybody ready?"

"We'll be too crowded in one car," Bootsie remarked casually. "I'll go with David and the rest of you can take Dennis's car."

"That won't be necessary." Melanie spoke up for the first time. "I'm not going."

"You've been cooped up in the house all day," David protested. "It will do you good to get out."

"I'm rather tired. I think I'll go to bed and read."

"I'd really like you to come," he said quietly.

"Don't be pushy, darling." Bootsie linked her arm in his and pulled him toward the door. "She's old enough to know what she feels like doing."

David looked as though he wanted to try further argument. But Bootsie didn't give him a chance, and Melanie wasn't receptive. Finally he allowed himself to be led away. They all left in a flurry of jokes and laughter.

Melanie stared after them, feeling depressed. David hadn't taken long to revert to his old ways. Once a playboy, always a playboy, she thought bitterly. He romanced whatever woman he was with at the moment, and dropped her as soon as the next one appeared on the scene. Melanie ignored the fact that David had asked her to come along.

Jean appeared in the doorway carrying a dress over her arm. She glanced around the room. "Where is Mrs. Hightower?"

"They've all gone into the village."

The nanny looked disappointed. "I wanted to tell her I got the spot out of one of her gowns, anyway."

"How wonderful."

Jean didn't notice Melanie's ironic tone of voice. "Yes, I had to be terribly careful. The fabric is so delicate." She held the dress up. "Isn't it gorgeous? They both have such exquisite wardrobes. Did you see that outfit her ladyship had on?"

"It was a sweater and skirt."

"But she looked so elegant in it. The peerage have a certain flair that's unmistakable." For the first time since she'd arrived, Jean's face was positively animated.

The woman was obviously impressed by titles. David had probably disappointed her by being so down to earth. Jean didn't know it was only an act, Melanie thought sourly.

"I'm going to bed," she said abruptly. "I'll turn out the lights down here and save Bevins the trouble."

"No, I'll do it. I still have to press her ladyship's clothes."

"That's not part of your job."

"Oh, I don't mind. I like doing it. She's ever so nice."

"I'll bet you could get an argument on *that*," Melanie muttered under her breath.

It had been a busy day, but Melanie wasn't really tired. After a warm bath that was meant to relax her, she got into bed with a book. That often made her sleepy, but not tonight.

She stared at the words, seeing images of David and Bootsie instead, disturbingly intimate images. Were they planning a romantic reunion for later tonight? How could she doubt it? They'd been apart for a long time.

Melanie turned off the light and closed her eyes determinedly. She certainly wasn't going to listen for them to come home! An hour later she was still wide awake—and David hadn't returned. At least not to his own bedroom.

It took a long time for her to fall asleep that night.

Melanie was up early in spite of her lack of sleep. She dressed and went down to breakfast reluctantly, dreading a repeat of last night's brittle chatter. Fortunately her fears were unfounded. The twins and their nanny were the only ones at the breakfast table.

"The upper classes always sleep in," Jean informed her after Melanie asked about the others.

"Is that supposed to be a virtue?" Melanie asked coldly. When a loud crash came from the kitchen she remarked, "I see Mrs. Crossiter's day off didn't do much for her disposition."

"Bevins just told her the Viscount has houseguests," Julia, the pretty housemaid, whispered as she refilled the coffee cups.

"I'll bet Bevins enjoyed that." Melanie grinned.

"Lady Addersley has stayed here before. She sleeps until noon and wants her breakfast in bed."

"You must have something better to do than gossip," Jean told the girl disapprovingly.

"When is Uncle David going to get up?" Ashley asked. "He told us he'd take us someplace today if it wasn't raining, and it isn't." The storm had passed over, leaving the sky a clear blue.

"We missed the fair, but there's another one in Stepfield Greens," Ariel said. "We could go there today."

"That would be neat!" her brother said. "I'll go upstairs and see if he's awake yet."

"You're not to disturb your uncle," Jean said firmly.

"If he doesn't get up soon it will be too late to go."

"You'd better find something else to do. The Viscount has houseguests. He's undoubtedly made plans with them for today."

"But he promised!"

"That was before the company came. You mustn't be selfish," Jean admonished. "Your uncle has spent enough time with you."

Melanie tried to control her temper. She had no authority to reprimand the nanny, even though the woman had as much sensitivity as a potted plant! The children looked both hurt and resentful.

"Maybe he'll be up soon," she told them gently. "It's still early yet."

"But Miss Morton says he won't take us," Ariel said with a woeful face.

"She doesn't know that." Melanie gave the nanny a baleful look.

"You shouldn't coddle children," Jean said. "They have to learn that adults have rights, too."

"The right to go back on their word?" Melanie demanded.

Jean pushed back her chair and stood. "I don't think this conversation is seemly. If you'll excuse me, I have some things to attend to."

The twins waited impatiently for her to leave. "Maybe you could take us," Ashley suggested to Melanie.

"Will you?" Ariel asked. Both children looked at her hopefully.

"I don't see why not."

Melanie decided she'd better get out of the house before she did battle with everyone in it! David certainly wouldn't miss her. She was doing him a favor. He and Bootsie could continue where they left off last night.

"Can we go right now?" Ashley asked eagerly.

"First I have to find out where this place is. Do you know how to get there?"

"We've been there lots of times," Ariel assured her.

"How far is it from here?"

"You mean how many kilometers?"

"I'd prefer it in miles, but never mind, we'll find it."

Melanie's confidence was misplaced. She did eventually find Stepfield Greens, but not without stopping several times for directions. It was also a lot farther than the children had indicated.

They didn't arrive at the fairgrounds until almost noon, but it was worth the many detours. The twins were ecstatic at all the noise and bustle. They raced from one exhibit to another, pulling Melanie along.

Her favorites were the craft displays, but the children weren't interested in hand-knit sweaters and needlepoint pillows, no matter how beautiful. They preferred the mouth-watering array of homemade cakes, tarts and cookies. Melanie bought a generous sampling without much urging.

They wandered through the grounds eating currant buns while the children chattered on excitedly. The time passed quickly and pleasantly.

"Can we go to the Punch and Judy show?" Ashley asked, after they'd watched the blue ribbon awards for prize livestock.

"Sure, that sounds like fun," Melanie said. "I didn't know they even had those anymore. Lead the way."

"It isn't until four o'clock."

"That's pretty late," Melanie said dubiously. "We have a long ride home afterward."

"Please!" both children implored.

"I'd have to phone your uncle and ask his permission."

"What if he says no?"

"Then we can't go. I don't think he'd mind, though," she said after a look at their disappointed faces. He was too busy to worry about his responsibilities, Melanie thought grimly.

When she found a pay telephone and called Castlebury Manor, the line was busy. She dialed repeatedly and got a busy signal each time.

"You can call later," Ashley said, impatient at the delay. "Come on, let's go watch that man playing the harmonica."

Melanie became annoyed when her frequent calls to David were unsuccessful. She saw no reason to disappoint the twins just because his girlfriend and her pals monopolized the phone all afternoon. Requesting permission was only a courtesy anyway. He wanted the children to have a good time.

Melanie felt she'd made the right decision when she saw how much the children enjoyed the performance. It was the perfect ending to a fun-filled day.

The ride home wasn't as pleasant. Melanie got lost again, this time where there was no one to ask for directions.

"If I come to one more roundabout, I'm going to say something you shouldn't hear," she exclaimed.

"I think you took a wrong turn at the last one," Ashley said.

"Thanks for noticing," she answered grimly.

"Are you mad at us?" Ariel asked in a subdued voice.

"No, darling, I'm annoyed at myself," Melanie said remorsefully. "It's almost time for your dinner and we're still miles from home."

"I'm not hungry," Ashley said.

"Me, either," Ariel agreed.

"I don't doubt it after all the junk we ate." Melanie smiled. "I don't think I'd mention it to Miss Morton."

"She isn't much fun," Ariel complained.

"I don't think that's one of the requirements for a nanny—which is a good thing in her case." Melanie immediately regretted the remark, accurate though it was. "I'm sure you'll like her a lot when you get to know her better."

"Did you have a nice nanny when you were little?"

"Not very many people in my country have nannies."

"Then who took care of you?"

"My mother," Melanie answered reluctantly, not wanting to remind the twins of their loss.

"Ashley says if Uncle David gets married, his wife will be kind of like our mother," Ariel said. "I don't think I'd like that."

"It would be all right if he married Melanie," Ashley said.

"In your dreams," Melanie muttered.

Ariel looked at her with a worried frown. "Don't you like Uncle David?"

"Of course I do, honey." She tried to sound sincere, which was difficult. At the moment Melanie wasn't crazy about him.

"A lot of ladies like Uncle David," Ashley said. "When we stayed with him at his town house in London, they rang up all the time. Lady Addersley called almost every day."

"I'm not surprised." Melanie stared straight ahead at the road. "She might even be your new mother."

Both twins considered it. Then Ariel said, "I'd rather have you."

"I'm very flattered, but that isn't possible."

"Why not?"

"People have to fall in love before they get married," Melanie explained carefully.

"Like Beauty fell in love with the Beast?"

"That was okay, but I liked the Lion King better," Ashley said. "Especially the part where he gets back at the bad lion."

Melanie breathed a sigh of relief when they started to argue the merits of their favorite movies and forgot about her.

It was quite late when they finally reached Castlebury Manor. Melanie was prepared to apologize; she wasn't prepared for what awaited her.

David shot out of the library at the first ring of the bell, like a fighter raring to do battle. He beat Bevins to the door and threw it open, towering in the doorway like an avenging angel.

His eyes glittered with blue fire as he confronted Melanie. "Where the hell have you been?"

After a shocked glance at their uncle, the children scampered past him and up the stairs.

"I'm sorry we're a little late, but—" Melanie began.

"Is that what you call it? A *little* late? I was about to alert the police!"

"Don't you think you're overreacting just a trifle? I tried to—"

"I'm sorry if my concern upsets you," he interrupted. "What did you expect me to do? Simply overlook the fact that you disappeared with my niece and nephew?"

The injustice of the situation infuriated Melanie. "If you'd kept your promise to take them somewhere today, I wouldn't have had to."

"Oh, so now it's *my* fault."

"Well, *I* wasn't the one who stayed up all night doing who knows what, and then couldn't bother to get up in the morning."

"For your information, I came downstairs only slightly later than usual. And if you'd come with us last night you'd have known what I was doing."

"Your love life couldn't interest me less. As far as I'm concerned, you can do whatever you like."

His firm mouth thinned even more. "I'm gratified that I have your permission, but I'd prefer that you stick to the subject. Why didn't you tell someone where you were going?"

For the first time, Melanie was on shaky ground. She'd been so annoyed at David that she'd forgotten to leave him a message. He had to know the children were with her, though. Melanie's annoyance returned.

"Miss Morton had breakfast with us. She knew the twins were clamoring to get out of the house after being cooped up all day yesterday. Did you want *me* to let them down, too?"

His jaw clenched at the implied accusation. "I *expected* you to act responsibly. You're lucky I didn't call the police."

"I wish you had," she answered flippantly. "They could have given me directions. I got lost."

"Where did you go?"

"To a fair at Stepfield Greens."

"That's way to hell and gone from here! Whatever possessed you to go there?"

"I didn't know it was that far. Ashley said they were having a fair, and both kids were disappointed over missing the one here. So, I just thought it was a good idea," she finished lamely.

"Couldn't you at least have telephoned when you knew you were going to be late?"

"I *did* phone! I wore a path to that blasted booth, but your line was always busy. If you're looking for somebody to blame, try your long-winded girlfriend."

"Putting the blame on an innocent person to excuse your own thoughtless and negligent behavior is reprehensible," he said coldly.

Melanie's temper flared out of control at his defense of the other woman. "I didn't realize it was forbidden to criticize her ladyship. Of course *you* have reason to overlook her faults. I don't."

"Why are jealous women so irrational?" he muttered impatiently.

"Jealous?" Melanie howled in outrage. "Of what? She doesn't have anything I want."

His expression chilled even more. Before he could lash back, Bootsie came down the stairs. "What on earth is going on down here?" she asked.

"Melanie and I are having a discussion."

"It sounds more like a small-scale war." Bootsie laughed merrily. "I could hear you all the way upstairs. What are you two fighting about?"

"We are not fighting," David answered in a clipped tone. "Would you please excuse us for a few moments while we settle something."

"I've said all I have to say." Melanie's body was taut with fury.

He faced her with equal anger. "But *I* haven't."

Bootsie hugged his arm against her body. "I've never seen you like this, darling. I'm getting positively turned on."

"Don't say I never did anything for you." Melanie gave them a disgusted look and ran up the staircase, brushing by Dennis and Pamela who were coming down.

Dennis turned to stare first at her retreating back, then at David. "What the devil was that all about?"

"Just a slight misunderstanding." David forced a smile. "Why don't you all go into the library for cocktails? I'll join you in a few minutes."

Bootsie tightened her grip on his arm. "You'd better let her cool off first. Americans are so excitable."

"That's true," Pamela agreed. "You always read about them pulling out a gun and popping away at someone."

"That's ridiculous!" David exclaimed.

"Bootsie's right, though." Dennis took his other arm and propelled him toward the library. "I stay far away from Pammy when we have one of our little dust-ups."

"And sometimes when we don't," his wife said dryly.

"What we all need is a good, stiff drink," he said hastily.

Melanie slammed her bedroom door hard, needing to vent her rage on something. The nerve of the man, shouting at her because she was a few minutes late bringing the children home! At least *she* was trying to make a couple of lonely kids happy, while *he* was sleeping off a night of revelry.

She refused to admit that what cut the deepest was David's defense of Bootsie. He'd downplayed their relationship, but his feelings were undeniable if he refused to allow the slightest criticism of her.

Melanie tried to tell herself they deserved each other. The twins would be the losers, but that wasn't really her problem. It was a shame, because they were nice kids who'd gotten a terrible break, but who ever said life was fair? The sooner she got on with her own life the better.

Melanie went to the closet for her suitcase. David had made it impossible to stay here any longer. She'd get a room at an inn someplace and continue her interrupted journey in the morning. With any luck, she wouldn't have to see him again.

Melanie uttered an exclamation of annoyance when she discovered her suitcase wasn't in the closet. Bevins must have taken it to a storeroom somewhere. Muttering unflattering words about officious servants, she strode to the door and flung it open. David was standing outside with his hand up, ready to knock.

She scowled at him. "What did I do *now?*"

"I want to talk to you," he said quietly.

"The feeling isn't mutual."

"Please, Melanie, we have to talk and I prefer not to do it in the hallway." He took her arm and urged her back into the bedroom, closing the door.

She pulled her arm away and held herself stiffly. "We have nothing more to say to each other. If you came for an apology, forget it! I didn't do anything wrong."

"Will you at least admit you could have told somebody where you were going?"

"Well, I suppose so," she conceded grudgingly. "It simply slipped my mind. I just assumed you'd know the twins were with me when we were all missing—I mean, when we weren't here."

"I did make that assumption, but when it got late and there was no word from you I became frantic."

"I explained that, but you were so busy defending your girlfriend that you wouldn't listen. She tied up the telephone all afternoon."

"I was on the phone, too. The contractor called several times to discuss the renovation of the stables."

"I understand. Nothing is ever *her* fault," Melanie said sarcastically. "I'm the one who's to blame."

David took a deep breath. "There isn't any blame involved. I overreacted out of concern. I was afraid something had happened to you."

"To the children, you mean."

"And also to you. You're unfamiliar with the countryside and our driving customs. When it got later and later, I was sure you'd had an accident."

For the first time Melanie realized what he must have gone through. He'd lost his brother and sister-in-law that way, very recently. "I'm sorry," she said penitently. "I guess it was thoughtless of me."

"I should have guessed you got lost." His sober face lightened in a smile. "You have a terrible sense of direction."

She couldn't deny the truth. "I wouldn't have taken them if I'd know it was so far. The little devils didn't tell me that. They really had a wonderful time, though, if it's any consolation."

"I wish I could have gone with you, but it would have been difficult to get away. Houseguests rather complicate matters, especially when they're unexpected."

The reminder of his jet-setting friends and the pointless life they all led, effectively doused Melanie's sympathy. "Well, first things first."

David sighed. "That's not really fair. I can't help it if people descend on me unannounced. What was I supposed to do, turn them away?"

"Are you asking for my advice?"

He ignored her derisive tone. "I've spent a lot of time with the twins lately. I don't think one day's defection on my part is going to undermine their security."

"Especially since you have me to pinch-hit. Well, don't count on my help anymore. I'm leaving."

"Because of a disagreement where we both said things we didn't mean?"

"People's true feelings come out when they're angry, but that's beside the point. It's time for me to move on. You have a full house, and five is an awkward number."

Something flickered in his eyes. "You're leaving because of Bootsie."

"I didn't say that!"

"What else can I think? You obviously don't care for her."

"It has nothing to do with *you,* if that's what you believe. I simply find her shallow and boring. I'm sorry if that offends you," Melanie said stiffly.

"I wish I knew how to convince you that Bootsie and I aren't involved."

She shrugged. "Why does it matter?"

"Because I don't want you to go," David answered in a deepened voice. "And neither do the twins," he offered as an added inducement.

Melanie's heart had leapt for a moment. It plunged abruptly. "I'll miss them." She stressed the pronoun slightly. "But I'm still leaving. You'll just have to ask Bootsie to share you."

"I give up!" A muscle twitched in David's square jaw. "You are the most close-minded woman I've ever encountered."

"Then you should be glad to get rid of me."

"Very possibly," he snapped. "Unfortunately I'm stuck with you for the next couple of weeks."

"Is your hearing going, along with your taste?" she stormed. "As soon as I locate my suitcase, I'm out of here."

"You forget we have a business arrangement," he said coldly. "I hired you to overhaul my bookkeeping system."

"You have to be kidding! That was when we were still on speaking terms. I wouldn't work for you if you were the only client on the globe!"

David folded his arms over his broad chest and looked her up and down. "What a hypocrite you are. You condemn Bootsie for being selfish and self-centered when you're no better. I hired you in good faith to solve a serious problem for me. You accepted the job, and now you want to leave me in the lurch because your feelings are hurt over some supposed slight. Very professional, Miss Warren."

"That's not fair! I'm not the only C.P.A. in the country. You can get somebody else."

"I already opened my books to *you*. I hope I can rely on your discretion, but judging by your present behavior, I'm not counting on it."

"Are you implying that I'd talk to anyone about your finances?" she asked furiously. "That's insulting! Nobody has ever questioned my professionalism."

"Have them check with me."

Melanie clenched her fists in an effort to calm down. "Be reasonable, David. Don't you see how difficult it would be for us to work together now?"

"It might be difficult to be lovers. But we're talking about a business relationship. Unless of course you anticipate something more," he drawled.

"Not in this lifetime," she gritted.

"All right, Melanie, I'll look for another accountant." He turned away. "Hopefully this time I'll get one without an attitude."

"Wait." She stopped him reluctantly. "I'll do your damn job. In record time," she added grimly. "Just don't ever call me unprofessional again."

"I hope I won't have occasion to." He paused at the door. "We're having cocktails in the library. Join us after you change."

"I'm an employee now, Viscount," she answered tautly. "Although I don't know a lot about the peerage, I do know the hired help doesn't mingle with the guests."

"I understand." He smiled condescendingly. "Bootsie makes you feel inadequate. It's all right, I wouldn't want to put you through that."

Melanie clenched her teeth so hard her jaw hurt. "I have a feeling you're manipulating me, but if there's even a chance that you believe that ridiculous statement, I'm going to show you how wrong you are. I'll be down in fifteen minutes."

"Whatever you say." David shrugged, but his face wore a look of satisfaction as he went out the door.

Chapter Five

Melanie held her head high when she entered the library where the others were assembled, aware that she didn't have a friend in the room. It promised to be an uncomfortable evening with Bootsie and David both sniping away at her.

Dennis greeted her pleasantly enough. "There you are. We were beginning to think you weren't going to join us."

"I'm sorry I'm late," she answered. "But I just got back a short time ago."

"You could have taken time to change," Bootsie said blandly. "We would have waited for you." She and Pamela were both wearing very expensive cocktail dresses.

Melanie had grabbed the nearest outfit in her hurry to get dressed. It happened to be a cream colored silk blouse and a matching skirt. They were becoming but tailored, nothing like the finery on the other women. A person with good breeding wouldn't have called attention to the disparity, but Bootsie's comment was deliberate. She knew Melanie *had* changed, since she'd seen her in the entry hall earlier.

"I think she looks lovely," David said. "We're a lot more casual here in the country."

"I suppose there is something to be said for the simple life," Dennis remarked.

"Don't be such a hypocrite," his wife chided. "Your idea of austerity is having to park your own car."

"I'll be reduced to selling it if you go on any more shopping sprees. I can never understand why women would rather be staked to an anthill rather than wear the same gown to two parties in the same season."

"That reminds me, darling." Bootsie turned to David. "Don't forget about the Florentine Ball."

He gave her a startled look. "When is it?"

"On Saturday. You *did* forget!"

"No, I . . . uh, I didn't realize it was coming up so soon."

"Time does fly by. This will be the first social event of the new season. Did you get your invitation from the Sunderbys for their cocktail party beforehand?"

"I don't know. It might have gone to my town house."

"Well, don't worry. I accepted for both of us."

"I wish you hadn't done that," he said slowly. "I doubt if I'll be able to make it."

"I asked you to this affair months ago," Bootsie exclaimed. "I'm one of the chairwomen. You can't disappoint me at the last minute like this."

"That would be really bad form," Pamela commented disapprovingly.

"I suggest you stay out of this, my love," her husband advised.

"I can express an opinion."

Melanie listened to their wrangling with a sardonic expression on her face. David was uncomfortably aware of it.

"We'll discuss it later," he told Bootsie.

"No, we'll settle it *now!* What's so urgent down here that you can't get away for a weekend?"

"I have some business to attend to," he said, glancing at Melanie.

"Is she the reason you can't come to London?" Bootsie asked David sharply.

"Melanie is a certified public accountant. I hired her to put my books in order," he explained.

"Which I can't do without you. I agreed to do the job, but that doesn't include waiting around until you fulfill your social obligations. So I guess you'll just have to hire another accountant," Melanie said without bothering to hide her glee.

"We made a deal," he said grimly.

"Then you'll have to make a Solomon-like decision. Maybe you could divide yourself in half." She grinned. "That way, Bootsie and I would each get the half we preferred."

As Dennis smothered a chortle and his wife and Bootsie looked outraged, Bevins appeared in the doorway.

"Dinner is served," he announced solemnly.

It was an uncomfortable meal. Bootsie continued her efforts to pin David down, despite his evasive tactics. When she was finally forced to accept defeat—for the moment, at least—it did nothing to improve her disposition. After a period of sulky silence, she deliberately began to talk about people Melanie didn't know. David and Dennis tried to steer the conversation to general topics, but it didn't work.

By the time dinner was over, Melanie wasn't lying when she pleaded a headache. While the others discussed plans for the evening, she went to her room.

Melanie's headache was gone the next morning, but not her resolve. She planned to have a talk with David at the first opportunity. If he intended to go to London for the weekend, there was nothing to keep her here. What she'd said was true. She couldn't do his books without frequent conferences with him.

She brushed aside the poignant thought that this was probably her last day at Castlebury Manor. Bootsie had undoubtedly made him see things her way as soon as she got him alone.

Melanie was surprised to see David at the breakfast table when she came downstairs that morning. She had expected to take the twins out alone again—leaving a note this time.

"You're up early," she remarked tepidly.

"The same time as usual," he replied.

"Uncle David said we can get the horses from Mr. Thompson today," Ariel told Melanie excitedly. "We don't have to wait until Saturday."

"The black one's going to be mine." Ashley's face was lit with equal joy.

"That's nice," Melanie answered somewhat absent-mindedly. "We need to talk," she said to David. "If you've made plans to go to London I might as well leave today."

"You can't go now," Ashley exclaimed in dismay. "You haven't even seen the horses yet."

"I'll let you ride mine," Ariel wheedled. "She has a white star on her forehead and she's ever so gentle."

"I'll see them before I leave," Melanie promised.

"But why do you have to go?" Ariel asked. "Can't you make her stay, Uncle David?"

"Getting Melanie to do anything she doesn't want to do is a tall order," he said wryly. "I thought I had her convinced, but I was mistaken."

"Sure, make *me* the heavy," Melanie muttered angrily.

"It's *your* decision."

"Maybe I can stop on my way back," she told the children. It was a cowardly ruse, but she couldn't bear their sorrowful faces.

"When will that be?" Ariel asked.

"Not for quite a while," she answered honestly.

"We might not even be here then," Ashley complained. "We have to go away to school."

David looked at him closely. "Don't you want to go?"

"I guess so," the young boy answered without enthusiasm.

"Would you rather stay home and go to the village school?"

The twins looked at each other with dawning excitement. "Can we?" they chorused.

"If that's what you want."

"We could ride our horses every day," Ashley rhapsodized.

"And see Uncle David all the time, not just at holidays," Ariel said. "Guess what? We're not going away to school," she told Bevins, who had just entered the dining room. "We're going to live right here and go to school in the village."

The butler looked to David for confirmation. When it was forthcoming, something like amusement flitted across his face. David didn't seem to notice, but Melanie did and she was puzzled. What was Bevins up to now?

Mrs. Crossiter made a rare and unexpected visit to the dining room a short time later. Her lips were compressed in a bloodless line, making her expression even more forbidding than usual. "I'd like a word with you after breakfast, sir."

David looked at her warily. "If it's about the houseguests, Mrs. Crossiter, I know they've been extra work for you. Perhaps Miss Morton could help out."

"It isn't about the guests, sir. They'll be gone in a couple of days." She stressed the pronoun slightly.

Suddenly Melanie got it. Bevins must have told the housekeeper that the twins weren't going away to school, knowing it would annoy her. It had probably given him a great deal of satisfaction. They would all pay for her displeasure in the days to come, though. The twins would do well to stay out of her way.

Melanie rose, beckoning to the children. "Why don't you both go down to the stables and make sure everything is ready for the horses." They didn't need any urging and she followed them out of the room.

The doorbell rang as Melanie was passing through the front hall. She answered it, since she was right there. Bevins would thank her, she thought ironically. He was undoubtedly eavesdropping on Mrs. Crossiter's talk with David.

Sylvia Tyndall was standing on the doorstep with a basket of homegrown vegetables over her arm. A large hat shaded her face, but Melanie recognized her from their encounter in the restaurant.

"It's a ghastly time to come calling," the older woman said. "But any household with children is up with the birds."

"Yes, we just finished breakfast—except for David's guests, of course." Coolness crept into Melanie's voice.

"Oh?" Lady Tyndall's interest quickened. "Who would that be? My grapevine must be withering."

"They dropped in unexpectedly, night before last. His girlfriend Bootsie and a couple named Hightower."

"Hasn't Bootsie given up yet? She's been chasing David for years."

"Her diligence paid off." Melanie's mouth drooped unconsciously. "I think she finally caught him."

Sylvia gazed at her comprehendingly, but she kept her tone brisk. "Stuff and nonsense. David is much too bright to be taken in by that empty-headed little goose."

Melanie brightened. "You think so? She certainly seems to have him wrapped around her little finger."

"Don't you believe it. He simply has beautiful manners. Where is David now?"

"He's having a talk with Mrs. Crossiter."

"Another winner," Sylvia sniffed. "Poor David, it's a good thing he has you."

"I'm afraid you've gotten the wrong impression," Melanie said carefully. "There's nothing between us. We don't even get along very well a lot of the time."

"I'm sorry to hear that. You make such a stunning couple. How did you happen to meet?"

"It's a rather funny story. I'll tell you about it if you'll come outside with me. I want to watch for the twins."

"Don't they have a nanny anymore?" Sylvia asked as they walked to the back of the house and the terrace beyond.

"Yes, but she's more interested in the titled guests." Melanie instantly regretted her frankness. "The children don't really require her services, so it's thoughtful of Miss Morton to offer to help with the extra work."

"Mmm-hmm." Sylvia made a noncommittal sound. "Tell me about you and David," she said, settling into a patio chair.

Melanie related the story of her arrival at Castlebury Manor, including the incident with the frog in her bed. She omitted the part about David coming to her rescue. The memory, however, brought color to her cheeks.

Sylvia noticed, but she didn't comment on the fact. "I'm glad to see the twins are acting like normal children again. They were so subdued after the accident that it broke my heart."

"I'm sure it was horrible for them, but they seem to be bouncing back. David and I have taken them all over this week and they acted like regular, happy kids."

"You must like children."

"I haven't known enough of them to make a judgment call. I suppose they're like adults—some you like and some you don't."

"But you like Ariel and Ashley?"

"Tremendously. We established a rapport right at the very beginning." When she became aware that the other woman was looking at her speculatively, Melanie said, "I haven't used them to get in David's good graces, if that's what you're thinking. That's Bootsie's mentality."

"I never thought you did. But they do need a mother, and you would fill the bill nicely."

"If and when I do marry, it will be for love," Melanie said evenly. "Not because the man needs somebody to take care of his children."

"Even at my advanced stage of maturity I can see that David would be very easy to love."

Melanie forced herself to keep a light tone. "I have impossible conditions. He would have to love me, too."

"So far, I don't see any stumbling blocks. A discerning man like David shouldn't find that difficult."

"I didn't come here looking for a husband," Melanie said helplessly.

Sylvia smiled. "That's the nice thing about life, it's so full of surprises."

David came onto the terrace in time to hear her statement. "Some of them not so pleasant." He sighed.

"What's the matter?"

"Mrs. Crossiter just gave notice."

"That should be cause for rejoicing," Sylvia commented. "The woman is about as pleasant as a tight girdle. You should be glad to be rid of her."

"God knows she was difficult, but where will I get another housekeeper? The agencies have a limited number of qualified applicants who are willing to live in the country."

"Why did she give notice so abruptly?" Melanie asked. "I hope I'm not partially to blame. Was it the extra guests?"

"No, it's the twins. Mrs. Crossiter only tolerated them in the first place because she thought they'd be away most of the time. When she found out they'd be going to the village school instead, it was the last straw."

"They're not going to public school?" Sylvia asked.

"No, Melanie thought—and I agreed—that it would be better for us to spend at least a year as a family."

"Sound thinking." She looked at Melanie with renewed interest.

"Father took care of Mrs. Crossiter in his will, so she can afford to retire," David said. "She hasn't been happy working for anybody else since he died."

"At least she won't sour any more households," Sylvia observed.

"And you won't have to try and figure out how to give her a good reference without lying." Melanie grinned.

"Since you two can see the bright side of the situation, perhaps you can also do the cooking when she leaves," David said. "Where am I going to get another housekeeper?"

"Not to worry," Sylvia said. "My woman has a sister who just lost her job. Her employers moved to the south of France. Mrs. Beavey asked me just yesterday if I knew of anyone who was looking for help. I'll talk to her as soon as I get home."

"What do you know about the sister?" David asked warily. "I'd need to check her references before I hired her."

"You're remarkably picky for a man who just spent several months with a dragon like Crossiter. Try this one. If you don't like her, you can fire her. At least she's a warm body when you need one."

David laughed and slanted a glance at Melanie. "I didn't know it showed."

"The twins will be happy, anyway," Melanie said hastily. "I hope this new woman will let them into the kitchen."

"She has to be better than what you've been putting up with," Sylvia said.

"That's certainly true," David agreed. "When can I talk to her?"

The older woman stood. "I'll go home now and make the arrangements."

"I didn't mean to chase you away."

"You aren't. I want to make some phone calls. I've decided to have a few people in for dinner tonight. Come and bring Melanie—the others, too, of course."

"It sounds good to me," he said. "How about you, Melanie?"

She hesitated, remembering her decision to leave. But she didn't know for sure yet that David was going to London. It would also be deserting him at a time when he needed someone reliable. Maybe he didn't deserve her help, but the twins did. Melanie made up her mind.

"I'd love to go," she said.

"You're doing me a big favor, Sylvia," David remarked. "I was running out of ways to entertain my houseguests."

"That London crowd is very blasé." She smiled suddenly. "I'll try to make things interesting."

David's guests weren't thrilled when he tendered the invitation some time later. They didn't come down for brunch until noon.

"I'm sure the old girl meant well, but tell her we have other plans," Dennis said.

"Absolutely! She's the rudest woman I ever met," Bootsie said.

Melanie couldn't help herself. "I wouldn't say that," she drawled.

Before Bootsie could react, Pamela said, "I agree with Dennis. Who wants to spend all evening with a bunch of old fogies?"

"Sylvia is a very kind and warm person," David said with restraint.

"Not to me she isn't." Bootsie scowled.

"I don't understand it," Melanie remarked sweetly. "She's been very friendly to *me*."

David stepped in hastily. "You're all free to do whatever you like. Melanie and I are going to Lady Tyndall's."

Anger flashed across Bootsie's face and was masked instantly. "Oh, well, I suppose it won't be so bad."

"Compared to what?" Dennis asked. "You and Melanie can go, David, but I think Pammy and I will see what excitement we can scare up on our own. You're welcome to join us, Bootsie."

"No, I can tell David wants me to go, so I'm going to be a good little guest."

"Naturally I'd be delighted to have your company, but I can't ask you to suffer through a boring evening," David said smoothly.

"You always find a way to keep me interested, darling." She gave him an intimate smile.

As he searched for a suitable answer, Jean came into the room and approached Bootsie with an expression of fawning respect. Melanie wouldn't have been surprised if she'd curtsied! Her adulation of the peerage was both comical and annoying.

"When I was pressing your gowns this morning I noticed some beads were loose on the beautiful white chiffon. I took the liberty of sewing them back in place. I hope that was all right." Jean had the anxious look of a poodle hoping for a pat on the head.

"Aren't you a dear!" Bootsie smiled graciously. "I hope you're paying this woman what she's worth, David."

"I doubt it," he answered dryly.

Jean was pink with pleasure. "Your things are hanging in your closet, Lady Addersley. If there's anything else I can do for you, please don't hesitate to call on me."

After the nanny had left, Dennis said, "I wish our servants were that anxious to please."

"It's the title that awes those repressed, mousy ones," Pamela said.

"Are you implying that I'm not naturally lovable?" Bootsie laughed. "David can tell you differently, can't you, sweetie?"

Melanie sat in stoic silence, regretting her softhearted decision to stay. Why was it so hard for her to make up her mind and stick to it? Nothing was worth putting up with Bootsie! If David was, indeed, going to London for the weekend, then he had to release her from her obligation.

He had evaded the issue last night, but it was showdown time, either yes or no. The problem was getting him alone for a private talk. It was foolish to think Bootsie would leave him alone for a moment, but the matter was going to be settled today, Melanie decided grimly. This was the last evening she intended to spend with Bootsie.

In spite of Melanie's firm resolve, she couldn't find an opportunity to speak to David. When his guests didn't claim his attention, the twins did. She also had more than a slight suspicion that David was avoiding a showdown with her. For whatever reason, the afternoon slipped away without any change in their status quo.

Under different circumstances Melanie would have looked forward to the dinner party. Lady Tyndall was certainly not dull, and her husband had a nice sense of humor. Bootsie could be counted on to take all the fun out of the evening, however. Melanie resigned herself to the fact.

She dressed simply that night, in a blue silk sheath and high heeled pumps. Her only jewelry was a pair of small gold earrings and a thin gold chain around her neck.

Bootsie's diamond-and-ruby earrings, bracelet and ring were as flamboyant as her outfit. She wore a high-fashion gown of scarlet peau de soie with a very revealing neckline. It was skintight and the skirt was above her knees.

David blinked when he saw her. "I hope you're not expecting too much from tonight. Sylvia's parties tend to be fairly simple."

"You don't like my gown?" she pouted.

"That's not it at all. I think it's…spectacular. I just didn't want you to feel overdressed, that's all."

"Only insecure women dress so nobody will notice them." Her lip curled slightly as she flicked a glance at Melanie. "I always say, if you've got it, flaunt it."

Melanie's green eyes sparkled dangerously, but she kept her tone amused. "And if you don't—wear something low cut."

David wore the resigned look of a referee trying to keep two pumped up boxers from maiming each other. "Shall we go, ladies?"

Bootsie got her revenge. Maneuvering in front of Melanie, she slid into the front passenger seat, leaving Melanie to ride in the back alone.

The Tyndall estate was even grander than David's. A huge Tudor brick house had walls covered with ivy, and mullioned windows of leaded glass. An imposing front door could have guarded the entrance to a castle.

A butler showed them into a formal drawing room furnished with period French furniture and paintings in heavy gilt frames with picture lights above them. Other guests had already arrived and were having cocktails.

After greeting them, their host said to David, "You're a remarkably lucky young man to have two such beautiful lady friends."

"I'm indebted to Melanie for keeping him amused until I could get here." Bootsie linked her arm with David's and gave him an intimate smile.

"It was no hardship. He kept *me* amused, too," Melanie drawled.

"Yes, well . . . do come and meet the others," Lord Tyndall said.

Three other couples were sipping champagne a short distance away. They were contemporaries of the Tyndalls. Bootsie kept firm possession of David's arm as their host led them to the group and made the introductions. He excused himself a few moments later with a mumbled pretext.

"What on earth were you thinking of?" Lord Tyndall asked his wife after pulling her aside. "I was looking forward to a pleasant evening with friends."

"That's exactly what we're having," she answered.

"Not for long. If you wanted excitement, why didn't you arrange for a fireworks display on the back lawn. Or better yet, set up a minefield. The person who navigates it successfully gets to go home—and I'll go with him!"

"Why do you automatically assume the winner would be a male? You're such a chauvinist, Charles."

"Don't try to change the subject. I've been remarkably patient, but this time you've gone too far."

"What have I done?"

"You know jolly well! How could you tell David to bring both of those women? They were barely inside the door before they started sharpening their tongues. We'll be fortunate if that's the only weapon they use on each other."

"Don't be ridiculous, Charles. They're both ladies."

"Who happen to detest each other. I don't find verbal attacks any more palatable than physical ones. The evening is going to be a fiasco!"

"You worry too much," Sylvia said dismissively. "It's nice to have young couples around for a change."

"Your arithmetic is faulty. Two women and one man aren't a couple, they're a recipe for disaster."

"Is that all that's bothering you? Not to worry. I've invited an extra man to round out the numbers."

"Why doesn't that reassure me?" he asked dryly. "What are you up to this time?"

"Just trying to see that everyone has a good time. Come along, Charles, we must join our guests. They'll think we don't enjoy their company."

"Remind me that I'm having fun," he muttered.

Melanie had distanced herself from David and Bootsie as soon as possible. She was willing to be polite, for the duration of the party anyway, but Bootsie made that all but impossible.

Melanie was talking to a very pleasant couple, Delia and George Blake, when Sylvia brought over a newcomer to join them. He was about David's age, but that was one of the few similarities. His hair was blond instead of dark, and he was tall and slender without having David's powerful physique.

"You know the Blakes," Sylvia said to him, indicating the other couple. "Melanie, I'd like you to meet Lord Clive Westcourt."

"Just Clive, please." He smiled charmingly, extending his hand. "I'm so delighted to meet you. Do you live in the county? I haven't seen you around before."

"She's visiting from America," Sylvia explained.

"How nice. I hope you'll allow me to show you around," he said to Melanie.

"That's awfully kind of you, but I expect to be leaving soon," she answered.

"What a shame! I wish you had introduced us sooner, Sylvia. Can't you persuade her to stay longer?"

"She isn't my houseguest. Melanie is staying at Castlebury Manor."

"I see." Clive's expression held regret. "David is a lucky chap."

"We hardly know each other," Melanie said carefully. "I was hired to do some work for him, but then his plans changed. That's why I'm leaving."

"I don't know what you do, but you can come to work for me." Clive laughed.

"What kind of work *do* you do?" George Blake asked.

"I'm a certified public accountant," Melanie replied. "I had a preliminary conference with David on his estate matters, but I don't think our schedules are going to mesh." That was close to the truth, anyway.

"The opportunities women have today are quite wonderful," Delia Blake remarked. "Our daughter is studying to be a surgeon. In my day, we never would have thought it possible."

"That's because operations are usually scheduled at dawn, and you loathe getting up in the morning." Her husband chuckled.

"You see what I mean?" Delia asked indignantly. "The women of my generation weren't taken seriously!"

"You were fortunate in another way," Melanie said tactfully. "Today's woman doesn't have the luxury of staying home and taking care of the children, even if she wanted to. Most of us know we'll have to work, so we prepare ourselves for it if we're wise."

Their hostess had been restraining herself with difficulty. As Delia prepared to pursue the subject Sylvia said, "Your wife's glass is almost empty, George. Be a dear and take her to the bar for a refill. I need Charles to help me with something."

As the older couple excused themselves, urged on by their hostess, Charles murmured to his wife, "Nobody could ever accuse you of being indirect. Why didn't you just offer Clive and Melanie the upstairs bedroom?"

"Don't be lewd," she chided. "Anyone could see he wanted to be alone with her so they could get acquainted. I was simply fostering a friendship between two young people who have a lot in common."

"Like what? She's an American and he's a Brit, for starters. Besides, I thought you had plans for her and David. Have you given up on that notion?"

"Not necessarily. You never know what might happen."

"Ah, now I see the plot. Clive is bait to make David jealous." Charles looked at his wife with a raised eyebrow. "Isn't this situation remarkably like our early days? I was going with Esther Hepplewhite when we met. Did you have anything to do with our breakup?"

"She would never have made you happy," Sylvia said serenely. "Go talk to the Smythes, darling. We really must mingle with the guests."

When Clive and Melanie were alone, he said, "It's rotten luck that we had to meet at the end of your visit. When exactly are you leaving?"

Melanie glanced over to where Bootsie was still clinging to David like a barnacle. "As soon as possible," she said with unconscious grimness.

"You don't like the country?"

"That's not what I meant at all. It's just that I feel a little awkward about staying on at Castlebury Manor if David doesn't need me. I mean, if I don't have any business there," she corrected herself, which didn't sound much better.

"I'd invite you to be a guest at *my* house, but I don't suppose that would be proper on such short acquaintance," he said ruefully.

"You don't know anything about me." She smiled. "I could be the guest from hell."

"I'd be willing to take my chances." He chuckled. "Are you?"

Before she could reply, David joined them—along with the ever present Bootsie. His face was impassive as he gazed at their apparent rapport.

"It's been a long time, Clive," David said. "Sylvia didn't tell me you were going to be here."

"She had a surprise for *me,* too. I'm just sorry that Melanie is leaving before we got to know each other." Clive smiled at her.

David's expression changed to a frown. "Did you tell him you were leaving?" he asked her.

She shrugged. "There's nothing to hang around for any longer. I told you I couldn't do the books without you."

"I thought we settled that matter last night. You made a big speech about professionalism, as I recall."

"I was willing to fulfill my part of the bargain," she said angrily. "*You're* the one whose social life takes precedence over everything else."

Bootsie's eyes narrowed at the extent of their emotionalism. Controlling her own temper, she intervened playfully. "You two can't be around each other for five minutes without arguing. How could you possibly hope to work together?"

"For once your girlfriend is right," Melanie said curtly.

"We'll discuss it later," he rasped. "This is not the place."

"There's nothing to discuss. Are you going to London or aren't you? If the answer is yes, I'm out of here."

"Of course he's going." Bootsie gave him a steely look. "Tell her, David."

Sylvia joined them, ignoring the tension that was obvious between three of the foursome. "I didn't mean to neglect you young people. Are you and Melanie hitting it off, Clive?" she asked blandly.

"I certainly hope so," he answered. "She's charming. I don't know how Melanie feels, but I'm in your debt."

Melanie's bruised feelings received a boost. Clive was a charming, cultured man—everything David was, only with better taste.

She gave him a brilliant smile. "I can't thank Sylvia enough for introducing us. I'd always heard English men were delightful, and now I've discovered it for myself."

"Now it's your turn to say something nice about English women," Bootsie prompted David coquettishly.

Mastering his smoldering anger, he put an arm around her waist. "What can I say that I haven't already told you, my dear?"

She slanted an intimate look at him. "You're right. I'd rather hear it when we're alone."

"Isn't this lovely?" Sylvia looked gratified. "Everything's turning out just as I hoped."

* * *

The long table in the dining room seated twelve comfortably. It was set with delicate china, heavy silverware and a lovely floral centerpiece. Place cards directed the guests to their seats.

Sylvia and Charles sat in host chairs at opposite ends of the table. On her right and left she had seated the two young couples. Melanie found herself across the table from David, a less than desirable arrangement. Every time she glanced up she found herself looking at him.

The conversation was general at first, but the older couples at Charles's end of the table gradually began to talk about local events. Sylvia found other topics more interesting.

"Melanie tells me the twins have come around nicely since you and she have been spending so much time with them," she said to David.

"Those poor, sweet babies." Bootsie sighed. "David is wonderful with them—a real father figure. But they need a mother, too."

"That's true." Sylvia nodded. "It would be ideal if David could find a wife who enjoyed living in the country."

"That's not a requirement," Bootsie protested. "He doesn't have to stay here once the children are in school."

"Oh, haven't you heard? They're not going away. He intends to enroll them in the village school. That means he'll have to be here a sizable part of the time, especially on holidays. It's too bad you'll miss all the festivities in London, David."

"I'll survive." He looked at her in amusement, as though realizing what she was up to.

"We'll work something out, darling," Bootsie told him. "I won't let you pine away here all alone."

"I wish you'd take pity on *me*," Clive said to Melanie. "Christmas is quite wonderful in the country. Could I entice you into coming back?"

"Stranger things have happened," she said complacently, aware of David's steady gaze. The evening wasn't turning out so badly after all.

"Splendid," Sylvia said. "We'll have a series of parties at different houses. Christmas Eve will be at your house, David, to include the children. I'm getting quite excited thinking about it. Plan to come early and stay over New Year's, Bootsie."

"It's a little soon to start making plans," Bootsie hedged.

"Not for Christmas. People's calendars fill up quickly."

"David and I will talk about it." Bootsie turned hastily in her host's direction. "This Pinot Noir is delicious, Charles. You must tell me what year it is."

At the end of the evening, Clive wanted to drive Melanie home, but David pointed out that Clive's house was in the opposite direction from his. When that argument didn't fly, David insisted that she was his obligation, since he had brought her and she was staying at his home.

Melanie was less than thrilled to be considered an obligation, and she wasn't keen on staring at the back of Bootsie's head all the way home—although it was preferable to looking at either of her two faces, she decided. Bootsie wasn't any more delighted to be in Melanie's company, but neither woman could change the outcome.

Clive leaned in the back window as David started the car. "It was a wonderful evening," he said, squeezing Melanie's hand. "I'll phone you."

"I'll look forward to hearing from you," she answered softly, knowing David was listening.

As they drove away, Bootsie said, "You made quite a conquest tonight. Clive is filthy rich."

"He's also very nice." It was true, but Melanie's answer was deliberate.

David didn't comment. In fact he barely spoke on the ride home. Melanie was equally silent, but Bootsie made up for both of them. She kept up a running commentary during the entire drive.

Pamela and Dennis had beaten them home, although it was only around eleven o'clock. "Thank God you're back," Dennis exclaimed. "There is absolutely nothing to do around here. We might as well have gone with you to the party."

"Tell us it was truly awful," Pamela begged. "Misery likes company."

"Melanie had a good time," Bootsie said. "She snared herself a very eligible bachelor."

"We're having a nightcap. Fix yourselves one and tell us all about it," Pamela said.

"Not for me, thanks," Melanie said. "I'm going to bed."

"I am, too. Help yourselves to anything you want," David told the others.

An immediate chorus of protests broke out. "It isn't even midnight yet," Dennis complained. "I'm worried about you, old man. You used to party hearty."

"Don't go," Bootsie urged. "This is the last chance we'll have to be together until the weekend. We're leaving for the Metcalfs' tomorrow."

As Melanie started up the stairs they were also renewing their pleas for David to attend the house party with them. She didn't wait around to hear whether they were successful.

Melanie told herself she was glad to be leaving the next day. David couldn't very well blame her. He'd obviously made his own decision. When Bootsie said she'd see him in London on the weekend, he hadn't even tried to get out of it.

Her shoulders drooped and she suddenly felt very weary. It was only fatigue from all the tension, she assured herself. After a good night's sleep she'd be her old self.

As she was hanging her dress in the closet there was a knock at the door. She grabbed a robe and slipped into it hastily.

The knock sounded again, then David's muffled voice came through the thick panel. "I know you're not asleep yet, Melanie."

She opened the door and confronted him. "I intend to be shortly. Whatever it is, make it brief."

"I want to talk to you. May I come in?"

"Certainly not!"

"Would you prefer to come to my room?" Before she could refuse he continued, "Whether you like it or not we're going to talk, and I'd rather not do it here in the hall where we're bound to be joined by the others. Now, where is it going to be?"

Melanie could tell by the stubborn glint in his eyes that he didn't intend to give up. She reluctantly stood aside for him to enter. Anything was better than another sniping match with Bootsie.

"I don't see why this can't wait until morning," she grumbled.

"Because you're planning to leave."

"We've been through all this, David," she said impatiently. "I agreed to stay only if you did, too."

"I've known Bootsie for a long time," he answered indirectly.

"Fine! I hope you'll be very happy together."

"You persist in jumping to conclusions. I didn't say either of us was madly in love with the other. At the risk of sounding unchivalrous, Bootsie likes to imply that our relationship is more meaningful than it is."

"Maybe it is to her."

David shook his head. "I fulfill her eligibility requirements. Or at least I did before I acquired a family."

"Okay, what's her attraction for *you?*" Melanie challenged.

He smiled wryly. "You've only seen the downside of Bootsie. We've actually had some good times together in my former, free-spirited days. She's an entirely different person when she doesn't feel threatened."

"By me? How could I possibly make her feel insecure?"

"She knows I'm attracted to you. It's evident to everyone except you. Why do you think Sylvia invited Clive tonight?"

"To be my dinner partner."

"A man handpicked for charm and eligibility. Her real purpose was to make me jealous, so I'd see how much more suitable you are than Bootsie."

"Anybody would be." Melanie reacted predictably. "I've been telling you that all along."

"I got the message." He smiled.

"Then why are you letting her run your life? You don't really want to go to that ball. At least, I don't think you do," she added uncertainly.

"That's correct. But I agreed to go quite some time ago. It wouldn't be very kind to let her down at the last moment. I know you can't understand it, but this event means a lot to Bootsie."

"Then I guess you don't have any choice," Melanie said evenly.

"Unfortunately that's true. I dislike losing a friend, but I'm afraid she isn't likely to forgive me for this."

"I don't understand. Does that mean you're not going?"

"How can I if it means you'll leave?"

"You can get another accountant," she said helplessly.

"It's more than that. You've become part of the family." David smiled appealingly. "Who else would listen to all my problems and come up with solutions? I've grown to depend on you."

Melanie was immensely pleased, even though gratitude wasn't the emotion she would have preferred. "I'm glad if

I could come through when you needed me, but I don't want to create a new set of problems for you.''

He shrugged. "It can't be helped.''

"Maybe I was a little unreasonable,'' she said slowly. "I guess I could wait until you got back.''

"I couldn't ask you to do that. You were perfectly right to refuse.''

"I really wouldn't mind.''

David hesitated. "I'd feel guilty about leaving you here alone, but one solution does occur to me. We could all go up to London for the weekend. It would be a last fling for the children before they have to start school, and you might enjoy going shopping and to the theater. We can stay at my town house. Does any of that appeal to you?''

"I don't know.'' Melanie was too startled by the unexpected turn of events to have an opinion.

"It was just an idea—probably a rotten one.'' He turned toward the door. "We'll start work tomorrow, after Bootsie and her crowd clear out.''

"No, wait! I know the children would love a weekend in the city, and so would I. It would solve the matter to everybody's satisfaction.''

"You're being very understanding.'' He took both of her hands in his. "I'll make it up to you, I promise. This will be a weekend to remember.'' He leaned forward unexpectedly and kissed her cheek.

David was gone before she could react, which was probably a good thing. Melanie felt like a teenager after her first kiss—and it hadn't even been on the lips!

Her whole body heated at the memory of his strong hands and firm mouth. Fortunately she was frozen to the spot at his first touch, or she might have flung her arms around his neck and pulled his head down for the deep kiss she craved.

Melanie finally admitted what she'd tried so hard to deny. She was hopelessly in love with David. The big question was, did he feel anything but desire for *her?* That had been present between them since the first night.

Still, he *had* offered to give up his trip to London to keep her here. Or had she let herself be manipulated one more time? David was good at that. But he didn't have to go to such lengths to get a woman. Especially one who was so much trouble.

Finally Melanie stopped trying to undermine her own happiness. The man of her dreams really existed and she was going to spend a wonderful weekend in London with him!

Chapter Six

David's guests didn't leave until noon, and it took the efforts of the whole household to attend to their last minute requirements. Everybody was glad to see them go, with the exception of Jean.

She hovered around, savoring her last contact with a lady of the peerage. Her face was radiant when Bootsie said a few words to her and handed her some bills. It was the least she could do after all the extra duties Jean had performed for her. Although Melanie knew Jean valued the personal attention far more than the money.

Before leaving, David's friends made a last, but concerted effort to get him to go with them. "It isn't too late," Dennis said.

"Just throw a dinner jacket and a few casual things into a suitcase," Bootsie said. "We'll wait for you."

"Yes, do come," Pamela urged. "What will you do around here after we leave?"

"I expect to be very busy," David answered. "I have to hire a new housekeeper and enroll the twins in school, to start with."

"Good lord, man!" Dennis exclaimed. "You're starting to sound like one of those dreary suburbanites. Next you'll be telling us you have to mow the lawn and take out the garbage!"

"It might come to that if my help keeps giving notice." David laughed.

"I hope you know you're turning into a family man," Dennis said disgustedly. "I never thought I'd see the day."

"I didn't either, but don't knock it until you've tried it. Domesticity has its rewards."

Bootsie looked at him with dawning pleasure. "That's definitely a good sign."

"Well, if you're sure you can't join us, we'd better push on," Dennis said.

"I *will* see you on Saturday?" Bootsie asked David, a trifle sharply.

"I'm looking forward to the weekend immensely," he replied.

Life at Castlebury Manor improved greatly after the guests left. Another reason was the unlamented departure of Mrs. Crossiter. The housekeeper Sylvia sent over was not only pleasant and capable, she was willing to start immediately.

Mrs. Stanhope won over the twins on the first day when she baked them a chocolate fudge cake and let them scrape the bowl and lick the spoon.

She received Melanie's seal of approval for making her domain look like a kitchen instead of a laboratory. The bare counters gradually acquired a collection of potted plants, cookbooks and baskets of fruit. Even Bevins couldn't find anything to fault her on.

With his household problems under control, David was able to spend a lot of time with Melanie and the twins.

"We really should get started on the books," she remarked halfheartedly when he suggested taking the children somewhere.

"It would be foolish to get all involved and then have to stop in the middle. The weekend is almost here. We'll accomplish a lot more if we wait until we return and then really dig in."

That made sense, so Melanie simply concentrated on enjoying herself. The days were packed with activity and the nights alone with David were strenuous in a different way. The strong sexual attraction between them was always just under the surface of their easy camaraderie, waiting to explode.

Melanie frequently wondered why she kept resisting what would be, at the very least, a memorable experience. But a brief affair was contrary to her nature—and that was all David had to offer.

Clive called several times after the dinner party, without finding Melanie at home. She was gratified by his interest, but she didn't want to go out with him or anyone else. It was so nice having David all to herself again.

Enrolling the children in school was a poignant experience. They were subdued at first by the strange environment, but that soon wore off. While David and Melanie were taking care of the formalities, the twins asked permission to explore the schoolyard.

"They have lovely manners," the woman in charge remarked as she watched them leave. "You must be very proud parents."

"We are proud of them, even though we aren't their parents." David explained the circumstances.

"What a tragedy for the little ones," she said. "I did hear about the accident, now that I recall. Are you a relative, also?" she asked Melanie delicately.

David answered for her. "Miss Warren is a very dear friend of the family. The twins are devoted to her."

"I see. Well, they're fortunate to have people who care about them."

When the woman left briefly to get some forms, Melanie said, "You didn't have to lay it on so thick."

"How did you want me to describe you?" His eyes brimmed with mischief. "A sexy siren who tells us what to do and makes us like it?"

Melanie laughed. "Okay, I'll settle for friend of the family."

The woman returned just ahead of the children. Ashley ran to David, and Ariel clasped Melanie's hand.

"They have a thing you can climb up real high on in the playground, Uncle David," the young boy said.

"And lots of other things, too," Ariel said. "Come and see, Melanie."

"In a few minutes, honey," Melanie replied.

When the twins had scampered out again, the woman said, "They seem to be adjusting beautifully. You both deserve a lot of credit. It's so important to provide children with parental figures and a secure home environment, especially after a traumatic loss."

"We're working on it." David gave Melanie a big smile.

While he supplied the children's vital statistics, a new set of doubts began to gnaw away at Melanie. Was most of her allure the fact that she and the twins got along so well? David felt a deep responsibility for them. Was he shopping for a suitable wife? It was a little suspicious that he was suddenly extolling the benefits of domesticity, when he'd never shown an inclination to get married before.

Melanie had shrugged off her misgivings, but they were there, just under the surface. That evening she and David had their coffee in the library after dinner as usual, sitting companionably together on the couch. Normally she would have been pleased when he took her hand and laced their fingers together. Now, she was wary.

He stretched out his long legs and crossed them at the ankle. "It's nice to have houseguests, but it's even nicer when they leave."

"Is that a hint?" Melanie asked lightly.

His expression changed subtly as he turned his head to gaze at her. "I don't think of you as a houseguest."

"What would you call me, an employee-to-be?" Her laughter was a little edgy. "I haven't done anything constructive yet. You might even regret hiring me if I find you owe back taxes. Nobody likes an accountant who costs them money."

Melanie knew she was babbling, but the look in David's eyes told her the situation was becoming too intimate. If she didn't do something to defuse it he was going to kiss her—and she was afraid of her own response.

"I have plenty of money," he said. "What I've never had is someone like you."

"That's hard to believe, considering all the women you've dated."

"I wish I could convince you that I'm not the womanizer you think I am."

"Does it matter?" she asked carelessly.

"It matters a great deal. Your good opinion means a lot to me."

"You already have that. I respect you for putting your life on hold for the sake of the twins."

"That's something anyone with a spark of decency would have done. I want your approval of me as a man."

"You have that, too." She laughed awkwardly. "Outside of having rather questionable taste in women, I'd say you were quite a guy."

He cupped his hand around her neck and urged her face closer to his. "I had sense enough to recognize that you're the best thing that ever happened to me."

David's husky voice was resonating deep inside her where desire ruled. She couldn't seem to drag her eyes from his chiseled mouth, only inches away from hers.

"You really shouldn't..." Her voice trailed off, along with her resolve.

His long fingers stroked her cheek. "Don't fight it, darling. You're only delaying the inevitable. You know that, don't you?"

"I'll admit I'm attracted to you," she answered haltingly.

He laughed softly. "That's a pretty pale description of how I feel about *you.*"

When he slowly lowered his head, Melanie was powerless to move away. She was mesmerized by the brilliance of his blue eyes, burningly aware of his taut body so tantalizingly close.

A discreet cough ripped the intimate moment like a rude expletive. They both turned toward the door with varying emotions. David was clearly annoyed, while Melanie felt a mixture of regret and relief.

Jean was standing in the doorway, looking at them impassively. "I'm sorry to bother you, sir. I was wondering if you wanted me to accompany you to London this weekend to look after the children."

"Couldn't that have waited until morning?" David asked with unaccustomed curtness.

"Yes, of course. I didn't realize I might be intruding." She flicked the barest glance at Melanie.

He took a deep breath. "It's all right. I should have told you I wouldn't be needing you this weekend."

"I really wouldn't mind, and you'll need someone to take care of the twins."

"Thank you, but I've already made arrangements. Is that all, Miss Morton?" David's tone was pleasant, but he left no doubt that the discussion was closed.

The nanny left with a murmured reply and the same closed expression she always wore.

David turned back to Melanie with a wry face. "Talk about your rotten timing."

Melanie had used the short respite to get a grip on herself. "Perhaps you *should* take Miss Morton to London. I'll be happy to look after Ariel and Ashley, but I'd like to get some shopping in and I'm afraid they'd be bored dragging through the stores."

"I didn't ask you along to be their baby-sitter. They'll be with me when you're off on your own, and there are reliable agencies I can call on to stay with them in the evening."

"It was just a thought." Melanie stood and said casually, "Well, I think I'll call it a night."

"This early?"

"I'm reading a very exciting book. I can't wait to finish it."

"I'm sorry I can't provide more competition," he drawled, without trying to persuade her to stay.

It was further proof to Melanie—if she needed any—that David's feelings for her were solely sexual. He was annoyed and mildly frustrated, but nothing more.

Clive finally reached Melanie on Saturday morning as she was packing her bag. "I can't believe I finally got you!" he exclaimed. "I was afraid you'd left town, but the maid said you were still here."

"Yes, I'll be around for awhile. David and I were able to rearrange our schedules, so I'll be working for him after all."

"That's wonderful! I hope you'll have dinner with me one night soon. Like tonight, if possible."

"I'm sorry, Clive, but I'm leaving shortly to go to London for the weekend."

"No problem. We can have dinner there."

"Don't tell me you have to go all the way to London to get a date, because I won't believe it."

"For you I'd be willing to. Actually I have some business in the city that I really should take care of. You're giving me the impetus I need. Is it a date?"

There wasn't any reason to refuse. David was going to a fancy ball, why should she stay home like Cinderella? "I'd love to have dinner with you," she answered.

"Fantastic! I'll call you when I get in. Where are you staying?"

"At David's town house."

"Oh?"

She laughed. "You can lower your eyebrows. He has a date in the city and he's taking the twins. I'm only going along for the ride."

"David must be out of his mind, but it's my good fortune," Clive said warmly.

In all the rush of getting the children and the luggage in the car, then running back into the house for forgotten items, Melanie didn't have a chance to tell David about her date with Clive. Not that she needed his permission. It was probably just as well not to mention it she decided, when it occurred to her on the drive. They'd been getting along so beautifully. Why rock the boat?

David's town house was as elegant in its own way as Castlebury Manor. A graceful staircase led from the marble-floored entry to the upstairs bedrooms. Opening off the entry hall were a formal living room and an equally dignified dining room, both filled with exquisite pieces that looked like family heirlooms.

A paneled den was less formidable. It had couches and comfortable chairs, just right for conversation or watching television. One wall held all the latest entertainment equipment.

"Everything is spotless," Melanie marveled. "Why doesn't your house get dusty like a normal person's?"

"You'd know how normal I am if you'd ever let me show you." He grinned mischievously. When she frowned and glanced pointedly at the children, he said, "I rang up and told my charwoman to give the place a special going-over. She comes in regularly."

"Can we watch television?" Ashley asked.

"As soon as you unpack. I'll take the rest of the luggage upstairs. I've put you in the blue room at the end of the hall," David told Melanie.

After he left, Ariel said, "Look, Uncle David has some messages." She pushed a button on the telephone answering machine.

A woman's voice came on. "Hi, David, it's Marilyn. I heard you were going to be in town for the weekend and I'm so thrilled. Call me the minute you get in, darling."

After a beep, another woman said, "Stephanie here. It's about time you came home, luv. I'll be waiting to hear from you."

David returned as the machine beeped again and yet another female voice left a message. Melanie didn't wait to hear this one.

"I'm going upstairs to unpack," she said.

He followed her out the door. "I hope you'll find everything you need. The spare bedroom is rarely slept in."

"Why doesn't that surprise me?" she asked coolly. Without waiting for a reply she ran up the stairs.

The blue room might not have been slept in, but some of the former occupants had left little souvenirs of themselves. There was a bottle of perfume on the dresser, and a pair of earrings and some new panty hose in one of the drawers.

The most irritating thing was the small collection of clothing in the closet. A pink satin robe was perhaps understandable. It could get chilly after a shower, wrapped only in a towel. But a slinky black dress with matching shoes? Anyone who kept part of her wardrobe in a man's house had to be a regular visitor. She would have brought something less elegant to go home in the next morning.

Melanie knew her annoyance was irrational. David was an attractive, unattached male. Naturally he'd have a lot of women interested in him. The sheer number of them was a little daunting, however.

Her spirits rebounded when they took the children out a short time later. David had left it up to them to choose the day's activities, starting with where to have lunch.

"What do you bet it will be pizza?" Melanie teased.

They surprised her by opting for Chinese food instead. David took them to a well-known Chinese restaurant that was crowded and noisy. It also had the best dim sum that Melanie had ever tasted.

Waiters bustled between the tables pushing carts with wicker baskets filled with steaming morsels of food. Each selection was served on a separate, small white plate. The variety was endless. Some carts offered sesame prawns, spring rolls and little squares of duck with plum sauce. If those didn't appeal, the next cart might have crab balls, pouches of paper-wrapped chicken and small green onion pancakes. A diner simply pointed to his selection. At the end of the meal the dishes were counted to determine the amount of the bill.

"I like dim sum." Ariel picked up a crab-stuffed lobster claw from her child-size plate. "It's like playing house."

"You two continue to amaze me," Melanie said. "I never knew you had such sophisticated palates." Both children had chosen knowingly from the bewildering offerings.

"Don't compliment them too soon." David chuckled. "I haven't converted them to French food yet."

"He tried to make us eat eels," Ashley said indignantly.

"I didn't *make* you. I just suggested you try it."

"I don't blame you," Melanie told the boy. "Who wants to eat something that slithers around on its belly?"

"How will I ever make gourmets out of them if you plant pictures like that in their minds?" David complained.

"Wait until they grow up," she advised. "Otherwise sensible adults will eat anything if it's expensive enough or hard to get."

"*You* don't, and you're all grown-up." His scrutiny was unmistakably male.

"Only on the outside," she answered lightly. "My preference in food runs to tuna fish sandwiches and jelly doughnuts."

David's eyes wandered over her delicate features. "With a face like yours, you can have anything you want."

"Are you in love with Melanie, Uncle David?" Ariel asked. Both children were staring at them with fascinated curiosity.

Melanie and David turned to look at them in startled astonishment. Before either could answer, Ashley said, "We saw this television show and the man was in love with the woman, but she didn't love him back. They gave each other these long dopey looks and kissed a lot, but she only wanted his money. She was really in love with his brother."

"It wasn't his brother," Ariel corrected. "It was his cousin. Remember, he needed the money to pay his solicitor because he ran over somebody when he was drunk and they wanted to put him in jail."

"That sounds like a soap opera," Melanie exclaimed. "Did Miss Morton know what you were watching?"

"I don't know. She was busy doing something for Lady Addersley."

"I think I'd better have a talk with Miss Morton," David said. "What else did you watch on television this week?"

"Not very much," Ashley answered evasively. "Can we go to the park now? You said we could ride the paddleboats."

The children were in such a hurry to change the subject that Melanie suspected they'd watched a lot of unsuitable TV. Fortunately it had taken their attention off David and herself. He had looked as shocked as she felt. Which didn't exactly delight her.

They were a little reserved with each other on the way to Regent's Park, but it wasn't noticeable because the twins monopolized the conversation.

When they reached the park it became even easier. David took Ashley out on the pond in one paddleboat, while Melanie and Ariel shared another. The children naturally wanted to race, which erased any remaining tension in the adults.

By the time they returned to shore they were all laughing and squabbling about which team could beat the other at different sports.

The happy mood ruptured when they returned home and Ariel asked, "What are we going to do tonight, Uncle David?"

"Let's go to the cinema," Ashley suggested.

David cleared his throat, looking uncomfortable. "You've had enough activity for one day. I want you to go to bed early tonight."

"But we're on holiday!" Ashley said indignantly.

"You've been on holiday all summer."

"Not in London."

"We could go to an early show and still be home by bedtime," Ariel wheedled.

"Not tonight." When they prepared to argue, David said reluctantly, "I have an appointment this evening."

"Can Melanie take us?" The twins turned to her expectantly.

She hesitated. Clive didn't say when he'd pick her up, and she hadn't heard from him. If for some reason he didn't show up, she was in for a long, dull evening. It was still fairly early, though. She had to give him the benefit of the doubt.

"There's a cinema not far from here," Ariel urged.

"Maybe tomorrow night," Melanie answered as the doorbell rang.

It was a Mrs. Hoskins from an agency David had called earlier. After introducing her to the children, he took the woman into the kitchen to show her where everything was.

The twins went along. They'd accepted defeat on the movie and were now negotiating to stay up later and watch television.

When David returned to the den, Melanie said, "I expected to make dinner for the kids."

"I didn't bring you here to work."

"You're just afraid I can't cook," she teased.

"You don't have to. You have other talents."

"Shame on you. That's a very chauvinistic thing to say."

"I was referring to your expertise in the business world," he replied smoothly.

"Which you only have my word for, so far." She smiled. "I could be leading you on shamelessly to get free room and board."

"I wish you wanted more than that from me," he murmured.

I do—and a lot of good it's going to do me, Melanie thought silently. She turned away. "Hadn't you better get ready for your date?"

David suppressed a sigh. "Yes, I suppose so."

Melanie was glancing at the paper when David returned a short time later, looking stunningly handsome in his elegant dinner clothes. The snowy white shirt emphasized his deep tan and the startling blue of his eyes.

Melanie felt even more like Cinderella in her slightly rumpled skirt and blouse. It had seemed pointless to change, since there'd been no word from Clive.

David paused in the doorway. "I hope you won't be too bored this evening," he said tentatively.

"Don't worry about me," she answered evenly. "I'll be fine."

"You don't have to ride herd on the twins. Mrs. Hoskins will see that they get to bed on time—or reasonably thereabouts." He gave her a smile which she didn't return.

"They're in good hands," she said. "Go and enjoy yourself."

"Yes, well . . . I probably won't be too late."

She couldn't help smiling. "You don't have a curfew."

"I wish I didn't have to go at all," he said in a muted voice.

Did he expect her to believe that? David would shrug off domesticity like a pair of old jeans as soon as he returned to his former environment.

"It's getting late," she said pointedly.

"I know." He hesitated for a moment, as though wanting to add something. When she didn't offer any encouragement he said quietly, "Good night, Melanie."

The telephone rang a few moments after David left. What he needed was a social secretary, Melanie decided grimly. She picked up the receiver grudgingly, in no mood to take a message from one of his endless girlfriends.

Clive's voice was apologetic. "I hope you're not too angry with me, although you have every right to be."

"No, I'm not angry. Where are you?"

"I'm in London—*finally!* It's been a nightmare getting here."

"What happened?"

"I got a late start this afternoon, but I still had plenty of time to make it. Except that a tire blew out in the middle of nowhere and I didn't have a spare. The reason for that is another story." He sounded harried. "I had to hike miles to a petrol station and then wait around until they could send someone back with a new tire. I would have called to tell you

I was running late, but the phone was out of order. The whole affair was a blasted comedy of errors!"

"It's all right, Clive, calm down."

"I was afraid you wouldn't be speaking to me."

"That would be juvenile. Things happen sometimes and there's nothing you can do about it."

"You're an angel! Give me ten minutes to change clothes and I'll be right over."

"Don't hurry, I'm not ready yet, either."

Melanie's spirits rose as she ran upstairs to get dressed. Clive's major effort to keep their date was a gratifying change from David's ambivalence. If Clive was given a choice between herself and Bootsie, that witchy redhead wouldn't even be in the running!

Melanie was putting on her makeup when the twins came to her room.

"Mrs. Hoskins wants to know when you want dinner," Ashley said.

"Tell her I'm going out to dinner," Melanie replied.

"Where are you going?"

"I don't know yet."

Ariel was watching with interest as Melanie outlined her mouth with a brush. "How old do I have to be before I can wear lipstick?"

"When you're in your teens," Melanie answered.

"That's too far away," the little girl protested. "Why can't I wear it now?"

"Because it would be wasted on you." Melanie smiled at her. "You don't need cosmetics to make you beautiful."

"Neither do you, but it looks nice on you." Ariel stared appraisingly at the hint of green eye shadow that made Melanie's eyes sparkle like emeralds. She had also added a touch of blush to emphasize her high cheekbones.

Ashley was bored by girl talk. "If you wanted to go out tonight, why didn't you go with Uncle David?"

"I wasn't asked." Melanie immediately regretted her cool tone of voice. "He's seeing his old friends and they have a lot to talk about," she added brightly.

"He has a date with Lady Addersley," Ariel told her brother knowingly.

"I like Melanie better," he said. "Couldn't you fall in love with Uncle David so you could get married and live with us all the time?"

"No, I couldn't." She stood and shooed them out of the room. "I have to get dressed now."

Melanie was determined to have a good time that evening and she did. Clive took her first to a three-star restaurant with a dining room grand enough for a palace. The windows were draped with deeply swagged maroon velvet, and crystal chandeliers cast a soft glow over the diners.

A platoon of serving people surrounded them from the moment they arrived. A formally dressed maître d' escorted them to their table, an equally elegant waiter presented huge, tasseled menus, a sommelier consulted with Clive over his wine selection, and a busboy filled their water glasses and put butter pats shaped like clover leaves on their bread-and-butter plates.

When they had a brief moment alone, Melanie said, "This would be a great place to come if you didn't know anybody. You wouldn't have a chance to feel lonesome."

"They do tend to lay it on a bit thick," Clive said ruefully. "I always felt the food was worth it, but if you'd rather go somewhere else we can just have a quick drink here and leave."

"Oh, no! I wasn't complaining. I'm delighted to be here."

"You couldn't be as happy as I am. This is worth everything I went through to get here."

"I'm really flattered. If I'd found myself in the same situation, I might have been tempted to turn around and go home."

"The idea never entered my mind," he said, raising his glass to her.

Clive's obvious admiration warmed Melanie even more than the excellent champagne he ordered. He was really a very nice man, utterly open and charming. Unlike David who was always playing games with her. She was instantly annoyed at herself for even thinking of David. Clive deserved her full attention, and that was what he was going to get.

When it came time to order, Melanie discovered the menu was all in French. Her high school French was usually equal to most menus, but this one defeated her. There were things on it that couldn't possibly be what they seemed.

"What appeals to you?" Clive asked.

"I haven't gotten around to making a decision yet. I'm still trying to decipher the menu. This *pied de cochon farci aux morilles,* for instance. *Pied* is foot, *cochon* is pig, and I think *morilles* are mushrooms, but what does it all add up to?"

"Pig's foot stuffed with foie gras and mushrooms."

"You're joking! Who would expect to find pigs' feet in an elegant restaurant like this?"

Clive chuckled. "It's acceptable if you gussy them up and give them a French name. Would you like to try it? It's one of their specialties."

"No, thanks. I'm not partial to things most people throw away."

"Does that include escargots?"

"Especially snails—anything that slithers or crawls." Melanie started to laugh. "I must tell the twins they had pigs' feet on the menu."

"They're junior gourmets?" He looked puzzled.

"Just the opposite. They were outraged because David wanted them to try eel. I told them I wouldn't, either."

Clive paused for an instant. "You seem quite fond of those youngsters. Did you know them before you came here?"

"No, I guess we just hit it off right away. They're really terrific kids."

"That's encouraging. I like to think they're the reason you extended your stay, not David."

"I told you why I'm staying on. It's strictly business."

Melanie regretted having mentioned anything to do with David. She could see where someone might get the wrong idea. It was also bad form to talk about one man when you were out with another. Clive was too nice to be short-changed.

"Tell me about yourself," she said. "Do you like living in the country? You seem so at home in this environment."

"The truth is, I can take it or leave it—the city, I mean. I'm not a party animal like David."

"I guess it takes all kinds," she said brightly.

"That doesn't mean I don't enjoy what London has to offer. I frequently miss restaurants like this one and all the extensive nightlife."

"I've heard London really swings if you know where to go. Those places don't seem to be in the guidebooks for tourists."

"Fortunately you have your own personal guide tonight." Clive smiled. "What's your pleasure, gambling, disco, a jazz club, cabaret?"

"They all sound fabulous. You'll have to choose."

"All right, we'll see how many of them we can fit in."

They started with a very exclusive disco, open only to members. A brawny man in a tuxedo carefully examined the credentials of anyone he didn't recognize. Clive was greeted by name and they were waved inside.

In spite of being a private club, the place was packed. Music blaring at megadecibels was the same as any disco, but the patrons looked like a convention of celebrities.

Melanie didn't recognize any of them, but they all appeared to be movie stars or diplomats, or maybe royalty. She didn't know which were more gorgeous, the men or the women. Their clothes were the kind of high-style creations that were seen in fashion magazines rather than on real people.

Her eyes widened when a woman walked by in a thigh-high, orange vinyl skirt, knee-length patent leather boots and a sheer black blouse worn without a bra. The man with her was wearing kilts and had his hair tied back in a ponytail.

Clive grinned at Melanie's expression. "You'll have to admit it isn't touristy."

"These people look like they're all from Central Casting. What do they do in real life?"

"The man in the kilts is an earl, and you'd never guess what the woman with him does for a living."

"I could make a guess," Melanie said dryly.

"You'd be wrong. She's an industrial designer."

"I guess it's true. You can't tell a book by its cover—or lack of, in this case."

"You don't like her outfit?" he teased.

"I always wondered who wore those wild getups pictured in the fashion magazines. Now I know—people with a lot of money and no inhibitions."

Not everyone had gone to extremes. There were many stunning gowns, and a fortune in expensive jewelry. Clive told her who a lot of the more notable people were, and paused for a few words with many of them.

Melanie found the whole scene fascinating. This was indeed a world that tourists didn't see. But when Clive suggested moving on, she was ready. The noise and frantic activity became a little much after a while.

The gambling casino he took her to next was also a private club, but it was quieter and the patrons weren't as flamboyant. They were all well dressed, but their object wasn't to see and be seen. They were more interested in the dice tumbling across green felt-covered tables, or the little white balls spinning on roulette wheels. An atmosphere of excitement pervaded the large room as thousands of pounds changed hands.

Clive bought a stack of chips for each of them, insisting that Melanie play, instead of simply watching as she wanted to.

"I don't know much about gambling," she protested.

He laughed. "Neither does anybody else. The house always wins if you keep playing long enough."

"Then what's the point?"

"Are you having a good time?" he asked, in a seeming digression.

"I'm having a wonderful time."

"Then think of it as a cover charge."

Melanie wagered cautiously, losing her chip more often than not, but winning a few now and then. At the end of an hour or so, she still had some chips left, while Clive had lost his entire stack.

"You'll have to teach me your system." He chuckled. "I need to buy more chips."

"You've proved your point about the house always winning if you play long enough." She glanced at her watch and gasped. "Do you know what time it is?"

He shrugged. "We got a late start. Where would you like to go now?"

"It's almost three o'clock in the morning!"

"There are a lot of after-hours places. Would you like a drink?"

"Thanks, but now that I know how late it is, I'm tired. May I have a rain check?"

"Any time, any place," he answered fondly.

Most of the houses in David's neighborhood were darkened at that hour. The sound of the taxicab door closing sounded very loud in the stillness. After telling the driver to wait, Clive walked Melanie to the door.

"It's been a wonderful evening," she said.

"The first of many, I hope."

"What are you going to do for an encore?" she teased. "We did everything except wash an elephant."

"You didn't say you wanted to." He grinned.

"I'm sure you could have arranged it. I've never met anyone so knowledgeable about London."

"You see, David isn't the only one who knows his way around."

Melanie's smile faded at the reminder of David. She'd managed to forget about him for most of the evening—or at least put him out of her mind temporarily. Now he was back in living color.

When they reached the front door Clive framed her face between his palms and gazed at her with unmistakable desire. "I hate to see the evening end."

"It's been great fun," she murmured, knowing he was going to kiss her. In a way, she welcomed the idea. Maybe that would break David's spell.

"That's the understatement of the year," he said, in answer to her comment.

Lowering his head slowly, Clive took her in his arms. His kiss was gentle at first, then more urgent when she didn't draw away.

Melanie wanted to respond. Clive wasn't merely the answer to a problem, he was a thoroughly nice man who was delightful to be with. Any sensible woman would be thrilled to have him interested in her. When his kiss deepened, Melanie was forced to admit the truth. She really liked Clive—as a friend. There was no magic. Only one man could provide that.

Suddenly the front door flew open and David stood towering in the entry, his face dark with anger at the sight of them in each other's arms.

Fixing his glare on Melanie, he demanded, "Where the hell have you been?"

Chapter Seven

Melanie and Clive were frozen in each other's arms. For a moment they could only stare at David in surprise. Then they moved apart.

"Do you realize what time it is?" David asked in outrage.

"I'm sorry, old boy," Clive said awkwardly. "It was my fault for keeping Melanie out this late."

"You don't have to apologize to him!" she said irately.

"Then I suggest *you* explain where you've been all this time," David said.

"I don't have to explain anything. Especially not to *you!*"

Anger radiated from their taut bodies as they stood toe-to-toe, glaring at each other. Clive gazed from one to the other, looking uncomfortable.

"Why don't we all just calm down?" he asked.

"Stay out of it," David rasped. "This is between Melanie and me."

"I can't let you talk to her like that. I don't see that we've committed such a grievous sin, but if you're looking for someone to blame, I'm the one you should be shouting at."

Melanie thrust out her chin. "Neither one of us has to answer for our behavior."

"Exactly what kind of behavior are we talking about?" David asked ominously.

"See here! If you're implying what I think you are, you're way out of line." Now Clive was starting to get angry.

As the two men balled their hands into fists, Melanie took a deep breath. "It's all right, Clive, I can handle this. Why don't you call me this afternoon?"

"I'm not going to leave you here alone with him!"

A muscle bunched in David's square jaw. "At least *I* can be trusted to act like a gentleman."

Clive took a step toward him. "Are you saying that I can't?"

Melanie put a hand on his arm. "Please, Clive, don't make things any worse. I promise I'll straighten him out." She urged him toward the waiting cab.

"Well, if you're sure," he said reluctantly.

"Very sure. I'm just sorry it had to end like this."

"It isn't over." He cupped her cheek in his palm and gazed into her eyes. "This is just the beginning."

Melanie was conscious of David standing only a few feet away ready to explode. She contained her own temper until Clive left. The door had hardly closed before David remarked with barely restrained rage, "How touching! Maybe you should have gone with him."

She didn't dignify that with a denial. "How dare you embarrass me like that?"

"Clue me in on what you're embarrassed about. Staying out all night with a man you barely know—or getting caught at it?"

"Even if what you were accusing me of was true, I don't see that it's any of your business."

"So you're admitting you slept with Clive."

Melanie was too angry to see the bleakness behind David's outrage. "I don't have to tell you anything! *You* owe *me* an apology!"

"For what? Interrupting your good-night kiss? It was pretty chaste considering the kind he must have given you earlier. Or is that the best good old Clive can do?"

"That's about what I would expect from someone who equates manhood with the amount of notches he can carve on his bedpost."

"Hey, *I'm* not the one who scored on his first date."

"Your preoccupation with my love life is puzzling, considering how active your own is," she said witheringly. "I'd almost think you struck out with Bootsie tonight—if I didn't know her better."

"Your antipathy toward Bootsie is downright irrational. I can't understand why she provokes such an extreme reaction from you."

"You're very clever at changing the subject when you don't want to talk about something," Melanie said, doing the same thing. "Don't think I'm going to forget about your disgraceful behavior tonight. Why were you waiting up for me in the first place?"

"I wasn't waiting up," he answered carefully. "Your voices during that prolonged good-night woke me."

"You couldn't have been asleep for very long." She noticed for the first time that David was fully dressed, although he'd removed his tie and unfastened the top button of his shirt. "You weren't even in bed! I'll bet you just got home yourself."

"For your information, I've been here since midnight."

"Then why on earth didn't you go to bed?"

"Because I was worried about you. I came home and found Mrs. Hoskins still here. She said you didn't want any dinner, and she presumed you'd gone out. When she finished cleaning up in the kitchen and went to ask if there was anything else for her to do, you were nowhere around.''

"I guess I forgot to tell her I was going out. But the twins knew.''

"Presumably they didn't mention it to her, and when I got home they were asleep. I thought perhaps you'd gone to a movie or something, but when it got later and later, I became understandably upset.''

"I'm really sorry,'' she said penitently. "It never occurred to me that you'd worry about me.''

A flicker of emotion softened David's hard expression, then disappeared in an instant. "I didn't know you were in good hands.''

Melanie's remorse died a sudden death. "What is that supposed to mean?''

"Only that I had no reason to believe you were out on a date. It was quite a coincidence that Clive knew where to find you,'' David drawled.

"He phoned the house before we left this morning. I told him where I was going.''

"Oh, I see. Then the coincidence is that he just happened to be going to London, too.''

"You can knock off the sarcasm,'' she flared. "Okay, we had a date. Are you satisfied?''

"Hardly. Why didn't you tell me?''

"I don't know. I guess it just slipped my mind.''

"Even when I was apologizing for leaving you alone?''

"We made a date, but I hadn't heard from Clive,'' she said defensively. "I thought maybe he forgot.''

"You knew damn well he didn't! He's been pawing the turf since the first night he laid eyes on you at Sylvia's party.''

"You're exaggerating. Clive is a perfect gentleman.''

David's eyes glittered. "Was that passionate kiss I interrupted proof of his good manners?''

"It was only a good-night kiss!" Melanie exclaimed in frustration. "That's what people do after a date. It's like shaking hands."

"You and I had dinner in the village together, but evidently that doesn't qualify as a date. When we came home we went to our separate bedrooms without even a handshake," he said mockingly.

She clenched her fists in an effort to stay calm. "I really should let you picture us having an orgy, but it isn't fair to Clive."

"It certainly wouldn't do to be unfair to Clive," David agreed satirically.

Melanie glared at him before continuing. "I had a very exciting evening, only not the kind you imagine. After dinner in a fabulous restaurant we went to a private disco filled with celebrities. From there we went to a casino and gambled. I was having so much fun I never even thought about the time. I'm sure you've spent a lot of nights like that, but it's all new to me. Is that a crime?"

David's mocking expression turned somber. "No, it's perfectly understandable. I didn't realize how selfish I was being. You didn't come to England to bury yourself in the country with a couple of demanding kids."

"Could you just *try* not to be sarcastic?" she asked in exasperation.

"I'm being completely serious." He thrust his hands into his pockets and turned away. "I'm really dense. I should have gotten a clue when I saw how much you enjoyed Sylvia's party."

"You *are* serious, aren't you?" Melanie looked at him uncertainly. "Of course I enjoyed myself. It was a lovely party. But that doesn't mean I've been unhappy with you and the twins."

"You don't have to be polite."

"You're overreacting," she said impatiently. "You know how fond I am of Ariel and Ashley. That has nothing to do with enjoying a little nightlife without them. *You* spent a glamorous evening out, and I'm sure you had a good time. That doesn't mean you hate to go back to Castlebury Manor. Or maybe it does," she added hesitantly.

"Not at all. One thing has nothing to do with the other."

"That's exactly what I just said! But even if I *was* getting a little restless, I don't see why you were so angry—once you saw that I was all right."

He turned to give her a sober look. "Don't you know why?"

"No, I honestly don't."

"How about finding you in Clive's arms?"

"You're a sophisticated man, David. You can't tell me you were shocked at seeing two people kiss good-night."

"You can't be that blind, damn it! You have to know by now that I'm in love with you."

Melanie stared at him incredulously. "If you're not joking, that has to be the best kept secret in town."

"Don't pretend you didn't notice. I've been very open about my feelings for you."

"We're talking about love now, not sex," she said tartly.

"They go together. Of course I want to make love to you. What red-blooded man wouldn't? You're a beautiful, alluring woman. But my feelings for you go a lot deeper than that."

Hope was making Melanie's heart pound, but caution warned her not to be gullible. David hadn't made a move toward her. "Why didn't you ever mention the fact to me?"

"Because I knew you didn't share my feelings." He paced the entry restlessly. "Every time I tried to get close you backed off, even though you admitted you were attracted to me. That's the only thing that gave me any hope. And then you met Clive," he said flatly.

She managed to keep her voice dispassionate, although excitement was racing through her veins. "You had Bootsie clinging to you like ivy. She doesn't encourage competition.''

"I told you what the situation is between us. You weren't interested. I didn't want to believe it, but I guess I have no choice. I apologize for making a scene. It won't happen again."

"You give up awfully easily for a man who's supposed to be in love," Melanie said artlessly.

"What do you want from me? I acted like a raging idiot tonight, insulted a friend and bared my soul to a woman who couldn't care less. What more can I do?"

She smiled enchantingly. "You might try kissing me."

He stopped pacing and looked at her warily, as though suspecting a trap. "You don't need an excuse to leave. I won't try to stop you."

She walked slowly toward him. "It's no wonder all those women chase after you. If they waited for you to make the first move, nobody would have any fun at all."

David's face lit with incredulous joy as she put her arms around his neck. "Does this mean what I hope it does?"

"I didn't expect to have to spell it out for you, but if that's what it takes." She pulled his head down and parted his lips for the insertion of her tongue.

David's arms closed around her convulsively as his uncertainty vanished. He kissed her with all the pent-up longing that had been building for so long. While his mouth devoured hers, his hands moved restlessly over her back, urging her against his taut body.

The extent of his desire was equaled by hers. Melanie pressed even closer, crushing her breasts against the hard wall of his chest while uttering tiny cries of satisfaction.

"I can't believe this is really happening," he muttered, burying his face in her scented hair. "It's like a dream come true."

She laughed softly. "I'm glad I'm in your dream."

"You've never been out of it. Do you know what hell it's been, seeing you every day and not being able to touch you like this?"

"I know." She sprinkled tiny kisses over his face. "We've wasted so much time."

"We have all the time in the world, my love. I'm looking forward to holding you in my arms all night, every night."

Melanie held her breath. Was David asking her to marry him?

His eyes darkened as he pulled her close again and cupped her bottom in both hands, lifting her so their hips were joined. "I want to make love to you a hundred different ways—starting right now."

The prospect was so mind spinning that it drove all other thoughts out of her head. When he lifted her in his arms she buried her face in his neck, feeling a warm tide of passion rising inside her.

David carried her up the stairs, murmuring arousing words that made her heart race. The anticipation escalated when they reached her room. He paused for a moment by the bed to give her a deep kiss that was like a promise of what was to come. Every nerve and muscle in her body responded to his overwhelming masculinity.

When David tried to place her on the bed, she refused to release him even for an instant. He tumbled on top of her and the weight of his body pressed heavily into hers. They were welded into one person with a single, thundering heartbeat. Before he could move, she clasped her legs around his hips and arched her body into his hard arousal.

David made a deep primal sound and gripped her hips in both hands while his tongue plundered her mouth. But when Melanie moved against him rhythmically he drew a sharp breath and released her. With a tremendous effort he rolled over onto his side, carrying her with him.

"It's too soon, sweetheart," he said with difficulty. "I want it to be good for you."

"How can it get any better than this?" She unbuttoned his shirt with trembling fingers.

David chuckled deeply as he shrugged off his shirt and slid her zipper down. "Wait and see."

After lifting her slightly to remove her dress, he unclasped her bra. Melanie shivered with anticipation as he feathered her breasts with his fingertips, gazing at them with glowing eyes.

"You're as beautiful as I knew you'd be," he said huskily.

Lowering his head, he strung a line of kisses from one rosy nipple to the other, then paused to capture one between his lips. She twisted restlessly as he curled his tongue around the little bud and pulled gently.

When she cried out with pleasure he said, "Is that good, angel? I want to make you happy."

"You do, darling," she whispered.

"So happy you'll never leave me?"

Melanie barely heard him. He had removed her panty hose and was stroking her thighs erotically. When he reached the damp triangle of curls, she lost control. Ripping open his slacks, she reached for his vibrant manhood.

David's control vanished along with hers. Shredding his clothes in a blur of activity, he clasped her in his arms and entered her in one swift, fluid movement. It was more wonderful than she could have imagined. He filled her completely, and it still wasn't enough. She was greedy for him, wanting more and more, which he gave gladly.

His deft thrusts grew more rapid as the limit of their endurance approached. Melanie could feel David's body pulse and her own responded joyfully. His surge of power spread liquid fire through her. She clung to him tightly as the flames burned hotly, then smoldered, and finally subsided to a warm glow.

Neither felt like moving afterward. They remained twined together, utterly content. When Melanie finally summoned the energy to open her eyes, she found David gazing at her with such love that her heart swelled.

"I knew it would be like this," he murmured.

"*I* didn't." She smiled. "If I'd known, I never could have resisted you all this time."

"I'll let you make it up to me," he teased.

She smoothed his hair lovingly. "It will be my pleasure."

"No, darling, it will be mine."

"Are we having our first argument?" She laughed.

He pulled her close and kissed her sweetly. "I don't ever want to argue again."

"That's kind of unrealistic, considering our tempers. Although, yours is worse than mine. I do believe I saw smoke coming out of your ears tonight."

"You weren't exactly calm, yourself." He chuckled.

"Okay, so we're both hotheaded, which isn't necessarily such a bad thing." She grinned. "If we'd been politely distant to each other, we'd both be wearing pajamas right now."

David stroked her bottom, sending a little ripple up Melanie's spine. "You looked very sexy in the little blue chiffon thing you wore that first night, but I prefer you like this."

"You looked pretty sexy yourself, pal."

"For one stupid moment I thought you'd staged that fall to get me into your bedroom. But then I realized I couldn't be that lucky."

"You almost were." She tilted her head to look up at him wonderingly. "I think I fell in love with you that first night."

He kissed her tenderly. "I wish you'd let me in on it. I've been spending a lot of sleepless nights because of you."

"Including this one. You'd better go back to your own room. It's almost morning."

"I have no intention of leaving you." He scissored his legs around hers, joining their bodies more closely. "This is a very historic occasion."

"Which we've just celebrated."

"That was only the warm-up," he murmured, caressing her breast.

Melanie's body sprang to immediate life, but she tried to ignore it. "The twins will be up soon. You don't want them to find you here. They're too young for sex education 101—although you'd be a wonderful teacher."

David chuckled wickedly. "And I haven't even demonstrated all I know yet."

"You can further my education tonight."

"How about a little homework before the test?" He parted her lips with the tip of his tongue.

Melanie was powerless to resist that kind of inducement. She curled around him in willing compliance, ravenous for him once again.

David fed her hunger with his hands, his lips, his body. He strung a line of kisses from her breasts to her navel, pausing to dip his tongue into the little depression. Her passion mounted as his mouth moved lower, searing her with its heat. She drew in her breath sharply when he parted her legs and kissed the satiny skin of her inner thigh.

"You're so exquisite," he groaned. "Every inch of you is beautiful."

Melanie uttered a tiny cry when he stroked her intimately, she trembled when his mouth touched the core of her desire. Reaching for him desperately, she pulled him on top of her.

Their mating was just as urgent this time, their need for each other unquenchable. They were swirled in a vortex of passion, then tossed free to soar into the heights together. When it was over they were totally and completely satisfied.

Melanie was the first to stir. She wanted to stay in David's arms forever, but that wasn't possible. "You have to go back to your own room," she whispered.

"I don't want to," he grunted, like a sleepy little boy.

She smiled. Recent experience had taught her how wrong that description was. David was a magnificent male in his prime.

She poked him gently. "Okay, stay here, but don't think *I'm* going to tell the twins what you're doing in my bed."

He sat up reluctantly. "You're a cruel woman."

"How soon they forget." She laughed.

"I could never forget anything about you, my love." He kissed her tenderly before swinging his long legs out of bed. "After I get a few hours' sleep, I'll refresh my memory, just in case."

"What do you plan to do with the kids? They're a little young to send off to the movies alone."

As David stood and stretched, the muscles rippled in his splendidly nude body. "I'll think of something. Never underestimate the ingenuity of a man in love."

By the time Melanie arose the next morning, David had given the twins breakfast. She'd had only a few hours' sleep, so he must have had even less, although he didn't show it. David looked as vital as always.

"We already had breakfast." Ariel gazed at Melanie disapprovingly. "Uncle David said we shouldn't wait for you."

"You didn't have to get up," he said. "I planned to bring you breakfast in bed."

"Is Melanie sick?" Ashley asked.

David smiled. "No, I just thought it would be nice to show my appreciation for all she's done for me."

Melanie returned his smile. "I'd say we're about even."

As usual, Ashley was more interested in plans for the immediate future. "What are we going to do today?"

"How would you and Ariel like to go to the zoo? And maybe a trip to Madame Tussaud's Wax Museum afterward, then tea at the Ritz. You can have those little chocolate things you like so much."

"Yay!" Both children jumped up and down.

"Hurry up and get dressed, Melanie," Ashley said.

She groaned inwardly, hoping she had the stamina to get though such a strenuous day after only a few hours' sleep. But David had a surprise for her.

"Melanie and I won't be going along," he said. "You'll have your own car and driver today."

"You can't send them off alone with only a chauffeur to look after them," Melanie protested.

"You know I wouldn't do that. I phoned a company in London that specializes in taking children on tours when their parents have more adult things to do." David's eyes twinkled. "The driver doubles as a guide. He skips the museums and churches in favor of places kids enjoy."

"What a clever idea for a business," Melanie said.

"I thought so." David couldn't hold back a grin.

The twins weren't so sure. "We want to be with you and Melanie," Ariel said.

"You certainly can if you like," David answered smoothly. "We're going to spend a quiet day at home."

"That's no fun," Ashley objected.

"It depends on your point of view. What's it going to be? If you don't want to go to the zoo I'll have to phone and cancel the car."

The children conferred briefly. "Okay, we'll go," Ashley said grudgingly. "But I don't see why you can't come, too. It would be a lot more fun than just staying home."

"What are you going to do all day?" Ariel asked.

"Just rest," Melanie answered hastily. She didn't trust the mischief brimming in David's eyes. "We were both out late last night."

"We'll probably spend most of the day in bed," he remarked with an innocent expression.

The twins got over their disappointment rapidly. Sean, the driver-guide, was a young man who'd had a lot of experience with children. By the time the three of them left the house, Ariel and Ashley were completely won over.

When the door closed behind them, Melanie said, "They seem happy. Now I don't feel so guilty."

"There's nothing to feel guilty about. We're all doing what we want to do. Or at least we will be soon." David put his arms around her. "Let's go back to bed."

"Shouldn't we at least wait until Sean starts the car?" She smiled at his impatience.

"Why waste precious time?" He teased her lips apart and inserted his tongue suggestively.

As Melanie clasped her arms around his waist, the phone rang. David made a sound of annoyance.

"I'm going to take that damn thing off the hook!" he growled.

"You can't do that when you have children. They might need to get in touch with you."

"Not yet, they just left. Okay, I won't answer it. There's nobody I want to talk to, anyway."

"Has it ever occurred to you that it might be for me?" she teased.

David's face darkened at the reminder of Clive, the only person who knew where to find her. "Whoever it is, he's damned insistent." He strode toward the den.

Melanie followed, trying to decide what to say if it was, indeed, Clive. He deserved to be let down easily, but how? She needn't have worried.

"Hello," David said gruffly. His scowl faded and he looked obliquely at Melanie before lowering his voice and turning away. "No, I was just...uh, you didn't wake me. I've been up for a long time."

It didn't take a rocket scientist to figure out he was talking to Bootsie or one of his other girlfriends, Melanie thought cynically. She turned and left the room, as much for her own sake as David's. It was painful to be reminded of what a playboy he'd been. Could he really change? She went into the kitchen and poured herself a cup of coffee.

David followed a few minutes later. "Sorry for the interruption, darling." His glance was wary. "I'm all yours now."

"That's debatable."

"You don't really believe that." He put his arms around her from behind and nibbled on her ear. "You know you're the love of my life."

"Your current one, anyhow."

He turned her in his arms and tipped her chin up, forcing her to look at him. "Don't ever say that. Didn't last night tell you anything?"

"I don't have any complaints about last night. It's the competition today that keeps me from being a true believer." She tried to keep her tone light.

"My dearest love, you're the one I've been looking for all my life. I don't deny that I've known a lot of women, but that was before I found *you*. You have to believe me."

"I want to," Melanie answered wistfully. "But why should I think I'm any more than your current favorite? You must have felt the same way about all of them in the beginning."

"You're wrong. I've never been truly in love before. You saw how I acted last night when I found you with Clive. That kind of jealousy is reserved for more than a passing fancy."

Melanie wavered. David *had* been almost frightening last night. And he'd never lied to her. Why should she question her own happiness? As she opened her mouth to say she believed him, the telephone rang again.

He swore pungently under his breath. "Let it ring," he rasped.

She moved out of his embrace. "You can't ignore it all weekend. She'll just call again—or one of the others will."

Melanie started to leave him alone as she had before, but David caught her around the waist, forcing her to remain. He pinned her to his side, so close that she could hear the person on the other end of the line when he picked up the kitchen phone.

"David Crandall here," he answered curtly.

"Goodness, darling, you sound so businesslike." Bootsie giggled. "You were much friendlier last night."

"How friendly was I?" He held the receiver slightly away from his ear to be sure Melanie could hear both sides of the conversation.

"Not as friendly as I'd hoped," she replied in a pouting voice. "How about coming over this afternoon and making it up to me?"

"We have to talk, Bootsie."

"That's not very imaginative. I can think of better things to do," she said seductively.

"You're a good friend," he persisted. "So I feel I must be honest with you."

"I don't like the sound of that." Her voice was suddenly hard, all the coquettishness gone.

"I think you should know that I've fallen in love with someone," David continued doggedly.

"It's Melanie, isn't it?"

"Yes."

"I knew that scheming little opportunist was out to take you away from me. Oh, she's clever all right. Pretending to be so crazy about Ariel and Ashley. Men are so stupid! She isn't interested in them. What she's really after is your money and your title."

"It's nice to know they're the only things that make me attractive," he remarked sardonically.

"Not to *me!* I care about you, darling—and I know you care about me, too."

"As a friend," he said firmly.

"How can you say such a thing? You're infatuated with Melanie right now because she's a novelty, but that won't last. You and I belong together."

David's impatience was beginning to show. "We had fun in the old days when I didn't have any responsibilities. Don't try to make it into a grand passion."

"It is for me," Bootsie said dramatically.

He sighed. "That isn't true, but there's no point in arguing about it. I just wanted to tell you about Melanie and myself before you heard it from somebody else."

"If you think you're going to dump me for that devious little witch, you're very much mistaken." Her shrill voice filled with venom when she realized he meant what he said. "I'll be a laughingstock among all our friends."

"You're welcome to tell them you dumped *me,*" David said dryly. "Although nobody but you considered us a steady item."

"That's a lie! Everybody will think you're a cad for treating me like this."

"I guess I'll just have to live with it. Goodbye, Bootsie." He hung up before she could argue further.

Melanie was a little shaken by the depths of the other woman's spiteful anger. It was obvious that what David had maintained all along was true. Bootsie didn't love him. She was only concerned with her own image.

Melanie shivered. "I hate to think of the things she's going to say about you."

"That doesn't bother me. All I care about is convincing you that Bootsie doesn't mean anything to me. Did I succeed?"

"Yes," she said softly, feeling a glow of happiness.

"I hope that goes for any other woman who might call here today."

"What did you used to do, write your phone number in telephone booths?" she teased. "You get more calls than information."

"I was a very friendly fellow." He grinned.

"As long as it's past tense."

David put his arms around her and pulled her close. "Shall I show you how much you mean to me?"

"I was kind of hoping you would," she murmured.

"Feel free to ask, any time." His chuckle had a deep masculine sound.

They walked up the stairs holding hands and gazing into each other's eyes.

Melanie quivered with anticipation when David closed the door and turned to her with glowing eyes. She was still wearing the robe she'd come downstairs in. Underneath it was one of her short chiffon nighties, pink this time.

David parted her robe and gazed at her in wonder. "How can one woman look so sexy?"

She smiled. "It's a gift."

"Straight from heaven."

He slipped the robe off her shoulders and took her in his arms. Their kiss was unhurried. They murmured tender words of endearment and caressed each other slowly, gratifying all their senses.

But when David lifted the hem of her gown and stroked her bottom erotically, the tempo increased for both of them. Melanie slipped her hands inside his slacks and raked her nails lightly over his buttocks.

He groaned with pleasure and arched his body into hers, then drew back. "I promised myself I wouldn't rush things today."

She smiled seductively as she unfastened his slacks. "Fortunately I didn't promise myself anything."

"Please, darling," he pleaded while she pushed his slacks and shorts down his hips. "You know I can't resist you."

"I'm counting on it."

When she caressed his pulsing manhood he reached for her convulsively. After a passionate kiss, she took his hand and led him to the bed. But when David would have settled her against the pillows, she urged him down instead and straddled his hips with her knees. After unbuttoning his shirt, she leaned down and kissed the hollow in his throat, then each of his flat nipples.

He uttered a hoarse cry. "You don't know what you're doing to me, sweetheart." His body was rigid as he fought for control.

"I think that's pretty evident," she murmured.

He stripped off her gown and urged her forward until her breasts brushed his face. His mouth devoured them like a starving man. Suddenly the tables were turned and Melanie was the one with a raging need.

When neither could endure the tantalizing pleasure any longer, David lifted her slightly and centered her on the throbbing proof of his passion. It was a tumultuous coupling, tossing them on waves of sensation that mounted in intensity until the final implosion. Melanie collapsed in his arms and he held her tightly as the final spasms coursed through their joined bodies.

They drifted off to sleep afterward, thoroughly fulfilled.

It was afternoon before they awakened. Sunlight was shining through the window. Melanie could feel it on her closed eyelids. She smiled and cuddled closer to David, too content to open her eyes.

"I wonder what time it is," she murmured.

"Who cares?" His embrace tightened. "We aren't going anywhere."

"We have to be out of bed before the children come home."

"That won't be for hours yet."

"How do you know, if you don't know what time it is?" she asked.

"Just an educated guess."

Melanie turned her head to look at the bedside clock. Her eyes widened and she sat up in bed. "Evidently you didn't go on to higher learning. It's almost four o'clock."

David tried to urge her back. "I want to hold you a little longer. We'll get up in a few minutes."

"There isn't time for that."

His arms closed around her. "I'll bet I could make you change your mind."

"I know you could," she said fondly. "That's the trouble."

"I wish all my troubles were like that."

"You don't have any."

"Not since I found you." He kissed her tenderly.

Melanie savored this last moment in David's arms. No matter how much time they spent together, it was never enough. Finally she drew away reluctantly.

"You can lie there if you like, but I'm going to take a shower."

"Good idea," he said. "I'll take it with you."

She laughed. "That comes under the heading of unclear on the concept. We don't want the twins to come home and find us making love, remember?"

"Were you thinking of seducing me in the shower?"

"I think it's a fair bet one of us would."

"I can't argue with you there." He chuckled. "All right, I'll use my own bathroom."

"I'd appreciate it." Melanie swung her legs over the side and stood.

David watched her from the bed, his eyes wandering appreciatively over the curves of her supple body. "If you had any compassion at all, you wouldn't tempt me like that."

"A little denial is good for the character."

"But indulgence is a lot more fun," he said wickedly.

"Just remember that when you're explaining the facts of life to two nine-year-olds."

"Oh, all right." He sighed, getting out of bed. "When we're together like this I forget I'm a parent. I need you to keep reminding me."

Melanie stood under the shower, smiling at David's reluctance to leave her. It would have been wonderful to make love again. They seemed to scale new heights every time. She still found it hard to believe that he shared her feelings—although how could she doubt it after their impassioned lovemaking?

But it was more than that for her. She wanted to live with him the rest of her life, to bear his children and watch them grow up, to be equal partners in everything.

Did David feel the same way? Melanie's smile faltered. He'd never mentioned their future together except in the most general terms. Was she just kidding herself that theirs was something other than a transient affair? All those women who called him were more than mere nodding acquaintances.

Melanie tried to shake off her uneasiness. Maybe David took it for granted that she knew he wanted her to be part of his life. He would say something soon. Her smile returned as she reminded herself that he'd had other things on his mind the last few hours.

Chapter Eight

Life at Castlebury Manor was unbelievably idyllic after their trip to London, a complete change from what it had been before. All tension was gone between Melanie and David, Mrs. Stanhope ran the house effortlessly, and the twins were happy and secure. Even Bevins had mellowed. He almost smiled on occasion.

Jean Morton was the only one who didn't succumb to the easygoing atmosphere. Perhaps she'd been too imbued with the necessity for dignity in a nanny. Jean wasn't unpleasant, as the former housekeeper had been, merely detached. She lived in a private, rather barren world. Outside of receiving several phone calls a week that seemed to make her happy, she never mentioned having anyone special in her life.

The rest of the household were too busy to think much about her. As soon as they returned from London, Melanie started work on David's books. He turned a small study over to her to use as an office, and it soon began to look like one. Ledgers and folders gradually covered the entire desk and spilled over onto every available flat surface.

David stood in the doorway one morning surveying the litter. "You aren't very neat," he teased.

"Neither was Einstein," she answered absentmindedly.

"How do you know that?"

"I don't, but people seldom linger to discuss it."

"Okay, I can take a hint." He grinned. "I only dropped by to give you a goodbye kiss."

Her preoccupation disappeared. "I can always stop for that. Where are you going?"

"To take the twins to school. You were certainly right on target. They can't wait to get there."

"I hope it lasts." Melanie laughed. "It just doesn't seem natural for kids to like school—except maybe for recess."

"Don't question a gift from the gods."

"I don't," she said softly.

"You should know better than to look at me like that." He stepped inside and closed the door. Walking over to the desk, he leaned down and kissed her. "How am I going to get any work done?"

"Keep thinking about tonight."

"Then I *really* won't get anything done." As he leaned forward to kiss her again a knock came at the door.

"Who is it?" Melanie called.

Jean's voice answered. "The children are waiting. Would Mr. Crandall like me to drive them to school?"

"No, tell them to get into the car. I'll be right there," David answered. He gave Melanie an annoyed look. "I swear that woman has radar. She always seems to know when I'm about to kiss you."

"I'm sure she couldn't care less. She's only trying to do her job. You wouldn't be happy if she neglected the twins."

"I suppose you're right. Well, I'd better go."

"Are you coming back afterward? I need you."

"Your place or mine?" he teased.

"I have to ask you about an apparent investment your father made. It's a good thing one of us has a sense of responsibility," she said with mock disapproval.

The days seemed to fly by. Melanie went into her office early and worked until the twins came home from school. Then she knocked off to spend time with them, unless they brought classmates home, which happened frequently. Both Melanie and David were overjoyed that things were working out as they'd hoped.

When the children didn't have playmates over they usually wanted to ride their horses. On those days, David and Melanie sat companionably on the railing of the paddock and watched them trot around the ring. That was fine in the beginning, but it only satisfied the twins for a short time. They wanted to explore wider vistas.

"If you and Melanie had horses, too, Uncle David, we could ride all over," Ashley said.

"I'm thinking of buying two more," he said. "I just haven't found time yet."

"Don't hurry on my account," Melanie said. "I'm a city girl. We don't ride animals, we take them for a walk on a leash."

"That's sissy stuff," he scoffed.

"Maybe so, but you can't fall off a poodle."

"I wouldn't let anything happen to you." David put an arm around her waist and smiled at her. "I've gotten rather fond of you."

"What if the horse didn't feel the same way?"

Melanie's head was resting on his shoulder as she laughed into his sunlit eyes. Neither were aware of being under scrutiny. Lady Tyndall's face wore a look of satisfaction as she watched from the terrace.

After a moment she walked across the lawn. "You two look very relaxed," she remarked.

Melanie drew away self-consciously. "I've been working on David's books all morning. I was just taking a breather."

"You don't have to explain to me, my dear, I'm not your employer." The older woman turned to David. "I hope you're providing pleasant working conditions for this girl."

"I'm doing my best." He grinned.

Melanie had an uncomfortable feeling that Sylvia knew about the fringe benefits that went with the job. She seemed to know everything that was going on in the county, although she never indulged in mean gossip.

"What did you bring us this time?" David asked, eyeing the basket over Sylvia's arm. She dropped in at Castlebury Manor often, usually with something from her garden or kitchen.

"It's a casserole Mrs. Beavey made for your dinner tonight. I know your housekeeper is off today, and that nanny of yours isn't good for anything."

"It's her day off, too."

"How can you tell?" Sylvia sniffed. "The woman is like a shadow. You're never sure she's there."

"Except when you don't want her to be." David shot Melanie a look of amusement.

"Well, I'll leave this in the kitchen on my way out." She gave them a benign smile. "I'm old enough to know when two's company."

Sylvia had never come right out and asked Melanie how things stood between herself and David, but she obviously knew they were more than friends. How much more? Melanie wondered.

David was a wonderfully passionate lover, and he seemed to want her to be a fixture in his life—but he never put it into words. Sometimes Melanie thought her main attraction, besides the sexual one, was her rapport with the twins. What would happen when his accounting job was finished and she had no reason to stay on? Would he ask her to marry him if it was the only way to keep her here? That wasn't what she wanted.

Most of the time Melanie avoided thinking of the future. The present was too fantastic. The days flowed by in a golden stream, unmarred by any friction. Even Jean seemed almost cheerful. She'd returned from her day off with a very pretty gold pin that she wore constantly. Melanie wished her well, but she couldn't help wondering what kind of man would be attracted to someone that cold.

The idyll, like most things in life, was too perfect to last. It developed a fracture one day about noon. Melanie had emerged from her office and was on her way upstairs to freshen up for lunch when the doorbell rang. She stopped out of curiosity, halfway up the staircase. They didn't get many drop-in visitors.

This one was about as welcome as the asp in the Garden of Eden. Bootsie stood on the doorstep, looking ravishing in a black cat suit and a very short plaid skirt. She peered over Bevins's shoulder at David, who was crossing the entry.

"Surprise, darling," she called, all smiles, as though they were still on the best of terms.

He walked slowly toward her as the butler returned to the kitchen. "This *is* a surprise. I didn't expect to see you here."

"Oh well, you know me. I like to do things on the spur of the moment."

David looked at her impassively. "Forgive me for bringing it up, but I thought I'd be the last person you wanted to see again."

"You mean that little tiff we had?" She gave a small trill of laughter. "I hope you didn't take that seriously. *I* certainly didn't."

"I see. Well, I'm glad we're still friends," he said awkwardly.

"And we always will be." Her smile turned rather chilling. "I have no intention of letting you go out of my life." Before he could comment she said, "Where did Bevins get to? I need him to bring in our luggage."

"You brought someone with you?" David asked warily.

An older woman was getting out of the car parked in the driveway. She was very attractive, with perfectly arranged blond hair that framed patrician features. It was difficult to tell her age. She was perhaps in her fifties, but her skin was unlined and her slender figure was a triumph of dieting and massages.

She smiled, showing perfect white teeth. "It's so good to see you again, David. How are you, dear boy?"

He gazed at her impassively. "What brings you here, Rosamund?"

"What kind of question is that to ask a grandmother?" Bootsie chided. "She came to see the children, naturally."

"Where are the little angels?" Rosamund asked. "I can't wait to give them kisses and hugs."

"They're in school," he answered.

She gave Bootsie a look of annoyance. "I told you we didn't have to start so early."

"It will give us time to unpack before they get home. You'll also have a chance to meet Melanie." Bootsie looked at David. "She *is* still here?"

"Yes, she's probably in her office." He looked around vaguely and noticed Melanie on the stairs.

She'd been too curious to move. Now it was too late. Melanie flushed with embarrassment at being caught eavesdropping. The only solution was to pretend she was just coming downstairs.

David introduced her to the older woman. "This is the children's maternal grandmother, Rosamund Faversham."

Rosamund looked her over with interest. "Bootsie has told me so much about you. She says you're a very clever woman."

"We share the same opinion of each other," Melanie answered evenly.

"Would you mind telling Mrs. Stanhope there will be two more for lunch?" David asked Melanie swiftly.

"And send Bevins back," Bootsie ordered. "We need him to take our luggage upstairs."

Melanie continued to the kitchen without replying.

"You're staying overnight?" David's face was expressionless.

"We'll be here longer than that," Rosamund answered. "I want to spend some time with my darling little grandchildren. It's been much too long since I've seen them."

"Or even talked to them," David said tersely. "They expected at least a call from you on their birthday last month."

"Did I miss that? Oh, dear! Well, I have a suitcase full of gifts for them, that should make it all right."

"Birthdays are very special events in a child's life," he said sternly.

"You're right. I wish you'd reminded me."

As David's face darkened, Bootsie said hastily, "Rosamund was out of the country at the time."

"Yes, I was sailing around the Greek islands on Stavros Agnotello's yacht. You have no idea how magnificent it is! I was so thrilled to be included, since I barely knew Stavros. My friend, Countess de la Tours wangled the invitation for me. You can't imagine how many influential people I met."

"I'll show you to your rooms," David said, without waiting for her to recite the guest list.

Lunch was served later than usual that day, to give Mrs. Stanhope time to prepare for the unexpected guests. Her extra effort was apparent when Bevins announced that luncheon was served.

Melanie and David usually ate outside on the terrace, or in a sunny breakfast room off the kitchen. Today the dining room table was set with the best china and silver.

The guests looked right at home in the elegant setting, Bootsie in her high-fashion outfit, and Rosamund in a simple, perfectly cut silk suit with a diamond-and-sapphire pin on the lapel. They made Melanie feel like a stable worker in her jeans and navy pullover. David was dressed similarly, but it didn't seem to bother him.

Rosamund remarked obliquely on their attire. "I don't remember it being so casual in the country when Marie was alive. I do hope you're not letting Ariel and Ashley go native."

"Not to worry. They don't run around in sarongs with a hibiscus blossom tucked behind their ears," David said dryly.

"Sarcasm doesn't become you," she chided. "Naturally I'm concerned about the way they're being brought up. Bootsie tells me you took them out of public school. Do you think that's wise?"

"It isn't written in stone. I simply decided to give it a try. They don't have any friends here in the country, so we thought—that is, *I* thought it would be good for them to get to know the local children. They need to be with their peers."

"Exactly. Children who've had their advantages. I don't want them to grow up without any social skills."

David's eyes smoldered dangerously. "The village youngsters don't eat with their fingers, and most of them even wear shoes."

"Nobody said they weren't nice enough children," Bootsie said impatiently. "What Rosamund means is that the twins should be preparing themselves for a different kind of life. If you were thinking clearly you'd see that."

"How much training does it take to sit on the deck of a yacht and guzzle martinis?" he demanded.

Rosamund uttered a little cry of outrage. "Are you referring to me?"

"Not specifically. The same thing could apply to your pack of peripatetic pals."

"How can you criticize me for trying to run away from reality? I just suffered a great loss, in case you've forgotten. If I keep up a frantic pace, it's to forget my pain," she declared dramatically.

Melanie found it difficult to keep from snickering. Now she knew why David didn't want his sister-in-law's mother to raise the twins. The woman was a worse snob than Bootsie, and that was saying a lot.

Melanie could hardly wait for lunch to be over. She folded her napkin and placed it on the table. "If you'll excuse me, I have to get back to work."

"That goes for me, too," David said swiftly.

"Surely you don't have to rush off," Rosamund protested. "We just arrived."

"Yes, what's so urgent that it can't wait?" Bootsie asked in annoyance. "You aren't being very hospitable."

"I would have tried to be if you'd given me advance warning."

"Warning?" Rosamund raised her eyebrows. "Are you putting us in the same class as a visitation of locusts?"

"You have quite a way with words, Rosamund," he drawled.

"That's not exactly reassurance. If I'm not welcome here I'll leave," she said stiffly.

Bootsie gave him a stony look. "Is that what you want, David?"

He lied manfully. "No, of course not. I can't offer you much in the way of entertainment, but you're welcome anytime."

Rosamund was placated. "Don't worry about me. I'm really quite exhausted from the cruise. I came here to rest and relax, and to see the children, of course."

In that order, Melanie thought cynically. She rose and left the room.

David followed her a few moments later. He closed the door of her office and slumped into a chair. "I don't know how I'm going to get through their visit. You'd better hide all the sharp knives and blunt objects in the house."

"Which one do you feel like maiming?"

"Both of them! This is Bootsie's revenge. She knows how I feel about Rosamund."

"She is a little . . . superficial," Melanie said cautiously.

"That's being generous! Rosamund Faversham thinks the world is made up of two kinds of people—her kind, and the ones who were put on earth to serve her. Thank God my sister-in-law took after her father."

"What was he like?"

"Rather ineffectual, but lots of personality. Everybody likes Dudley."

"You mean he's still alive? I got the impression that Rosamund was a widow."

"No, her ex-husband is still alive and well and living in Spain. Dudley and Rosamund have been divorced for years." David hauled himself up. "Well, I'd better go before they track me down in here."

Melanie found it hard to concentrate after all the new developments. She was glad when Sylvia phoned.

"I know I'm disturbing you, but I'll only keep you a minute," the older woman promised.

"It's all right. I was having trouble working, anyway."

"You have my sympathy. David's father was an individualist. I can just imagine what shape his books are in."

"That isn't what's preoccupying me at the moment. David has houseguests again."

"Who is it this time?"

"Bootsie is back for a rematch, and she brought the children's grandmother with her. The atmosphere is rather tense."

"You're right, that spells trouble," Sylvia said thoughtfully. "Rosamund must want something."

Fear clutched at Melanie. "You mean the twins?"

"Good heavens, no! When she went down the assembly line, they forgot to put in any maternal feeling. Most likely she wants money."

"How could that be? She looks terribly rich. The suit she has on must have cost a fortune, and she's wearing a gorgeous diamond-and-sapphire pin."

"Probably a copy of one from her more affluent period. Rose Dauber—that was her name before she married Dudley, not Rosamund, just plain Rose. Anyway, Dudley was a baron so she assumed he was rich. He *was* fairly well off, but poor Dudley had no head for business. He preferred to play polo and gamble at his clubs. When he'd pretty well run through his fortune, he went to live in Spain where things were cheaper.''

"She didn't want to live in Spain?"

"You have to be asked first." Sylvia laughed. "Dudley was tired of her extravagant spending. Rose's face-lifts alone would send several children through college."

"I didn't realize. She looks so young."

"She's my age," Sylvia said tersely. "Although she'd endure needles stuck into painful parts of her anatomy before she'd admit it."

"Well, at least she got her money's worth out of the face-lifts. I'm surprised she hasn't remarried."

"It isn't from lack of trying. Rose is really brazen about getting herself invited to the watering holes of the rich. She's up against a lot of younger competition, though, and it costs a great deal to keep up that front."

"What does she live on?"

"I guess she gets alimony from Dudley, but it can't be very munificent. The golden goose is on its last legs."

"Why would she ask David for money? He isn't really family."

"Rose isn't particular where she gets it from. But I suppose she figures they have a tenuous relationship through the twins."

"I'm relieved to hear she doesn't have designs on them. David would fight her tooth and nail for custody."

"That's one thing he doesn't have to worry about. They would be a liability. She might admit to being a grandmother while she's here, but you can bet she never refers to it among her upper-crust friends."

A click on the line told them a receiver had been picked up somewhere in the house. It was followed by a series of beeps as somebody dialed a number.

"Hello?" Rosamund said. "Are you there, Daphne?"

"I was using the phone," Melanie said.

"Oh, I'm so terribly sorry. I should have checked first. Will you be very long? I have to make a rather important call."

Sylvia broke the silence at her end. "You never change, Rose."

"Who's that?" Rosamund asked sharply.

"It's Sylvia Tyndall."

"Oh, how nice to hear your voice," Rosamund said tepidly.

"Yes, it's the high point of my day, too," Sylvia answered dryly. "What are you doing so far from London?"

"I couldn't stay away from my little ones any longer."

"It *has* been a while. When did you see them last?"

"Longer ago than I would have wished, but that's irrelevant. It's the quality of our time together that matters."

Melanie broke in abruptly. "I'll hang up now and let you two chat."

The twins were quite excited to hear their grandmother was visiting. Unfortunately she was resting when they got home from school.

Jean wouldn't let them disturb her. "The Baroness is exhausted and can't be awakened," she said.

"But we haven't seen her in ever so long," Ariel protested.

"Then another hour or two won't matter."

"That seems like a long time to a child," Melanie said mildly.

She didn't like to make waves, but Jean was carrying her romance with the peerage too far. She'd been doing little chores for Rosamund and Bootsie all afternoon. If she wanted to be their personal maid that was fine, but keeping the children from their grandmother wasn't.

"You could never get a job as a nanny," Jean said in a superior tone of voice. "You have to teach children to respect the rights of others."

Melanie's cheeks were pink with repressed anger. "At what age do they have rights of their own?"

An unpleasant scene might have ensued, but Rosamund appeared at the top of the stairs. She had changed into a pale green silk jumpsuit with a wide jeweled belt, and she looked refreshed after her nap. Every hair was in place and she'd reapplied her makeup.

Running gracefully down the stairs, she held her arms open wide. "My darling babies, come to Grandma-ma."

They rushed into her arms, but after kisses and hugs Ariel said, "We aren't babies, Grandma."

"Grandma-ma, with an accent on the last *a*," Rosamund corrected gently. "You'll always be my babies. I don't want you to ever grow up."

"We have to grow up," Ashley said.

"Yes, I believe thirty is the absolute cutoff for the seventh grade." David had come into the hall in time to hear their conversation.

"Ask her," Ariel whispered to Ashley.

"No, *you* ask her," he answered.

"What is it you want, angels?" Rosamund looked at them indulgently.

When the twins remained silent, David and Melanie exchanged a laughing glance. "I believe they want to know if you brought them anything," he said.

Rosamund tapped her forehead with the heel of her hand. "Of course, what a silly goose I am! Wait till you see what I have for you, my darlings. Go upstairs and get that large blue bag out of my closet," she instructed Jean. Turning back to David she said, "When are we having tea? I'm absolutely parched."

"I'll tell Bevins to serve it," Melanie said, looking for an excuse to leave.

As she started toward the kitchen, David frowned and caught her wrist. "You don't have to do that. You're not a servant. I'll ring for him."

"I don't mind." She gave him a mischievous grin. "I just remembered some pressing business I have to take care of in the kitchen."

He returned her smile ruefully, sliding his hand up her arm. "You'd better come back. I need somebody to hide the blunt objects."

Rosamund and the twins were too involved to pay any attention to their lowered voices and conspiratorial chuckles. But Bootsie was watching from the staircase with clenched fists.

She came down the last few steps, saying with a forced smile, "Isn't it nice to be together as a family again? I hope you won't feel like an outsider, Melanie."

"Not if *you* don't," Melanie answered sweetly.

Bootsie laughed merrily, linking her arm with David's. "I feel like family after all these years."

"I think of you that way, too," he said smoothly. "As a sister."

Melanie would have felt sorry for her if she really loved David, but that wasn't the case. Bootsie was simply determined to get him back, no matter what it took.

They had tea in the drawing room, in deference to the guests. The formal room was usually rather forbidding, but after the floor became littered with wrapping paper and ribbons from Rosamund's gifts, it looked more lived in.

She'd brought the twins lavish presents, an exquisitely dressed china doll for Ariel, an elaborate train set for Ashley, and electronic games for both of them. If Rosamund was short of money, it hadn't curbed her shopping instincts.

The twins were properly grateful. They expressed their thanks enthusiastically, before sitting on the floor to examine each other's gifts.

Tea was more elaborate than usual. In addition to sandwiches and cake, Mrs. Stanhope had provided large stemmed strawberries with clotted cream, and an assortment of iced petits fours. Ariel had several of the chocolate ones before returning to her doll.

"Look Grandma-ma," she said, lifting the doll's taffeta skirt. "She has lace on her panties." When Rosamund didn't respond, Ariel tugged at her pant leg for attention.

Rosamund glanced down at her with a smile that turned to a tiny shriek. "Look what you've done! You've gotten chocolate on my pants."

Ariel's eyes got very big. "I didn't mean to."

"Put some cold water on the stain," Bootsie suggested.

"No, that will only make it worse," Rosamund replied.

"I'll send it to the cleaners for you tomorrow," David said impatiently. "It's not the end of the world! It was an accident."

"I'm sorry, Grandma-ma," Ariel murmured.

"I know you are, darling." Rosamund kissed the little girl's cheek, avoiding her chocolate-smeared mouth. "It's all right, pet. Don't worry about it."

Rosamund wasn't really a bad sort, Melanie decided. She was just supremely self-centered. When something threatened her own well-being—even something as minor as a smudge on her pants—she didn't stop to consider anyone else's feelings.

Life at Castlebury Manor changed drastically after the arrival of the guests. If Melanie had thought Bootsie and her friends were demanding, Rosamund made them look positively saintly. But no matter how unreasonable her requests, Jean was delighted to fill them.

Rosamund slept until noon and required her breakfast in bed, which Jean gladly served. Then Rosamund took a lengthy bath. The maids couldn't get in to straighten her room until the middle of the afternoon. She also tied up the telephone, making lengthy calls not only to London, but to the Continent as well.

"I wouldn't want to pay your phone bill," Melanie remarked to David.

"If it keeps her busy so we can get some work done, it's worth it," he said.

Rosamund didn't bother them much during the day, but Bootsie made up for it. She seemed to be equipped with radar or ESP. As soon as David went into Melanie's office, Bootsie appeared.

David tried to be polite, but it became increasingly difficult. She would leave after he explained that they were working, but a short time later she was back again on the flimsiest of pretexts. Her constant harassment finally created friction between Melanie and David.

"I give up!" Melanie exclaimed after Bootsie had interrupted them for the third time that afternoon with some trivial question. "Why don't you just take her someplace—far away preferably. I'll make a list of the things I have to ask you about, and we can try to go over them when you get back."

"That's ridiculous! I don't have any obligation to an uninvited guest. We have work to do."

"Tell that to your girlfriend and see how far you get."

David gritted his teeth. "She isn't my girlfriend."

"Ask anyone in this house and I bet you'll get a different opinion."

Melanie knew she was playing into Bootsie's hands by snapping at David. That's what she wanted, to cause trouble between them. But it wasn't easy to be reasonable when they could never even express their affection for each other anymore. As for intimacy, forget it!

After resting all day, Rosamund and Bootsie were wide awake and looking for entertainment. Since there wasn't any, at least nothing up to their standards, they settled for the pub in the village. Every night after dinner they coaxed David into taking them.

Melanie was invited, too, but she declined. It was bad enough having Bootsie bug her all day, she didn't want to spend all evening fencing with her as well. Then by the time they came home, Melanie was asleep. Bootsie saw to it that they stayed until the place closed.

David came to Melanie's room the first night as soon as he returned. He tried waking her with a kiss, but by that time she wasn't responsive. Which of course made him feel rejected. They argued about it the next day.

"We finally had a chance to be alone, but evidently that wasn't important to you," he said stiffly.

"What was I supposed to do, wait up all night for you?"

"You could have come along."

"I had a better time sleeping."

"At least now we know where your priorities lie," he answered coolly.

She slammed a ledger down on her desk. "It doesn't take a brain surgeon to figure out what yours are!"

David's anger evaporated as he looked at her lovely, flushed face. "I'm sorry, darling, I didn't mean to snap at you. I'm just so damn frustrated! It seems like forever since I've held you in my arms."

"To me, too." She sighed. "How many weeks have they been here?"

He smiled wryly. "It's been three days."

"You're joking!"

"Would I joke about a thing like that?" He jammed his hands into his pockets and paced the floor. "The problem is how to get rid of them."

"How about just asking them to leave?" Melanie wasn't serious, but he answered as if she were.

"How can I? Rosamund is the children's grandmother, even if she isn't very good at it."

"I know. She either smothers them in kisses, or else she's too busy to pay any attention to them. I don't think they feel rejected, though. Kids are pretty good at figuring people out. They know she's fond of them in her own way."

"None of which solves *our* problem. How are we going to manage a night alone?"

"I don't suppose you could find boyfriends for both of them and send them off on a date?"

David grinned. "Rosamund's would have to be rich."

"At this point, I'd almost be willing to chip in."

He curved his hand around her neck and looked deeply into her eyes. "Save tonight for me. We're going to spend it together if I have to put knockout drops in their coffee."

Neither David nor Melanie thought life could get more complicated, but an unexpected visitor proved them wrong.

They were all having tea in the late afternoon when the doorbell rang. Bevins went to answer it.

He returned to announce, "There is a gentleman here to see Baroness Faversham."

Rosamund looked blank. "I wasn't expecting anyone. Who is it?"

"He says his name is Nigel Daventry."

Her reaction was curious. She flushed and slanted a glance at David, biting her lip. "I'll speak to him privately."

Before she could cross the room, a young man appeared in the doorway. He was startlingly handsome, with the kind of rugged good looks associated with surfers. His hair was blond and slightly shaggy, but it looked just right with his deeply tanned features. He was dressed casually yet expensively, in slacks and an open neck silk shirt under a sport coat draped over broad shoulders. Rosamund had really picked herself a winner, except for one thing. The man was at least twenty years younger than she.

He broke the small silence that greeted his arrival. "Am I too late for tea?" White teeth gleamed in a mischievous smile.

"How on earth did you find me, Nigel?" Rosamund exclaimed.

"I rang up your friend, Charlotte, when I couldn't locate you. She told me where you'd gone."

"Are you going to introduce us?" David asked.

"Oh...yes, of course," Rosamund said. "This is Nigel Daventry, my...that is, an old friend."

"He carries his age well," David drawled.

Nigel's eyes narrowed, but his smile didn't falter. "I try to avoid stress." He greeted Bootsie, whom he evidently knew, before turning to Melanie. His expression changed as he gazed at her. "I don't believe we've met."

The obvious approval of such a handsome man gave her spirits a boost, something they hadn't had much of lately. She extended her hand. "Hello, I'm Melanie Warren."

"Is there a Mr. Warren?" he asked softly.

"There is." She smiled. "He's my father."

David's eyes smoldered as he stared at their clasped hands. "Where are you from, Daventry?" he asked abruptly.

Nigel released Melanie's hand. "From London most recently. I've lived all over."

"Nigel has been advising me on my investments," Rosamund said.

David regarded her with a raised eyebrow before turning back to the other man. "You're a stockbroker?"

"Not exactly. I'm more of an investment counselor."

"I see. Did you put any of your clients in Cyberon before they merged with Tradex? I understand the stock split five for one."

"Well, to tell you the truth, I've been on vacation for the last month. I haven't been following the market."

"That's rather strange, isn't it?"

"You've heard the expression, all work and no play," Nigel answered smoothly. "I wouldn't want to be known as a dull boy."

"Nobody could ever accuse you of that." Bootsie laughed. "People are still talking about the way you livened up the Bedloes' garden party."

"I try to be an entertaining guest," he said modestly.

"You're just what we need around here," Bootsie declared. "Poor David has had his hands full trying to keep three women happy."

Nigel's glance glided briefly over Melanie. "I'd be delighted to be of assistance."

David's jaw set. "That's very decent of you, but I know you want to get back to London after being gone for so long."

"What's another week more or less?" Bootsie asked airily. "We need him here."

"If you put it that way, how can I refuse?" Nigel smiled charmingly.

David's face was stormy, but Bootsie had maneuvered him into an untenable position. He couldn't very well tell the man to leave, even though he hadn't invited him. Nigel was a friend of Rosamund's.

Surprisingly, she was less than enthusiastic about having him there. "Perhaps it *isn't* a good idea to neglect your affairs."

"They'll wait," Nigel said.

As she prepared to argue, the twins came dashing into the room.

David's face relaxed for the first time. "Where have you two been?"

"We were shelling peas for Mrs. Stanhope," Ariel answered.

"She needed us to help her," Ashley said importantly.

"Who is *he?*" Ariel noticed Nigel for the first time.

"A friend of your grandmother's," David answered.

Nigel stared at them incredulously before shifting his gaze to Rosamund. "You told me they were babies!"

As her face flushed, Ariel said indignantly, "We're nine years old—going on ten!"

"You just had your ninth birthday," Rosamund protested weakly.

Melanie felt sorry for her. Now she understood why Rosamund had tried to discourage Nigel from staying. She didn't want him to find out she had grandchildren that old—and who could blame her? Nigel was quite a hunk. They were still a rather unlikely couple, even though Rosamund looked a lot younger than her age. But more power to her, Melanie thought with amusement.

David seized the opportunity. "Now that you know all of our secrets, you might want to hightail it back to London," he told Nigel suavely. "It gets rather hectic with two active children in the house. Don't feel you have to stay."

"I get on well with children, and I wouldn't think of letting down three such lovely ladies," Nigel answered, just as smoothly.

David's affability fled. "You only have to worry about two of them. Melanie's free time is limited. I've engaged her to put my business affairs in order."

"I see." Nigel looked as though he did.

It would have been difficult not to. David was like a splendid stag ready to do battle to defend his turf. Melanie was torn between gratification and annoyance. David was always telling *her* how much he loved her, but if he announced it to the world there wouldn't be any doubt.

Bootsie wasn't pleased by David's all but open declaration that Melanie was off-limits. She got back at him slyly. "Melanie works much too hard. You really should teach her to play, Nigel."

Nigel was fully aware of his host's hostility and Rosamund's displeasure. He hadn't gotten to be the perfect guest by miscalculating. "I'm sure David could teach her more than I could," he said pleasantly.

The gathering broke up when Nigel left to bring his things in from the car, a sporty Jaguar two-seater. Rosamund went upstairs with him. When Bootsie started an intimate conversation with David, Melanie left the room. Feeling at loose ends, she wandered out to the terrace at the rear of the house, wishing they'd all go back to London.

David joined her there a few moments later. He was still simmering over Nigel. "I ought to hang a sign outside—

Castlebury Manor, Your Home Away From Home," he rasped.

Melanie couldn't help snickering. "That was pretty smooth the way he finessed an invitation out of you."

"I don't find anything admirable about him," he said coldly. "But you obviously do. Women never see through men like that."

"Don't take it out on me. *I'm* not the reason he came, your relative is."

"We aren't related, and I'm furious at her! I don't care what Rosamund does in her private life, but she should have the good taste not to entertain her studs here."

"Do you really think they're lovers? He's young enough to be her son."

"Foolish women like Rosamund are easy prey for unprincipled men like Nigel."

"Maybe we're not being fair to them. It could be a May-December romance. He can't be after her money, because you said she doesn't have any."

"No, but she has connections. Nigel is like the little fish that relies on the big fish for its meal ticket. It's a tidy arrangement. She gets herself invited places and brings him along as her escort. You can bet they're both looking for rich spouses."

"Then why are they wasting their time here?"

David shrugged. "They could be temporarily out of invitations. The opportunities here might not be ideal, but it beats paying for your own room and board."

"Poor David. It's too bad you're so civilized. A caveman would throw them all out and put up a No Vacancy sign."

"That's not half of what I'll do if that creep ever comes on to you again," he said grimly.

"At least he noticed me. That's more than you've done lately."

He pulled her close. "That isn't true, and tonight I intend to show you just how much I've missed you."

Chapter Nine

Nigel's arrival increased the tension at Castlebury Manor, even though he was a model guest. The young maids were captivated by his rugged good looks; they vied to clean his room. Nigel didn't demand extra service like Rosamund and Bootsie, and he never acted bored. When the two women complained about having nothing to do, he took them on little excursions around the countryside.

"You ought to be grateful to him for getting them out of our hair for the afternoon," Melanie said, when David made a snide remark.

"I *would* be grateful if he kept on going—back to London."

"You're letting prejudice get the best of you," she said impatiently. "Okay, so maybe he lives by his wits. At least he's pleasant to have around."

"I didn't expect *you* to join his fawning fan club," David answered coldly. "I thought you'd be discriminating enough to see through that phony charm."

"It's a pleasant change from Bootsie's lack of it—phony or otherwise."

"Isn't it funny that you can see all of Bootsie's faults, and none of Nigel's?" David asked sarcastically.

"Perhaps because he's polite to me."

"He'd like to be a hell of a lot more than that! But if I ever catch him trying it, he'll be doing his romancing in a considerably higher voice."

"There's an easier solution to the problem," she said artlessly.

"What do you mean?"

"Oh, never mind," she answered in annoyance. David could make sure other men knew she was off-limits. But the idea of marriage—or even getting engaged—had obviously never occurred to him. "Would you mind getting out of my office? I'd like to get some work done."

Tension in the house built, although Nigel was careful not to make any moves on Melanie. That didn't mollify David. His irritation grew each night as he watched Rosamund and Nigel go upstairs, presumably to their own rooms.

Melanie got into the habit of escaping into the side garden when she wasn't working. It was the only place she could relax and get away from all of them. Nobody else except the gardener ever came there.

One afternoon Nigel discovered her secret hiding place. Melanie was lying on a chaise with her eyes closed, enjoying the peace and quiet. Until someone blotted out the sun. She opened her eyes to see Nigel standing over her with a smile on his face.

"You looked like Sleeping Beauty lying there," he said. "I was tempted to waken you with a kiss."

"That's risky nowadays," she answered lightly. "You could be sued for sexual harassment."

"It would be worth it," he murmured, sitting down next to her on the chaise.

"Not if Rosamund caught you."

"You've gotten the wrong impression of our relationship," he protested. "Rosamund and I are merely good friends."

"You don't have to explain anything to me. It's none of my business."

"You don't believe me," he said reproachfully.

"Does it matter?"

"It matters very much." He arched an arm across her body and leaned his weight on it. "I was attracted to you from the first moment I saw you. You're an enchantingly beautiful woman."

"That's always gratifying to hear." Melanie wanted to stand up, but it would have put her in Nigel's arms. She was certain he wouldn't move aside.

"I think you're attracted to me, too."

"It's nice to know you don't have an ego problem," she remarked dryly.

"Why waste time playing games? We can't count on being alone for long. Privacy is harder to find around here than a virgin at an orgy."

"You'd know more about that than I would."

"Don't try to kid a pro. You've been around." He made a visual inventory of her curved body. "You might even be able to teach *me* a thing or two."

"I doubt if that's possible," she said with a straight face.

He took it as a compliment. "I haven't had any complaints."

"Maybe you just weren't listening," she said dryly. "Nobody has a perfect score every time."

"Would you like a demonstration?" He smirked. "Then you can make up your own mind."

Melanie was suddenly tired of him. Nigel was undoubtedly handsome. It was a pity that he had no other redeeming features. "I'm afraid I'll have to pass."

"You're missing a bet. We'd be quite wonderful together." He leaned in closer.

"I doubt it." She put her hands on his chest to hold him off. Their faces were only inches apart.

"Because of David? He doesn't have to find out. Believe me, I know how to be discreet."

"Okay, that does it!" David came striding toward them, his face a mask of fury. "I want you out of here, *now!* Pack your things and leave."

Nigel was startled and chagrined, but he recovered his poise. Rising gracefully he said, "Aren't you overreacting a bit, old chap? We were just having a conversation."

"If you're not off the premises in ten minutes I'll take great pleasure in throwing you out bodily," David gritted.

"There's no need to get physical," Nigel protested. "Can't we discuss this like gentlemen?"

"We're one gentleman short."

After warily eyeing David's balled fists, Nigel realized it would be useless to try to reason with him. "All right, I'm leaving."

"And take Rosamund with you."

"She's your problem, not mine," Nigel answered mockingly. "Try offering her more of an incentive if you want to see results. Threats won't do it." He sauntered away leisurely.

David swore pungently and headed for the house.

Melanie wanted to tell him that he needn't have taken such drastic methods. She could have handled Nigel herself. Now was not the time, however, when he was in such a towering rage. She followed him back to the house, a prudent distance behind.

David stormed inside, shouting for Rosamund. When she came hurrying down the stairs he didn't bother to take her someplace private.

"What on earth is going on, David?" she asked. "I don't appreciate being summoned in such a rude manner."

"I thought you'd like to know that I just sent your beach bum boyfriend packing."

"You asked Nigel to leave? But why? Surely there must be some mistake."

"My mistake was in letting that parasitic womanizer in here in the first place! What you do in private is your own affair, but you might have the decency to act your age in front of your grandchildren."

She lifted her chin in outraged dignity. "Exactly what are you implying?"

"I'm spelling it out for you," he said succinctly. "I think it's time you went back to London."

"You're turning me out?" Her face was incredulous.

"Let's just say, I think you'll be happier in the city."

"I can't believe this! That you would put me out of my dead daughter's home!" She produced a small lace handkerchief and dabbed at her eyes.

"Save the histrionics, Rosamund," he snapped. "I know them by heart."

"You're a cruel man, David. How can you keep me from my darling grandchildren?"

"You've spent precious little time with them since you've been here. I have no idea why you'd even want to stay." He rumpled his thick hair in frustration. "It's too quiet for you here. Why don't you admit it?"

"That's not true." She slanted a speculative glance at him. "I've enjoyed every single minute with the children, but I do have some things I should take care of in London. The problem is, my monthly check isn't due for another two weeks."

"How much do you need?" David asked stoically.

"Well, if it wouldn't be too much trouble." Rosamund named a sum. "It's only a loan, mind you. I intend to pay you back."

"Come into my office. I'll get my checkbook."

Two people had been silent witnesses to the confrontation, Melanie by the door to the garden, and Bootsie at the top of the stairs.

Rosamund came out of David's office all smiles. She was humming as she ran lightly up the stairs and encountered Bootsie.

"How could you let him buy you off like that?" Bootsie asked angrily. "You have a perfect right to be here!"

"My dear girl, David was correct about one thing—I don't belong in the country."

"So, it's a little quiet right now. We can liven things up. I'll call some of my friends in the city. We'll give a big party."

"Don't make the mistake of pushing David too far. You can't keep inviting people here whenever it suits you. This is his home, not a hotel."

"He doesn't really mind. David is bored here, but he won't admit it. I'm actually doing him a favor," Bootsie answered confidently.

"Well, you'll have to do it without me. *I'm* going back to London."

"You can't do that! I drove you down. What excuse will I have for staying?"

"If you're smart, you'll stop looking for one. You're playing a losing game."

"I'll never give him up," Bootsie declared passionately. "That woman thinks she's won, but she hasn't."

Their voices faded as they moved down the hall, still arguing.

Melanie emerged from the doorway and walked slowly into the entry. She met David coming from his office. Neither commented on what had just happened.

David watched with a sense of relief as Bootsie and Rosamund drove away.

Melanie had gone to her bedroom, not wanting to risk a last-minute scene with Bootsie. She turned as he entered the room after a brief tap. He closed the door decisively.

"Are they really gone?" she asked.

He nodded, giving her a wide grin. "Just in case they had second thoughts, I locked the front door—like this." He turned the bolt and walked toward her.

"The twins will be out of school soon," Melanie said halfheartedly as David took her in his arms.

"I told Miss Morton to pick them up," he replied, pulling her T-shirt out of her jeans and caressing her bare back.

"They always come looking for us when they get home."

"She can watch over them. That's what I pay her for." He stripped the shirt over Melanie's head and unclasped her bra.

She uttered a low sound of contentment as he stroked her breasts and curled his tongue around one nipple. "I've missed this."

"Not nearly as much as I have." His mouth closed over hers, parting her lips for an arousing kiss.

Melanie wound her arms around his neck and curved her body into his in mounting anticipation. She was unfastening his belt when a knock came at the door.

David stiffened. "Who is it?" he barked.

"I just wanted to tell you I'm leaving now to get the children," Jean said.

His jawline was rigid. "Fine. And when you come home I want you to keep them occupied. We don't wish to be disturbed. Is that quite clear?"

"Yes, sir," the nanny replied unemotionally.

Melanie's brow furrowed as the woman's footsteps receded down the hall. "How did she know you were in here?"

"Because she has an uncanny sense of how to irritate me."

"Doesn't it strike you as strange that she manages to interrupt us every time we start to get romantic?"

"I'd call it maddening, not strange."

"It almost seems as if she's looking after Bootsie's interests," Melanie said slowly. "You know how dazzled Jean is by her."

"Miss Morton's taste is in her mouth. You're the jewel in the crown." He unsnapped her jeans and urged them over her hips.

The rest of the world ceased to exist when David's hands wandered lovingly over her bare body, lingering knowingly where he knew it would please her most. Desire rose inside Melanie like a hungry beast demanding to be fed.

She pushed the shirt off his shoulders and unzipped his jeans. David cooperated eagerly, shucking off his clothes and kicking them aside. When he was splendidly nude, Melanie brushed the tips of her breasts across his chest, tantalizing him erotically.

David arched his body in reaction. "How much of that do you think I can stand?" he groaned.

She laughed softly. "We'll find out, won't we?"

"Sooner than you think!" He picked her up and wound her legs around his hips.

Melanie's simmering passion burst into full flame. Clinging to him tightly, she plunged her tongue into his mouth. After a sizzling few moments David shifted her body and sheathed himself inside her.

The excitement escalated as their damp bodies writhed against each other, bringing almost unbearable ecstasy with every thrust. Completion came in a molten stream that rocketed through both of them at the same time, bathing them in a warm glow.

David carried her to the bed afterward and they remained twined in each other's arms, too contented to move.

After a while he stroked her hair languidly. "I hope that drove any lingering thoughts of Nigel out of your mind."

"Who?" She snuggled closer, smiling.

"When I saw you in his arms I felt like killing him."

"I wasn't in his arms." She kissed the hollow in David's neck. "How could I want anyone else as long as I have you?"

He gathered her in a close embrace. "You'll always have me, sweetheart. I'll never let you go."

It wasn't a proposal, but Melanie was sure that would come in time. Now wasn't the moment to question her happiness. Not after what they'd just shared.

Life returned to normal at Castlebury Manor after the unwanted guests left. The twins took their grandmother's departure with equanimity. They were fond of her, but she'd never been a big part of their lives. David and Melanie were free from tension, and the servants had less work to do.

Everything was perfect for the next couple of days—until the phone call from Rosamund. The twins were in bed and Melanie and David were relaxing over coffee in the den.

His expression changed when he discovered who the caller was. "What is it now, Rosamund?"

"That isn't very polite," she chided. "Whatever happened to respect for one's elders?"

"You're right," he said remorsefully, making a wry face at Melanie. "I hope you had a pleasant trip home."

"Bootsie drives like a madwoman, but we arrived safely."

"That's good. What can I do for you?" He tried to sound pleasant.

"I'd like to speak to you about my grandchildren."

"Oh?" David was suddenly wary.

"Yes, I find I miss them terribly."

"That's too bad. Perhaps I can bring them to see you—say, around Christmastime."

"I had something more immediate in mind. I would like to have custody of the twins."

"*What!*" David sprang to his feet. "You can't be serious!"

"Never more so. Why does that surprise you? After all, I *am* their grandmother."

"When did the realization hit you?" he asked scathingly. "You've never shown any interest in their welfare before."

"That's not true! I couldn't take care of them until now because I was simply too overwhelmed by grief over the death of my only daughter. My health wouldn't permit it."

"But now you've recovered? What cured your grief—all those house parties and yachting trips? Too bad the poor will have to settle for dignified mourning."

"You can revile me all you like. The fact remains that I'm the children's grandmother and I intend to seek custody."

"You'll get them over my dead body!"

"I had hoped you'd be more cooperative."

"That shows how far removed from reality you are."

"I believe *you're* the one who isn't thinking clearly. Sympathy will be on my side."

"How many people will sympathize with a jet-setting grandma who has a lover young enough to be her son? What kind of example is that for nine-year-old children?"

"You're in no position to criticize anyone else's morals," Rosamund said coolly.

"What is that supposed to mean?"

"Simply that *your* affair with Melanie, right under the children's noses, is deplorable."

"Kindly leave Melanie out of this," he said frigidly. "She cares more about Ariel and Ashley than you ever could, and they adore her."

"That's not the point. We're talking about the propriety of having your paramour living right in the house with impressionable youngsters. I think any court would agree that they're better off with me."

David contained his anger with a great effort. "Melanie and I are in love. We are not having a tawdry affair, as you're implying."

"You can call it anything you like, but sex is sex, dear boy," Rosamund said airily. "That's what everyone would say if your conduct became public."

"Are you threatening me?" David asked ominously.

"Not at all. I just want you to consider all the consequences. Think about it and I'll call you tomorrow night." She hung up before he could say anymore.

Melanie had heard enough from his end of the conversation to know what it was about. Her face was anxious. "Rosamund couldn't possibly get custody, could she?"

"No, of course not," David replied, with more confidence than he felt. "She's just rattling my chain."

"Why would she ask for the twins if she didn't really want them?"

"Who knows? Possibly to get back at me for kicking her out."

"That seems rather drastic." Melanie hesitated. "I present a problem for you, don't I?"

Some of the strain left David's face as he pulled her into his arms and kissed the tip of her nose. "Are you joking? You're the best thing that ever happened to me."

"If I thought I was a threat to the twins, I'd leave."

"Don't ever say that! What would I do without you?"

Melanie put her arms around his waist and rested her head on his chest. The very thought of losing David was devastating, but she couldn't destroy three lives.

"Don't worry, darling." He stroked her hair tenderly. "Everything will work out."

A sleepless night showed on both their faces the following day. Melanie and David kept up appearances for the twins and the servants, but they couldn't fool Sylvia. She stopped by for the first time in a week.

"I thought you two would be celebrating," she said. "Your housekeeper told mine that the vultures have flown. So, why do you look like your pet hamster died?"

David managed a smile. "He was like one of the family."

"You never had a hamster. Tell me what's wrong."

"You're a good friend, Sylvia," he began carefully.

"I know, but I'm too pushy. Charles has been telling me that for years." The older woman's smile faded. "It isn't idle curiosity. I care about all of you."

"You've demonstrated that," David said gratefully.

"Sometimes it helps to talk things out. You can get too close to a problem to see the solution."

"I've spent all night looking for one." He told her about Rosamund's phone call.

"She wants those children about as much as I want an extra pound of fat on my hips," Sylvia said cynically. "I'd love to see her face if you offered them to her."

"I realize she isn't sincere, but I don't know what's behind this sudden demand."

"What do you care? She's just being a nuisance. Rose could never get the twins, not with her life-style. No court would take them out of the stable, healthy environment you're providing for them."

David glanced briefly at Melanie. "Some people might not consider it wholesome," he said with difficulty.

"David is referring to our relationship," Melanie explained, since he was reluctant to. "Rosamund is trying to make something tawdry out of it. If he doesn't knuckle under to her demands, she's threatening to tell everyone we're carrying on a steamy affair in front of the children."

"It isn't like Rose to resort to blackmail," Sylvia said thoughtfully. "That's a punishable offense."

"Her charge isn't true of course, but Melanie and I...that is, we..." He groped for the right words.

Sylvia finished the sentence for him. "You're in love. I knew that before you did. So what's the problem?"

"I just told you. I can't let Rosamund take the twins, but I won't let her drag Melanie through the mud."

"There's a simple solution. Why don't you two just get married? That would put a spoke in Rose's wheels." Sylvia's eyes twinkled. "A certain amount of affection is normal among engaged couples."

David turned to Melanie with an expression of dawning excitement, which she didn't share. A marriage of convenience wasn't acceptable. She'd tried to tell herself that he'd get around to asking her, but it was time to face reality. She didn't want a bridegroom who had no alternative.

"That's a very ingenious solution, but it has the disadvantage of being permanent," Melanie said evenly. "It would be a lot simpler if I cleared out and went back to my own country."

David looked as though she'd slapped him. "You could do that? Just walk away?"

"It makes more sense than getting married when you don't really want to."

His face was suddenly austere. "I suppose that's true. It's a lot to ask, even for the twins."

Sylvia was watching them with disgust. "How can two adults who love each other act like such children?"

Melanie's nerves were close to the breaking point. She turned on the older woman angrily. "If you were really so clairvoyant you'd see that David doesn't want to marry me."

"Where did you get an idea like that?" he exclaimed.

"Perhaps because you never asked me."

"I was on the verge of it a hundred times, but I was afraid you'd say no."

"That's a convenient excuse," she said bitterly.

"Darling Melanie, I've had so many strikes against me. You were convinced from the beginning that I was a womanizer and a playboy. Then when we went to London you were convinced of it."

"You did have women calling you nonstop."

He cupped her cheek in his palm, gazing at her tenderly. "I knew them all before I met you, and not one has ever meant what you mean to me. I wanted you to be so convinced of my love that you couldn't turn me down."

His words had the ring of truth that not even a good actor could fake. Melanie's heart soared like a bird as she clasped her arms around his neck. "You could have saved me a lot of sleepless nights if you'd just proposed. Half the time I was afraid I was only one more in a long line of your affairs, and the rest of the time I thought I only had the edge because the twins liked me."

"If you thought either of those things I've been unforgivably insensitive." He took her in his arms and kissed her with great feeling, oblivious to Sylvia who was watching indulgently.

"I wouldn't change one thing about you," Melanie said, misty-eyed.

"I hope that's settled to everybody's satisfaction," Sylvia remarked briskly, to cover her own emotion. "Now, can we discuss the wedding? I suggest that it take place soon."

"It can't be soon enough for me." David released Melanie, but kept his arm around her.

"How would you like to have the wedding in my garden?" Sylvia asked. "The chrysanthemums are coming into bloom and there are still some late roses. We could set up tables on the lawn for the reception afterward."

"It sounds perfect," Melanie said eagerly. "Ariel can be my flower girl and Ashley can be the ring bearer. They'll love it!"

"We'll have to start making lists," Sylvia said. "The first priority is your wedding gown. You'd better order it immediately."

"I'll be in my office. I don't think you ladies need my input." David chuckled.

"I'm glad you see it that way." Sylvia smiled. "The groom's only obligation is to show up on time."

"Scotland Yard couldn't keep me away." He gave Melanie a parting kiss.

After Sylvia left, David asked Melanie to take a walk with him. They wandered hand in hand through a clover-dotted meadow until they came to a large shade tree.

When they were comfortably settled on the grass, he brought a small velvet box out of his pocket and handed it to her.

Inside was a large, pure white diamond surrounded by smaller rose-colored diamonds. Melanie gazed at it with delight. "It's gorgeous!" she exclaimed.

"I hoped you'd like it. It was my mother's engagement ring. She would have been pleased to have her daughter-in-law wear it." He slipped the ring on Melanie's finger.

"Did your brother give it to Marie when they were engaged?" she asked uncertainly. "That wouldn't bother me, but it really should be handed down to Ashley's bride."

"Richard wanted to give it to Marie, but Rosamund felt she should have something more modern."

"Is that the way Marie felt, too?"

David shrugged. "Who knows? She was a sweet, gentle girl who wanted to please everybody."

"She certainly didn't get that trait from her mother," Melanie said tartly. Her face softened as she looked at the ring sparkling on her finger. "I love it, darling. I won't ever take it off."

They kissed tenderly, then with growing urgency. David eased her onto her back and strung kisses down her neck while he caressed her body. But when his hand slipped under the hem of her shirt and curved around her breast, she stopped him.

"It's all right now." He grinned. "We're officially engaged."

"It was all right before." She smiled. "In fact, it was perfect. But we don't want to give Rosamund any more ammunition."

David's face sobered and he sat up. "She's vain and foolish, but I never thought Rosamund would use her own grandchildren as pawns."

"Add thoughtless to your list of character flaws. I don't believe she actually meant to hurt them."

"I'm going to see to it that she never has a chance." David's eyes were steely.

"All Rosamund can do is cause you aggravation," Melanie said confidently. "So don't think about her anymore."

The twins were ecstatic at the news that Melanie and David were getting married.

"Did you fall in love with Uncle David?" Ashley asked. "You said you weren't going to."

"I was wrong," Melanie answered softly.

"What changed your mind?" Ariel asked.

"I convinced her." David smiled.

"How did you do that?" Ashley looked at him curiously.

"When you get older you'll understand." David laughed as Melanie's cheeks turned pink.

"Can I be a bridesmaid?" Ariel asked.

"If she gets to be one of those, can I be something, too?" Ashley asked.

"You're both going to be in the wedding party." Melanie put an arm around each of them.

"Will there be ice cream and cake?" Ashley asked.

"There's always a big wedding cake," Ariel said with the superiority of greater knowledge. "It's white, and they put a bride and groom on top."

"How can anybody stand on top of a cake?" Ashley asked derisively. "They'd squash the whole thing."

"I didn't mean a *real* bride and groom." Ariel gave her brother a look of amused condescension. "They use little dolls dressed up in bridal outfits."

"That's dumb," Ashley declared, to make up for his ignorance.

"It is not! You don't know anything at all about weddings."

"I know as much as you do!"

"Whoa! Hold it." David laughed. "This is supposed to be a happy occasion. Do you want Melanie to have second thoughts about becoming part of this family?"

Both children were instantly contrite. Then Ashley asked hesitantly, "Will she be our mother after you get married?"

"No, darling," Melanie said gently. "Your mother will always be the special person who brought you into this world. I'll continue to be Melanie—your best friend, I hope."

Ariel had been mulling over another problem. "What if you have children like us?"

"I'd be very proud if they turned out exactly like you," Melanie said over the lump in her throat.

"But would you still feel the same way about Ashley and me?" The little girl's hidden fears came out.

"We'll all be part of a family that loves each other equally," David answered, giving her a big hug.

Once the twins were reassured, their excitement over the wedding returned. They were all discussing the plans when the telephone rang. Melanie's nerves tightened and she exchanged a glance with David.

Very casually he said, "All right, children, it's time for bed."

They put up an immediate protest, only more determined than usual. "This is like a holiday or somebody's birthday," Ashley said. "We always get to stay up later when it's one of those things, and this is lots bigger than a birthday."

Ariel nodded in agreement. "I want to ask Melanie what a flower girl does, and what color my dress will be."

"You can ask her all those things tomorrow." David had his hand on the phone, but he didn't lift the receiver.

Melanie herded the children toward the door. "We'll have plenty of time to talk in the morning."

"But we have to go to school."

"Okay, after you come home then."

When the children were safely out of the room and Melanie had closed the door, David picked up the receiver.

"I was beginning to think you weren't home," Rosamund complained.

"I'm here, and I haven't changed my mind," he said austerely. "The twins are going to stay with me."

Instead of flaring back, she adopted a conciliatory tone. "I'm afraid things got rather out of hand yesterday. I never meant to imply that you don't love the children. I'm really grateful to you for taking care of them after that tragic accident."

"Somebody had to."

"You must realize that I was completely devastated at the time. Marie was my only child. Perhaps someday when you have children of your own you'll understand my feelings."

David didn't soften. "Did you ever give a thought to Ariel and Ashley's feelings? Their whole world collapsed. They needed comfort and love."

"I've always loved them! They know that."

"Because you bring them gifts? Where were you when they cried all night and walked around like little ghosts?"

"You're not being fair, David! If I failed them in the past I'm sorry. But now that I want to make amends you won't let me."

"It isn't in their best interests, that's why. This isn't some sort of personal vendetta I'm waging against you. If I thought they'd be happier with you I'd hand them over in a minute. How did you plan to take care of them—by turning them over to headmasters and nannies? And what about holidays? Would they come home to an empty house because you're on the Continent somewhere, partying with your friends?"

"I wouldn't neglect them as you're implying, but I'll admit there are some advantages to having them stay with you. At least, part-time," she added casually.

David stiffened. "Exactly what are you suggesting?"

"I'm proposing a solution that will satisfy both of us, joint custody."

"That's completely out of the question!" he shouted.

Rosamund remained unruffled, almost as if she expected him to refuse. "You're being very intractable," was all she said.

"You're damn right I am! Even if I considered you a fit guardian, there's no way I'd allow those children to be shuffled back and forth like merchandise in a store."

"A lot of children divide their time between two parents quite happily. This would be the same kind of arrangement."

"Don't even think about it, because it's never going to happen."

"Are you willing to let a court decide?" she asked softly.

David's knuckles whitened around the phone, but his voice remained confident. "Custody cases are expensive, Rosamund. Are you prepared to make that kind of investment? Remember, you could quite conceivably lose. Do you have money to throw away?"

"I realize you have a fortune at your disposal and I'm only a poor woman with meager resources." She sniffled slightly.

"That sounds a lot better with violins playing in the background," he said sardonically.

Rosamund's voice hardened for the first time. "All right, David, let's get down to business. You can't have things all your own way. I offered you two alternatives. I take the children to live with me, or I share custody with you."

"How many times do I have to tell you that neither choice is acceptable?"

"You have a lot to learn about compromise," she said impatiently. "If my terms are so repugnant, what do *you* propose?"

"That we leave things exactly as they are."

"Do you think that's fair? If I'm to be denied the comfort of my grandchildren, surely I should be compensated in some way."

Comprehension dawned, leaving David incredulous at first, then coldly furious. "Let me get this straight. You're offering to sell me the twins?"

"What a horrible way of putting it!"

"Excuse me for bruising your delicate sensibilities," he said in a voice dripping with sarcasm. "How much money would it take to heal them?"

"You're being purposely insulting and I don't deserve that," she said in an injured tone of voice.

"You wouldn't give up your claim to the twins if I paid you?"

"I don't consider it payment," she answered carefully. "You've convinced me that perhaps they'd be better off staying with you. I only want what's best for them, and I think they feel the same about me. Fortunately they were left very well-off, while I've had to struggle to make ends meet. I'm sure that would distress the children if they were old enough to understand. I know they'd want to share their inheritance with their grandmother."

"You really are some piece of work, Rosamund," David exclaimed disgustedly. "There isn't anything or anybody you wouldn't use to keep yourself in luxury."

"Don't be so holier than thou," she said angrily. "You don't know what it's like to be poor."

"Neither do you. Having to wear last year's ball gown is an inconvenience, not a sign of poverty. I suggest you look for an alternate source of income, because I'm not going to pay you one red pence."

"I'll make you wish you had," she said furiously. "I was willing to be reasonable, and all I got for my trouble was insults. Well, let's see how you like it when you and your girlfriend are splashed all over the tabloids!"

"They seldom cover weddings. It isn't spicy enough, unless perhaps the happy couple exchange their vows in the nude—which Melanie and I aren't planning to do."

"You're bluffing," Rosamund said uncertainly. "You don't really intend to marry her."

"If you doubt it, ask Sylvia. The wedding is scheduled to take place in her garden."

After a moment's silence Rosamund said, "It still doesn't excuse your lewd conduct. I have someone who will swear you two have been carrying on a torrid affair."

"Give it up, Rosamund. You're the one who was running a bluff, and it's going to cost you. From now on I want you to stay away from us—no more unexpected visits, no uninvited friends of yours. Forget how to get here."

"I have rights. You can't keep me from seeing my grandchildren," she blustered.

"I have no intention of trying. You're a poor excuse for a grandmother, but you're the only one they've got. I'll arrange for them to visit whenever it's convenient for all of us. Take what I'm offering, Rosamund," he warned. "It's the best deal you're going to get." He hung up without waiting for an answer.

Melanie had been listening anxiously. "Do you think she'll back off now?"

"What other choice does she have? Rosamund gambled that I'd pay anything rather than risk losing the twins. She was very clever about setting her hook, too. Giving me twenty-four hours to worry about it was a masterful stroke. Her real motive never occurred to me." David shook his head in wonderment. "Can you imagine putting a price on your own grandchildren's heads? What kind of woman would do a thing like that?"

"Someone who can delude herself into thinking she had just cause," Melanie replied uneasily. "That kind of person doesn't usually take no for an answer."

"She doesn't have any bargaining chips left. Our upcoming marriage makes the scandal angle absurd, and winning a custody case by claiming she's better able to take care of the twins is extremely iffy. Rosamund doesn't have the resources for a protracted legal battle, anyway.''

Melanie forced herself to relax. ''I'm glad it's all over.''

''Everything is just beginning for us.'' David took her in his arms. ''Wouldn't Rosamund be annoyed if she knew she was responsible for bringing us together?''

''Maybe you were too hard on her. We really owe her one.''

''I'm in a receptive frame of mind.'' He chuckled softly. ''Let's go upstairs and see if you can convince me.''

Chapter Ten

Sylvia called about noon the next day and asked Melanie and David over for lunch.

"I made up a tentative menu to give to the caterer," she said. "I want you to look it over."

"You don't need me for that," David said. "Whatever you and Melanie decide will be fine."

"You have to help me make up the guest list. She can't do that."

"Does it have to be today? I really have a lot of things to do, and we have plenty of time."

"Not that much. The invitations have to go out as soon as I get them from the printer."

"All right, we'll be there at one." David gave in with a sigh.

"Anyone would think you aren't interested," Melanie complained after he hung up. "If you're having second thoughts about this marriage, now is the time to voice them."

"You know better than that." He put his arms around her waist and nibbled delicately on her ear. "You couldn't get away from me if you tried."

"I hadn't planned on it."

She made a small sound of pleasure as his hands caressed her and he parted her lips for a stirring kiss. They moved against each other suggestively for a few moments before Melanie drew back reluctantly.

"Jean's timing is off today. This is when she usually interrupts us."

"Maybe she's finally decided to give us some privacy, now that we're engaged." David laughed.

"Or else she simply doesn't care what we do anymore. You must be a terrible disappointment to her." Melanie grinned. "A member of the peerage isn't supposed to take up with a commoner."

"The woman's a nutcase," he said negligently. "I'm thinking seriously of replacing her."

"I honestly don't know why you need a nanny at all, especially since the twins are gone for a good part of the day."

"She'll finally start earning her pay after we're married. As long as she's here to look after the children, we'll be able to get away for a few days alone now and then."

Melanie was sure they could make other arrangements for the twins, but she didn't argue the point.

David wasn't really interested in squab versus Cornish game hen, or how many tiers the wedding cake should have, but he listened indulgently while the two women discussed the subjects in depth.

When that was settled they moved on to the matter of floral arrangements, and then to clothes. Sylvia thought Melanie's wedding gown should have a train, but Melanie thought it might look pretentious.

"It's a garden wedding, after all," she protested.

"That doesn't mean it won't be elegant. Don't you agree, David?" Sylvia turned to him for support.

"She'd look gorgeous in anything, or nothing," he said fondly.

"I was looking for a more dispassionate opinion," Sylvia complained.

He grinned. "You came to the wrong person."

They finally got around to the guest list, but before they could finish, David looked at his watch and said they had to leave.

"We have to pick up the twins at school."

"Ring up their nanny and tell her to do it," Sylvia said.

"Normally I would, but Melanie promised we'd discuss the wedding plans with them this afternoon. I don't want them to feel left out."

"I suppose I can't argue with that, but we really must finish the list as soon as possible." Sylvia wouldn't let them leave until they promised to return the next day.

Melanie and David sat in the parked car watching the children streaming out of the schoolhouse. He reached over and took her hand.

"I never thought being a family man could be this satisfying."

"Don't get too satisfied. I'm hoping we'll add to our family," she said softly. When he gave her a startled look she laughed. "I didn't mean immediately, just sometime in the future."

"I hope it's a little girl, exactly like you," he said with deep emotion.

"Twins run in your family. Maybe we'll have a girl and a boy. Wouldn't that be neat? Then Ariel and Ashley would each have a little one to take under their wing."

They talked about the twins' reaction to their having children, and how best to handle it when the time came. After a while they realized that the schoolyard was almost empty. Only a few stragglers remained, giggling and pushing each other playfully.

"I wonder what's keeping the kids?" Melanie remarked.

"I hope they didn't have to stay after school. I'm in much too mellow a mood to punish them."

"You're a pushover even when you're not feeling mellow," she teased. "I guess we'd better go inside and find out what's up."

The third grade classroom was empty, except for the teacher who was stuffing papers into a briefcase preparatory to leaving. David and Melanie had made it a point to meet her when the twins started school.

"Good afternoon, Miss Pilgrim." David looked around the empty room. "Can you tell us where Ariel and Ashley are?"

The woman looked startled. "Mr. Crandall? I thought you'd be in London by now."

His smile faded. "Why would you think that?"

"Well, the twins' nanny came to get them. She said there was some emergency with their grandmother, and you were taking them to London to see her."

"When was this?" David asked sharply.

"Miss Morton arrived here about one o'clock, I believe. Yes, I remember, the children had just returned from lunch."

"You turned them over to someone in the middle of the day without checking with me first?"

"Miss Morton isn't a stranger. I mean, she *is* the children's nanny. I had no reason to doubt her story," the woman said diffidently. "I hope I didn't do anything wrong."

David grabbed Melanie's arm and headed for the door, too distracted to answer.

He drove home at breakneck speed, his face a mask of cold marble. "I should have expected something like this from Rosamund. There are no depths to which she won't sink."

"Are you sure she's behind this? Jean could have just used her as an excuse."

"That repressed little toady could never think up a stunt like this by herself," he said contemptuously. "It has Rosamund's devious mind all over it. But if she thinks she's going to get away with it, she's even crazier than I thought."

"What are you going to do?"

"First, I intend to have a certain nanny arrested for kidnapping. She's just lucky I can't get my hands around her scrawny neck!"

David braked to a stop in front of Castlebury Manor and raced for the door almost before the motor died. Melanie hurried after him, pale with apprehension.

"Bevins!" he roared. When the man appeared in the entry, David said, "Did I receive any phone calls from Baroness Faversham this afternoon?"

"No, sir. There were some other calls. I left the messages on the desk in your office."

Melanie had run upstairs as soon as they got home. She came down now to report what they both expected. "All of Jean's things are gone."

"Gave notice, did she, sir?" The butler's expression hinted that it was good riddance.

"Lots of it, but I wasn't picking up the signals." David strode toward the den.

"Did Miss Morton receive any phone calls around lunchtime?" Melanie asked Bevins.

"I believe she did, Miss. The phone rang and I picked it up, but Miss Morton was already on the line. I assumed the call was for her."

"Do you know who she was talking to? It's very important," Melanie said urgently.

"I didn't hear the other person's voice. Miss Morton said she would take care of it, so naturally I hung up. Is anything wrong, Miss?"

"Just about everything! She kidnapped the twins."

Bevins' face expressed real emotion for the first time since Melanie had known him. He looked shocked. "The poor little tykes. Have you notified the authorities?"

"I imagine that's what Mr. Crandall is doing now."

She was wrong. David came out of the den, looking even more furious, if possible. "Rosamund isn't answering her phone."

"Did you call the police?"

"I don't want the children frightened any more than they probably are already. Come on, we're going to London."

"But David, suppose this is a real kidnapping?"

"It will only take us an hour to reach the city. If I don't get any answers from Rosamund, I'll call the police immediately. Are you coming?"

Melanie grabbed her purse from the hall table where she'd dropped it and followed him out the door.

David drove like a race driver, berating himself all the way. "Why didn't I see what a danger Jean was?"

"How could you? She was such a cipher. Half the time we forgot she was even in the house."

"It's the other half that should have tipped us off. All those times she interrupted us when we started to get close. You mentioned it, yourself. It was no accident that she always seemed to turn up at an inopportune time. She was spying on us."

"For Bootsie." Melanie nodded. "She must have told her to keep us apart as much as possible. Jean would do anything for her." Melanie looked thoughtful. "You know, little things keep coming back to me. When Bootsie and the Hightowers left after that memorable visit, her ladyship had a private word with Jean and slipped her some money. I thought it was because Jean waited on her hand and foot, but what if it was for future services?"

"Nothing would surprise me anymore," David said grimly.

"Jean would have done it for nothing, but she must have been thrilled at Bootsie's gratitude. Remember when she came back from her day off with a gold pin? She wore it constantly, probably even on her nightgown. I'll bet Bootsie gave it to her."

"Jean should have put a higher price on her services," he remarked sardonically. "We ought to be worth more than a gold pin."

"The phone calls are beginning to make sense too," Melanie mused. "Those didn't start until after Bootsie was here. I thought they were from a boyfriend, because Jean was so giddy after she received one. But she never mentioned a man—or anybody else, for that matter. It's unnatural not to have at least a *few* friends."

"You said it yourself, she isn't normal."

When they reached London, David drove immediately to Rosamund's apartment. It was in one of the best neighborhoods in town. Bright-colored geraniums bloomed in boxes, and a doorman stood guard by the front door.

"For a poor woman with meager resources, she does pretty well," Melanie commented.

"Rosamund thinks she's roughing it," David said. "I'm surprised she didn't tell you about all the homes she used to own."

The doorman was getting mixed signals. David and Melanie were dressed casually, unlike the usual visitors to this neighborhood. But David carried himself with an unmistakable air of authority.

"Can I help you, sir?" the man asked uncertainly.

"We're here to see Baroness Faversham." David shouldered past him. "I know the way."

"Just a moment, sir! You can't go in there."

"Is she at home?"

"Yes, but I have to announce you."

David's eyes smoldered. "Don't worry about it. I'll announce myself—loud and clear." He took Melanie's hand and strode to the elevator, ignoring the man's protests.

Rosamund's apartment was at the end of a long, carpeted hallway. David's jaw was rigid as he rang the bell in short, urgent bursts. When there was no answer, he pounded loudly on the panels.

"I know you're in there, Rosamund. Answer the damn door! If you don't open up, I'm going to call the police."

After a few moments, the door opened and Rosamund glared at him indignantly. "*I'm* the one who should call the police. How dare you come in here and make all this racket?"

"You haven't heard anything yet," he answered grimly. Pushing past her, he stalked into the apartment.

She followed him, sputtering ineffectually while Melanie brought up the rear.

After a quick glance around, David disappeared to search the other rooms. They could hear him calling the twins by name.

Rosamund turned to Melanie. "Has he gone out of his mind?"

"Didn't you expect him to?"

David appeared in the doorway. "All right, Rosamund, what have you done with them?" he asked ominously.

"I don't know what you're talking about. You can't come in here and search my home! There are still laws to protect people."

A nerve pulsed in his forehead. "Where are Ariel and Ashley?"

"I presume they're at Castlebury Manor. Why aren't you there with them?"

His voice was low and deadly. "Don't play games with me. I want my children back, and I want them back *now!*"

"Why tell me? You can see for yourself that they aren't here." Her tone was disdainful, but she moved back prudently.

"*Where are they?*" Each word was like a bullet.

"They're in good hands," she answered grudgingly. "Which they obviously weren't with you."

"If you don't produce them instantly I'm going to call the police and charge you with kidnapping. And don't think I won't do it. I'll take great pleasure in testifying against you personally."

"Is that supposed to frighten me? The police will show you the door. Don't forget, I'm the children's grandmother."

"That doesn't give you the right to take them without my permission. Did you honestly expect to get away with it?"

"I tried to reason with you, but you refused to compromise. What else was I supposed to do? You left me no choice."

David stared at her in disbelief. "Putting aside the illegality of your actions for the moment, did you ever consider how damaging this is to the twins? They were happy, well-adjusted children again. Suddenly they're yanked out of school, taken far from home and told a pack of lies. That would be traumatic for an adult. God knows what it will do to two vulnerable children."

"I removed them from an unsuitable environment," Rosamund said piously. "In time they'll realize that I was simply thinking of them."

"That'll be the day! Will they also understand when they find out you only took them because I wouldn't pay your ransom demands?"

"That's too insulting to dignify with an answer," she replied distantly.

"If I were you, I wouldn't want to talk about it, either. All right, Rosamund, I can't let you victimize the children. It goes against every one of my instincts, but I'll give you your blood money."

"You needn't be so righteous. I don't want your money."

"That would be a first." He looked at her narrowly. "Are you telling me the price has gone up?"

"I'm not interested in bargaining with you. You should have settled when you had the chance," she said smugly. "Now I intend to seek sole custody."

"We went through this on the phone. You can't get it," he stated flatly.

"That's where our opinions differ. We'll just have to wait and see, won't we?"

David's body was taut with fury. "Don't be a fool! Do you know how much a trial like that will cost? Take what I'm offering before I change my mind."

"You can't intimidate me any longer. The odds have changed. I have resources of my own now."

"Who did you blackmail to get them?" he asked contemptuously.

"That's enough! I want you out of my house this instant."

"Not until you tell me where to find the twins."

"They're being well cared for. I knew you'd batter your way in here like a storm trooper, so I had them taken to a safe place. I didn't want you to frighten them with your ugly temper."

"You've only seen the tip of the iceberg." His voice was low and deadly. "If those children have been harmed in any way, I'll make you pay for it."

"Don't threaten me, David. The tables are turned. *I* hold the winning hand this time, so you'd better mind your manners. I'm not only suing for custody, I intend to have myself appointed administrator of the children's estate. All of their affairs will be transferred to me, leaving you no further function in their lives. If you continue to harass me, I might not even let you see them."

"The prospect of big money has gone to your head," he snapped. "I was prepared to pay you off just to get you out of our lives. You shouldn't have been greedy, Rosamund, because now you're going to wind up with nothing."

"I'm the one who has the children," she taunted.

As he started toward her in a black rage, Melanie grabbed his arm. "David, no! That won't solve anything."

"Listen to your lover, David." Rosamund smirked.

"You'd better quit while you're ahead," Melanie told her sharply. "He couldn't really bring himself to hit a woman, but I'm not hampered by any male British reserve. Let's get out of here, David."

"And let her get away with this?" he asked in outrage.

"There are better ways to deal with her."

"I'll put the kettle on." Rosamund gave them a malicious smile. "The police and I can sit down and have a good laugh over a cup of tea."

David protested all the way out of the building. But when Melanie finally got him inside the car, his shoulders slumped.

"The hell of it is, Rosamund is right about the police," he said. "They're not going to intervene in what they'd perceive as a family squabble."

"It would take too long anyway. We have to find the twins right away."

"That's what's driving me crazy." David pounded his fist on the steering wheel. "I keep thinking about how frightened they must be. Wherever Jean has them hidden, she must be keeping them there by force."

Melanie looked thoughtful. "You think they're with Jean?"

"Where else could they be? She and Rosamund are in this together. Rosamund undoubtedly promised her a big reward, based on the money she expects to get from the children's estate."

"Maybe, but I think there's someone else involved. Court cases drag on, sometimes for years, and they cost a lot of money. Where does Rosamund expect to get it?"

A gleam of hope lit David's gloomy expression. "You think she's bluffing?"

"Obviously not, since she turned down your offer without even bargaining for more. I think she found somebody to back her."

"For a share of the estate, you mean? If that's her plan, she and her partner in crime are due for a disappointment. If Rosamund did succeed in gaining control, she would only get a generous allowance. The twins' inheritance can't be touched until they're adults, and even then there are restraints."

"I don't think this whole thing is about money—at least not to the person who's backing her."

David braked for a red light and turned his head to look at Melanie impatiently. "If you have an idea, come out with it."

"I think Bootsie is bankrolling Rosamund in her bid for the twins," Melanie said slowly.

"You can't be serious!" he exclaimed. "Why would she do a thing like that?"

"To get even with you for marrying me."

"That's absurd. Bootsie hates to lose, but she wouldn't go to those lengths."

"You have a lot to learn about women scorned. You were totally honest with her about your feelings, but she refused to be discouraged. Bootsie has invested so much time and humiliation in trying to get you back that she can't let go."

"I'll admit she's hard to shake, but no normal person would resort to kidnapping."

"You've become an obsession. Think about it. Bootsie brought Rosamund to Castlebury Manor to make trouble. She tried to talk her out of taking the so-called loan in exchange for clearing out. When that didn't work, Bootsie dangled the whole estate in front of Rosamund's greedy eyes. They probably don't know she'd only get an allowance, although even that would be enough of an inducement for Rosamund."

"I don't dispute that part, but how would it benefit Bootsie if I lost the twins?"

"She knows how important they are to you. Maybe she hoped you'd be so busy fighting for them that you wouldn't have either the time or the inclination to marry me. And if it didn't work, well then she'd have revenge. You'd be made to suffer the way she has—in her own mind."

"I can't believe it. The whole thing is too bizarre. Bootsie may be willful and spoiled, but she wouldn't do anything this hurtful."

"Are you willing to bet Ariel and Ashley's future that I'm wrong?" Melanie demanded. "Go over to Bootsie's house. Confront her."

"What am I supposed to say—did you mastermind the kidnapping? Of course she'll say no."

"You might not have to question her. It's possible she has them there with her."

David was torn between hope and disbelief. But at this point he was willing to clutch at any straw. "All right, we'll go over and see her."

"I don't think it's a good idea for me to be there when you talk to her. Bootsie and I are like gasoline and matches when we get together," Melanie said. "You'll get a lot further if you talk to her alone."

"Maybe you're right," he agreed.

"Drop me off at the town house."

David's heart was racing when he rang Bootsie's bell. Could Melanie possibly be right? He prayed that the children would be there and this nightmare would be over.

A uniformed maid answered the door. She smiled, as though nothing was wrong. That was a good sign, wasn't it? David asked himself. If the twins were here and they weren't acting up, it meant they didn't realize they'd been kidnapped.

"Good evening, Viscount," the woman greeted him. "It's so good to see you again."

"Is Lady Addersley in?" He braced himself against disappointment that was unwarranted. Bootsie came running down the staircase.

"David, darling! What a wonderful surprise." She threw her arms around his neck and kissed him passionately.

He disentangled himself as soon as possible and looked around for some sign of the children.

"What are you doing in London, and why didn't you let me know you were coming?" she asked.

"It was a spur-of-the-moment decision," he answered absently, glancing past her into the living room.

"You keep looking around as if you've never been here before," she teased. "Although, it *has* been a long time. Come into the library and have a drink. We have a lot to talk about. It's so seldom I can catch you alone lately."

David ignored the barb and followed her into the other room, although he refused a drink.

"Living in the country is making you downright stuffy," she joked. "I intend to get you back to London if it's the last thing I do."

He had no time for small talk. "I need to talk to you, Bootsie."

"Of course, luv. You know you can tell me anything."

"It's about Rosamund. Have you spoken to her lately?"

"Not since we came home from your house. She's really a rather tiresome woman. We've never been what you'd call good friends. That's why I was surprised when she asked me to drive her down to Castlebury Manor."

"She asked *you?*"

"Of course, darling. I must say I thought twice about it. Correctly, as it turned out. Who knew her tacky boyfriend would show up? Honestly! At her age you'd think she'd have more sense. Anyone can see the man is a rank opportunist."

"He and Rosamund have a lot in common," David said grimly.

"I thought it was shameful that she asked you for money."

"She wants a lot more than that, now. Did Rosamund tell you she wants full custody of the twins?"

"No! When did she decide that?"

"I was hoping you could shed some light on the matter."

"Why me? As I told you, we're just acquaintances." Bootsie looked thoughtful. "Her proposal does make a lot of sense, though, when you stop to think about it."

"You just said she's a foolish old woman," he said sharply.

"Perhaps I was being a bit uncharitable. She isn't *my* cup of tea, but I'm sure the twins would be happy with her. Rosamund might be flighty in some ways, but she does love her grandchildren."

David's face was hard. "Let me tell you about this *loving* grandmother. She wants custody just so she can get her hands on the twins' inheritance."

"That's unkind, David," Bootsie protested. "I'm sure Rosamund simply feels it's time she took over responsibility for the children. Your sudden decision to marry Melanie undoubtedly triggered her concern. Very understandably, I might add."

"The twins are crazy about Melanie!"

"She made sure of that." Bootsie's rancor showed briefly through her sweet reasonableness. She quickly masked it. "That doesn't mean she'd make a fit mother for those dear youngsters. Men are so easily taken in by a pretty face—if that's the way you'd describe her. A clever woman can make a man believe anything she wants."

"I didn't come here to discuss Melanie," David said impatiently.

She eyed him coolly. "If you don't want to hear the truth, why did you come?"

"Rosamund had Ariel and Ashley spirited out of school and brought to London. I've just come from confronting her and she won't tell me where they are."

"You think *I* know?"

"I was hoping you could help me find out. The school released the twins to their nanny, and presumably they're still with her. Has Miss Morton contacted you? I know you became friendly with her."

"I would hardly consider us friends." Bootsie snickered. "She followed me around like a puppy dog. You know how people like that are. They're very impressed with titles. I found it amusing, so I let her perform a few small services for me, that's all.''

"Do you know if she has any friends or relatives in London?''

"Good heavens, no! How would I?''

"I have to find her! The twins aren't at Rosamund's, so they must be with Jean. But where? Think hard,'' David pleaded. "She must have mentioned someplace or somebody in London. Any tiny thing you can think of might help.''

"She never told me anything about herself. If Rosamund put her up to snatching the twins, then she's the only one who knows their whereabouts. Would you like me to talk to Rosamund for you?''

"I'll take any help I can get,'' he said gratefully.

"You know I'd do anything for you,'' Bootsie said softly.

He pretended not to notice her suddenly personal tone. "Could you phone her now? I'm really frantic about the children. I don't suppose Jean would actually harm them, but she must be restraining them in some way. They would try to get in touch with me, once they found out she lied about taking them to their grandmother's.''

"Maybe it would be better if I talked to Rosamund in person.''

"I can't afford to waste any more time,'' he protested.

"I understand your anxiety,'' Bootsie soothed. "But this has to be handled delicately. I can't come right out and ask her where Ariel and Ashley are. She would deny knowing anything about them.''

"She already admitted that she engineered the whole thing!''

"To you maybe, but she's not going to admit such a damaging thing to anyone else. I'll have to work up to it gradually.''

"I only hope I can restrain myself that long. Every instinct tells me to go over there and shake the truth out of her.'' David stood and thrust his fists into his pockets in an effort to control himself.

Bootsie rose gracefully and put her arms around his neck. "Leave everything to me, darling. I'm the one person you can always count on." When he tried to move away, she tightened her grip. "We belong together. You know it in your heart."

He put his hands around her wrists and removed her arms forcibly. "Please, Bootsie, I don't have time for this right now."

"Why won't you admit it? I'm the one you came to when you were in trouble. Doesn't that tell you anything?"

"I came to you as a friend."

She drew in her breath sharply. "I don't want your damn friendship! I'm in love with you."

"Be reasonable," he pleaded. "Can't you see how this thing is tearing me apart?"

"How do you think *I* felt all these weeks, seeing you carrying on with that little tramp, making me a laughingstock in front of all my friends!"

David made a mighty effort to rein in his temper. Melanie would be the first one to tell him that the twins' safety was more important than Bootsie's insults. "If I've embarrassed you in any way, I'm sorry. That was never my intention."

"I realize it wasn't really your fault. She used every trick of the trade to steal you away from me."

"Can't we discuss this later?" he asked tautly. "Every minute counts right now."

"And *I* don't?" Her eyes narrowed dangerously. "For someone who wants a favor, you're not going about it very cleverly."

"This isn't a game," he said sharply. "Do you want revenge, is that it? All right, you've got it. I'm at the end of my rope. Tell me what you want me to say and I'll say it."

She put her arms around his waist and gazed up at him seductively. "You could start by saying you love me—the way you used to."

"I never told you that."

"Then it's time you did." She laughed softly.

David moved away again. "This is surreal! What you feel for me isn't love, it's an obsession."

"I suppose you think Melanie loves you," she answered spitefully. "All she wants from you are social position and money. I have all that. I only want you for yourself. We belong together, darling."

"You need help," he said distastefully, taking note of her ragged breathing and flushed face.

Bootsie's hands curled into fists. "No, *you're* the one who needs help, and I'm the one who can give it to you—if you'll just come to your senses."

"Meaning, if I give up Melanie?"

"You shouldn't have to think twice, providing you really care as much about your niece and nephew as you profess to."

Masking his disgust, David managed to keep his voice dispassionate. "You're asking a lot for simply talking to Rosamund. How do I know she'll tell you anything?"

"She will," Bootsie said eagerly. "I know how to handle her."

"The only language Rosamund understands is money. Somebody is dangling a lot of it in front of her."

"Don't worry about it, just trust me. I guarantee I'll get the children back for you. Your precious Melanie can't do that." Bootsie grabbed his arm urgently. "You need me!"

"Like a fatal virus," he answered contemptuously. "The kidnapping was your idea, wasn't it? Rosamund isn't tricky enough to think up a stunt like that. Only someone as sick and twisted as you could put two little children through such an ordeal just to salve her own wounded pride."

"How about *my* ordeal?" she asked shrilly. "You care about everybody's feelings but mine. Well, you've trampled on them for the last time. Let's see how *you* like losing someone you care about. You'll never get the twins back! I only wish Rosamund could take Castlebury Manor away from you, too."

David looked at her in disgust. "Melanie was right about you. She said you were bankrolling Rosamund, but I didn't believe her."

"You always did underestimate me." Bootsie tilted her chin defiantly.

"Don't make the same mistake about me," he said grimly.

"You can't touch either one of us. Rosamund has rights as a grandmother, and you can't prove I had anything to do with taking the children out of school."

"I can have Jean arrested for kidnapping. Do you think she'll go to prison for you? I doubt if even *her* devotion is that great."

"Who do you think the police will believe if I deny any involvement? After all, what motive do I have?" Bootsie asked smugly.

"You won't get off scot-free, I promise you. If nothing else, you'll be tarnished by the scandal. I'm pretty sure Jean will sing like a canary when she finds out you turned against her and she's faced with a long prison sentence."

"You're bluffing," Bootsie said uncertainly. "You wouldn't want this to get into the tabloids."

"Don't you believe it! I'm not the one who will come out badly. I have every intention of pressing charges against Jean, if only to make sure she doesn't do this to some other unsuspecting souls."

"All right, take your petty revenge. A lot of good it's going to do you. Rosamund will still have the children," Bootsie said triumphantly. "It could take years for this to be settled."

David's eyes glittered with anger as he moved toward her. "If you know what's good for you, you'll tell me where they are."

"Or what?" She stood her ground. "You wouldn't resort to violence. I know you better than that."

His hands opened and closed spasmodically. "I've never struck a woman, but I'd sure as hell like to make an exception in your case."

"But you won't," she taunted. "You've lost and you know it. Go back and cry on Melanie's shoulder. She's all you've got left."

David stared at her with loathing. "I should feel sorry for you. You don't even know what love is all about. I couldn't conceive of a life without Melanie. When I look at her, my heart soars. Yes, I'm going back to her, and not you or anybody else will ever come between us."

"Get out of my house!" Bootsie shouted, the cords in her neck standing out. "Get out and don't ever come back."

"There's no danger of that," he replied contemptuously.

She picked up a china figurine and threw it at his retreating back. It missed him and crashed against the wall. Bootsie continued to scream and throw things, even after David had left the house.

Chapter Eleven

Melanie paced the living room floor nervously after David had let her off at his town house. There was no doubt in her mind that Bootsie was involved, even though David was reluctant to believe it. In the best case scenario, he'd find the twins with her and the whole ugly mess would be over with.

But was Bootsie stupid enough to incriminate herself by keeping them at her house? Rosamund could claim immunity because she was the grandmother, but anybody else was on shaky ground.

Jean was a more likely candidate to be hiding the children. She was stupid enough to take them in the first place; she might be dumb enough to let herself be talked into keeping them. She'd have her hands full, though. The twins weren't infants who could be plunked into a crib with the guarantee that they'd stay there. They would try to get in touch with David at the first opportunity.

Melanie didn't like to think about how Jean was restraining them—if indeed she was the culprit. The same problem might have occurred to Rosamund and Bootsie. Neither had a high opinion of the nanny's intelligence, although they weren't above using her. Who could they get who would be more reliable? A man would be a better choice. He could use force or intimidation.

Melanie stopped in her tracks as someone occurred to her. Rosamund's boyfriend, Nigel! He had all of the qualifications for a job this dirty. He was physically fit, chronically in need of money, and he wasn't bothered by scruples. If David struck out at Bootsie's, they'd tackle Nigel next.

Waiting for David to return was the hardest part. Melanie was tormented by visions of two frightened children being held hostage. Another thing worried her. If she mentioned her suspicions to David, he might go off the deep end and beat Nigel to a pulp without waiting for confirmation. All he needed was an excuse. Even if she was right about Nigel, it wouldn't help matters to have David land in jail for assault and battery. It would certainly prejudice the court against him in a custody battle.

After resuming her pacing, torn with indecision, Melanie knew she had to take action. The first step was to look in the telephone book.

She dialed Nigel's number and listened with a pounding heart to the repeated ringing at the other end. Finally when she was about to give up, he answered.

After identifying herself Melanie said, "I was beginning to think you weren't home. Did I get you away from something?"

"Nothing important. This is a surprise. I never expected to hear from *you*." He didn't sound overly pleased.

"You must be used to women calling you."

"Not ones who made it plain they weren't interested in me."

"We didn't meet under the best circumstances," she protested. "We both had someone watching us like a hawk."

Nigel didn't unbend. "We could have given them the slip if you'd wanted to."

"You're willing to take more chances than I am. You saw how jealous David is. If I'd been anything more than civil to you, I could have lost a good thing. He's really loaded."

"Are you going for the gold ring?" Nigel sounded a little friendlier. This was territory he understood.

"I'm just playing it by ear for now," she said.

"Well, I wish you luck. You're going to need it. The fellow went absolutely ballistic, and we weren't even doing anything. That was rather a mixed blessing." He laughed. "You might have been worth it. Too bad I'll never find out."

"You give up awfully easily," Melanie murmured.

"I'm a lover, not a fighter." After a moment's pause Nigel said, "Is David in London with you?"

"Yes, but he's off somewhere on business. I'm really awfully lonely," she added suggestively.

"I could do something about that. A man who would leave a beautiful woman all alone deserves what he gets." He hesitated. "Did David say when he'd be home? I wouldn't want him to burst in on us unexpectedly."

"Don't even think about it! We can't meet here. Why don't I come over to your place instead?" That was what Melanie had been angling for all along.

"Well, I . . . it isn't convenient right now."

A feeling of triumph filled her as her suspicions seemed to be confirmed. She fought to keep it from showing in her voice. "You have another woman there," she pouted.

"No, it's nothing like that. The fact is, I . . . uh, I have a roommate. We wouldn't have any privacy here."

"Too bad, but I'm sure we can work something out if we put our heads together. Why don't we meet for a drink someplace?"

"That's a great idea!"

"Give me half an hour. I want to look my best for you," she purred.

"You don't have to try very hard," he said deeply. "I remember how terrific you are."

Melanie hung up with a feeling of satisfaction. Everything was going according to plan. She reluctantly took off her engagement ring, but it was for a good cause.

After a quick dash to the drugstore to buy makeup, Melanie ran upstairs to fix her face and change clothes. The outfit some former girlfriend of David's had left behind was a godsend now, instead of an irritation. Maybe Nigel would have found her sexy in the jeans she'd worn to London, but an alluring dress would make her work easier.

First she applied makeup with a heavy hand. Eyeliner, a lot of mascara, and green shadow on her lids to deepen the color of her eyes. Time was too short to create a fancy hairdo, so she simply brushed her hair until it floated around her shoulders in a pale silken cloud.

Before donning the slinky black dress, she made liberal use of the forgetful guest's perfume and borrowed her gold hoop earrings.

The dress was a little snug. Either its owner was thinner than Melanie, or she wore her clothes tight to show off plentiful curves. That's what the dress did for Melanie. She wrinkled her nose at her reflection in the mirror, but Nigel was sure to find her sexy, and that was all that mattered. After a final spray of perfume she clattered down the stairs in her borrowed high heels.

Nigel was already sitting at a table when Melanie arrived at the pub they'd agreed upon.

"Sorry I'm late," she said breathlessly.

His eyes roved over her greedily. "It was worth the wait. You look sensational!"

She lowered her lashes slightly. "You look pretty terrific yourself."

He continued to examine her minutely. "I can't get over how different you seem from the last time I saw you."

Melanie didn't want him to dwell on the change. "You started without me," she said, eyeing his glass. "I need a drink to catch up."

"Don't worry, I'm not hard to catch." He circled her wrist with one hand and raised the other to summon a waiter.

When she had his attention again, Melanie said, "It's so good to be back in London. I miss all the excitement."

"It *is* pretty dead in the country. Will you have to live there if you marry David?"

"Not full-time, I hope. He has a house here in the city. We'd probably only go down to Castlebury Manor for a weekend or two if it weren't for the twins. I think David is a little *too* conscientious when it comes to them, but I'm not in a position to argue about it yet."

"That's right." Nigel chuckled. "Tie the knot first."

"Exactly. But when that day comes, look out world, little Melanie is going to live it up."

He fondled her hand. "You can have fun long before that."

"I intend to." She paused while the waiter set a drink in front of each of them, although Nigel's was still half-full. "Here's to good times," she said, raising her glass.

"I'll certainly drink to that." He drained his glass, set it aside and put the full one in its place. "We'll have to discuss the logistics, since your place is out."

"It's too bad you have a roommate. I wouldn't have expected that. Doesn't it rather cramp your style?"

"It's only temporary. A friend is down on his luck and I told him he could crash with me for a few days. I expect him to be gone soon."

Excitement raced through Melanie in a heady rush. "How soon?"

"Not anytime tonight, unfortunately. Let's talk about alternatives."

"A girl likes to be romanced a little first," she said coyly, gazing at him over the top of her glass as she took a lady-like sip.

"Anything your little heart desires, baby doll." He took a big gulp of his own drink.

"Tell me what you've been doing since I saw you."

"Is that your idea of romance?" he teased.

"I want to know more about you. Are you really a stock-broker?"

"I do a little investment counseling," he answered vaguely.

"I wish *I* could figure out a way to support myself in style without having to work regularly."

"You're not doing too badly."

She shrugged. "I get to live pretty well, but it isn't a free ride. Nobody seems to believe it, but I put in long hours auditing David's books, with no guarantee that I'm going to land him. I want to learn how to live it up like you and Rosamund do. From what I hear, she isn't exactly affluent, either."

"Not now, maybe, but she has dynamite prospects. And li'l old Nigel is going along for the ride."

While they were talking, Melanie pretended to keep up with him, drink for drink, but she managed to empty most of her drinks into a potted plant next to the table. As soon as her glass was empty she encouraged Nigel to order another round, which he did promptly. She was amazed at the amount of alcohol it took, but finally his speech started to slur slightly, and his tongue began to loosen.

"I invested a lot of time in the old girl, and now it's finally gonna pay off," he said with satisfaction.

"How is her good fortune going to benefit you?" Melanie asked artlessly.

He gave a tipsy laugh. "I scratch her back, and she scratches mine."

That could refer to any amount of services performed. Melanie tried to pin him down. "What makes you think she'll continue to be grateful once she comes into money?'' In her eagerness, Melanie went too far. ''Do you have something on her?''

Nigel looked at her suspiciously. ''Why are you so interested?''

She hid her chagrin under an enchanting smile. ''I'm always interested in rich men. And when they're as handsome as you, I get positively excited.''

He was instantly distracted. Putting his hand on her knee he said, ''That makes two of us, angel eyes. Let's get out of here. I know a small hotel just a couple of blocks away.''

''Checking into a hotel without luggage is so tacky. I have a better idea. One of my friends is a flight attendant. She keeps an apartment here in London and I have a standing invitation to use it any time I like.''

''Fantastic! What are we waiting for? I'll get the check.''

''While you're doing that I'll phone and ask her to tell the manager to let us in.''

''You don't have a key? What if your friend is off flying somewhere?''

''She isn't. I talked to her this morning. It might take me ten or fifteen minutes to locate her, though, so don't get impatient. I'll have to phone around to all her friends.''

''For you, baby, I'd wait forever.''

''You're sweet.'' She trailed a forefinger across his lips.

As soon as Melanie was out of Nigel's sight she headed for the door and went outside to hail a taxi. After giving the driver Nigel's address, she sat back tensely.

Melanie was sure that Ariel and Ashley were there, but she was almost afraid of what she'd find. Nigel couldn't just lock them in the apartment while he was gone. Even if he unplugged and removed the telephone, they could call for help by pounding on the door or yelling out the window. He had to restrain them in some way.

The thought was so unnerving that she almost hoped they wouldn't be there. But that was foolish. Nigel wouldn't actually harm the twins. Being an accessory to a crime that fell into a gray area was one thing, but violence was quite another. It could land him in prison for a long time.

Melanie knew her reasoning was sound, but it didn't make the taxi ride any more bearable. When they finally arrived, her entire body was taut with strain.

Nigel lived in a rather scruffy apartment house in a marginally good neighborhood. The brass panel that held the nameplates needed polishing, but the front steps of the building were swept clean.

Nigel lived on the fourth floor. After finding out the apartment number, Melanie went inside and knocked on the super's door. Even though she'd rehearsed her story thoroughly, butterflies were zooming around in her stomach. Could she bluff her way into Nigel's apartment? If not, she'd just have to break in, Melanie decided grimly, without allowing herself to wonder how.

The superintendent was a middle-aged man with cynical eyes and a pinched mouth. He looked like the kind of person who'd given up on humanity and was interested only in himself.

Melanie gave him a nervous smile. "I wonder if you can help me. Mr. Daventry told me to wait for him in his apartment, but I'm afraid I lost the key. I'm his accountant."

The man snickered. "Well, that's one I never heard." He looked her over, not missing a curve.

Her cheeks were very pink, but she kept her composure. "I was hoping you could let me in with your pass key." She took a bill out of her purse. "I'd be very grateful."

Her approval rating went up as he took the bill and pocketed it. "That's real generous of you, Miss. The people around here never think about the poor overworked super. They want plenty of service, but do you think they appreciate it? I could tell you stories."

He proceeded to tell her a long one. Melanie didn't want to antagonize him, but her nerves were screaming. How long could she count on before Nigel realized he'd been duped and came home, spoiling for a fight?

Finally she broke in on the man's monologue. "That's a really outrageous story. I can't believe anyone would act that way. Tell me the rest of it on the way upstairs."

He continued to talk all the way up in the creaking elevator and down the hall. After fumbling with a ring of keys, he eventually unlocked Nigel's door, but kept his hand on the knob. Melanie was reaching the limit of endurance, when there was a blessed interruption.

A tenant came out of the apartment across the hall. "I've been looking for you, Scruggs. When are you going to fix that drip in my bathroom? It's driving me crazy."

"I put in a washer last month. If you'd turn the faucet off tight, it wouldn't drip."

As the tenant and the super started to argue, Melanie slipped inside Nigel's apartment and closed the door.

An ominous silence greeted her. Two lively children could never keep this quiet. In a panic, she called out to the twins. There was no answer.

She ran into the bedroom. It, too, was empty. Nigel's slacks were thrown over a chair and a rumpled shirt had fallen to the floor as if he'd discarded both hastily. That was normal, though. He would have been in a hurry to change for their date. A newspaper lying on the bed and a depression in a pillow indicated Nigel had just been lounging around when she phoned. There was no sign of anyone else in the apartment.

"I was so sure," she groaned. "Oh, Ariel, where the devil are you and Ashley?"

Disappointment weighed Melanie down as she turned toward the door. A slight noise stopped her in her tracks. It was an eerie sound in the silent room, sending a shiver down her spine. It sounded like whispering. Melanie whirled around, but nobody was there.

Tiny hairs stood up on the back of her neck as she remained rigid, straining her ears. Gradually the whispering grew audible.

"But it's Melanie. We can't let her leave." It was Ariel's voice.

"We have to," Ashley answered. "You know what he said."

"She won't let him do it."

"Ariel? Ashley?" Melanie rushed to the closet. "Are you in there?"

"Please get us out." Ariel began to cry. "I'm scared."

"Don't worry, darling, everything's going to be all right. Melanie's here now." She turned the knob, but the door was locked. In sheer frustration she rattled the knob and pulled hard naturally without any result.

"What's taking you so long?" Ariel's voice rose to a wail.

Melanie forced herself not to show sympathy, so the little girl wouldn't have hysterics. "I'll have you out in a couple of minutes if you'll just be patient. Ashley, I want you to hold your sister's hand. I'm going to find something to break the lock and I'll be right back."

She rushed into the kitchen and pulled open drawers until she found one containing odds and ends of hardware. Grabbing a screwdriver, a hammer, a knife—anything that might be useful—she raced back to the bedroom.

Ariel was sobbing and Ashley was on the ragged edge. "Is that you, Melanie?" he whispered fearfully.

"Were you expecting Santa Claus?" she joked, although her face was strained.

"I thought maybe *he* came back."

"Don't worry about him—he's history." Melanie inserted the screwdriver in the doorjamb. "This will make some noise, so don't be frightened."

She hit the handle of the screwdriver with the hammer until the edge of the door splintered, exposing the lock. A few more blows separated it from the sash.

The two children burst out and threw themselves into Melanie's arms. She held their trembling little bodies close, crying along with them.

After an emotional few moments, both children started to talk at once, trying to tell her what happened.

"You can tell me in the cab going home," Melanie said, herding them toward the door. "Let's get out of this dump."

Melanie became coldly furious as the twins told their story in the taxi. She was afraid to think what David would do when he heard.

"Miss Morton came to school and told us Grandmother was sick and wanted to see us," Ariel said. "But when we got to London she took us to Mr. Daventry's apartment and left us there."

"He said we had to stay with him for a couple of days." Ashley took up the story. "We told him we wanted to go home, but he said we weren't going to live at Castlebury Manor anymore. That's when Ariel started to cry."

"I did not!" she said indignantly.

"Yes, you did," he insisted.

"Well, maybe just a little bit, but you were scared, too. Your voice got all squeaky."

Melanie stepped in hurriedly. "Did he say where you were going to live?"

"With Grandmother," Ariel answered. "When we told him we wanted to stay with Uncle David, he said we'd be lucky if she ever let us see him again."

Melanie was appalled at the cruelty of the man. "You must have known that wasn't true! Your uncle would never give you up."

Ashley looked at her with big eyes. "Mr. Daventry said there was nothing he could do about it, that Uncle David was going to find out what it meant to be a loser."

"He said this would teach him that he wasn't better than everybody else, even though he thought he was."

Nigel was in on this disgusting plot for the money, but revenge was icing on the cake, Melanie realized. David was everything Nigel admired and could never hope to be.

"I told him he couldn't talk about our uncle that way," Ashley said proudly.

"Mr. Daventry told him to shut up," Ariel reported. "He said he didn't have to take anything from a nine-year-old kid, and if we didn't behave ourselves we'd be sorry."

"I wasn't afraid of him," Ashley bluffed. "I whispered to Ariel that we should run away when he wasn't looking."

"Is that why he locked you in the closet?" Melanie asked.

"No, we never got a chance to try it. Mr. Daventry got a telephone call and he said he had to go out. That's when he put us in the closet."

Melanie looked at them in perplexity. "There's something I don't understand. After he'd gone out, why didn't you yell to attract somebody's attention? And especially when you heard my voice, why didn't you call out immediately? I almost left."

The twins exchanged an apprehensive glance. Finally Ashley said hesitantly, "Mr. Daventry said if anybody came to the apartment we had to keep perfectly quiet. He said if we didn't, he'd go to the police and tell them Uncle David did some very bad things. He said they'd send him to prison and he'd spend the rest of his life chained in a cell with only bread and water once a day."

Tears dampened Ariel's eyes again. "We couldn't let them do that to Uncle David."

Melanie almost choked on her outrage. Nigel had used psychological warfare to intimidate two nine-year-old children! His threats against David, coupled with incarceration in a small, dark closet, were almost guaranteed to frighten them into obedience. They'd do anything he said, to protect their uncle and avoid getting shut up in the dark again.

Nigel needn't have threatened David. It was gratuitous cruelty. Ariel and Ashley could have yelled until they were hoarse without any result. It would have been almost impossible for anyone to hear cries from a closet inside an apartment with all the doors and windows closed.

As the cab pulled up at the town house, Melanie started to worry about David's reaction when he heard what Nigel had subjected the twins to. Nobody could blame him for retaliating violently, but she didn't want Nigel's threat to come true.

The front door flew open as she was fumbling for her key.

"Where have you been? I—" Astonishment, then incredulous happiness spread over David's face as the twins rushed to hug him.

For a joyous few moments they all talked at once. David pulled them both into a close embrace, holding them so tightly that their words came out breathlessly. They clung to him the same way, clutching his shirt in their hands.

Finally David looked at Melanie over their heads. "Where did you find them?"

"It's a long story," she said. "I'll tell you after we put the children to bed. They must be exhausted."

"No, we're not," Ariel protested. She tightened her grip on David's waist.

"We want to stay with you two," Ashley agreed. He was similarly attached to David's other side.

Melanie understood their need for assurance. "You're safe now," she said gently. "But I think we could all use a cup of hot chocolate. You can answer all of your uncle's questions while I go into the kitchen."

It took nearly half an hour before the trio joined her. The twins seemed almost back to normal, but David's entire body was taut with fury. He tried to contain it for the children's sake as they chattered on about other things.

"When are we going home, Uncle David?" Ariel asked. "We have to go to Shirley Conover's birthday party this Saturday."

"I'm not going," Ashley declared. "It's mostly all girls, and Robbie Boles said they always play dumb kissing games."

"You're just worried that Shirley won't pick you to kiss her," Ariel teased.

"I am not! I just want to play soccer, that's all."

Melanie smiled at David. "They're going to be all right," she said softly.

"Thanks to you." He squeezed her hand hard.

The children talked about their friends at home and their plans for the weekend. The recent trauma they'd been through was all but forgotten. Eventually they started to yawn as the excitement wore off and the hot chocolate relaxed them. They voiced only token protests when Melanie again suggested bed.

Both she and David tucked the twins in. He was reluctant to leave them, as though fearful they'd disappear again.

When they were downstairs in the den his pent-up rage exploded. It was all the more frightening for being so deadly. "Do you know what I'm going to do to that man?" he rasped.

"I know what you'd like to do, but you're too civilized," Melanie pointed out carefully.

"Don't count on it! First I'm going to rearrange his face, then I'm going to damage the other equipment he uses to make a living."

"This wasn't Nigel's idea. It doesn't excuse him for his despicable acts, but he was only the muscle, not the brains—whether you want to believe it or not."

"I know that now," David said more quietly. "You were right about Bootsie. She was the mastermind behind this whole nightmare."

"Well, thank the Lord for small favors!" Melanie exclaimed. "I was afraid you'd still refuse to believe it when the children weren't with her."

"How did you know they wouldn't be?"

"I didn't. I was just considering all the alternatives, and I decided to chase one down before the kids got too traumatized."

A nerve throbbed in David's forehead. "That's what is unforgivable! This could mark Ariel and Ashley for life."

"It won't. You saw how quickly they snapped back. They might not want to hang up their clothes in the closet for a while, but then again, they might just use this incident as a good excuse." Melanie grinned.

His face remained sober. "How can I ever thank you?"

"You don't have to. I'm just glad Bootsie is finally out of our lives. How did she give herself away?"

"At first she pretended to be horrified at what had happened. She offered to intercede with Rosamund."

"That doesn't sound suspicious." When David's gaze shifted, Melanie made a shrewd guess. "The offer came with a price tag."

"She wanted me to come back to her," he admitted.

"She's wanted that all along. What made this time any different?"

"She guaranteed to get the twins back for me. The only way anyone could do that is if they were in on the scheme, so I realized you were right about Bootsie's involvement."

"Did you confront her with it? I hope you didn't let her off the hook this time."

David's jaw set grimly. "I made a lot of threats, which I may or may not carry out. What I find really incredible is how she can claim to be in love with me, and then put me through something like this. The woman is a certified mental case!"

Melanie put her arms around his neck. "Forget about Bootsie. I'll be happy to give you a demonstration of true love."

He kissed her hard, but briefly. "Hang on to that thought. I have to make a phone call first."

"Couldn't you make it afterward?"

His face relaxed in a smile for the first time. "I want to get all distractions out of the way, because what I have in mind for us is going to take all night."

She laughed delightedly. "When you put it that way, how can I object?"

David strode over to the telephone and rapidly punched out Rosamund's number. His eyes iced over as he listened to it ring.

"I've said everything I have to say to you," she announced after finding out who it was. "From now on you can speak to my attorney. I refuse to be harassed in this manner."

"Get used to it, Rosamund. This is only the beginning," he answered softly.

"Bootsie told me you threatened to air our private affairs in the tabloids."

"She didn't waste any time getting back to you."

"Bootsie is my friend. She called to warn me about what you might do. I can't believe you would stoop so low."

"As low as you did when you gave your grandchildren to a man who scared the hell out of them and locked them in a closet?"

"I have no idea what you're talking about."

"Did Bootsie omit that little detail? Maybe she hasn't found out about it yet, herself. Which one of you was Nigel supposed to report to?"

"What does Nigel have to do with any of this?" Rosamund asked warily.

"You really picked a rare pair for your gang members," David said contemptuously. "They'd both sell you out in a split second if it suited their own selfish purposes."

"You're just jealous because I have loyal friends on my side."

"Let me tell you about your good friend, Bootsie. She offered to return the twins to me if I took her back and sent Melanie packing."

"Bootsie would never do such a thing—even if she knew where they were, which she doesn't. You're trying to make trouble between us, but it won't work."

"She told you she'd still pay the cost of a lawsuit?"

After an almost imperceptible pause Rosamund said, "All right, she is loaning me the money to fight you in court. What difference does it make?"

"None to me, it's about what I'd expect from her. But there have been new developments. I wouldn't count on her continued financial support."

"You're grasping at straws," Rosamund said impatiently. "I see no reason for Bootsie to change her mind."

"Nigel, your other winner, is responsible for that."

"Why do you keep bringing Nigel into this?"

"Your trusty boyfriend has a roving eye, but that can't be news to you."

"Really, David, you're so transparent! First you try to make me doubt Bootsie, and now you attack Nigel. It shows how desperate you are, but your efforts are simply laughable."

"Let's see if you're still laughing when I tell you he made a date with Melanie tonight."

"You expect me to believe that?"

"I suppose not. You didn't notice when he was panting after her at Castlebury Manor. Why do you think I threw him out?"

"He told me why. It was because you didn't approve of—" she stopped abruptly.

"Of you two sleeping together?" David finished the sentence for her. "I couldn't care less—although even you could do better than that lazy leech. I threw Nigel out because he propositioned Melanie, and he did it again today."

"Now I know you're lying," Rosamund said triumphantly. "Nigel spent the day at home in his own apartment, taking care of—" She checked herself hastily, chagrined at what she'd almost revealed.

"He was *supposed* to be watching the twins, but Melanie phoned and asked him out for a drink. Faithful Nigel couldn't turn down an opportunity like that, so he locked Ariel and Ashley in a closet and left to convince Melanie that he was the greatest stud since Casanova. In case you're even remotely interested, the children are all right. They're with me."

"Nigel wouldn't . . . you're just . . ." Rosamund was almost incoherent as she dealt with a variety of emotions.

"You'll find out I'm telling the truth as soon as he has the guts to admit his stupidity. Unfortunately for all of you, the twins are old enough to tell exactly what was done to them and by whom. You've broken enough laws to send you all to prison for a long time."

"I'm the children's grandmother," Rosamund said faintly.

"That doesn't entitle you to endanger their lives. What would have happened if they'd suffocated in that locked closet?"

She started to cry. "I didn't know Nigel would do anything that terrible."

David massaged his forehead wearily. "That didn't help Ashley and Ariel a great deal."

"Are you really going to bring charges?" she asked fearfully.

"That depends on you. I intend to get a statement from Nigel and Jean, confessing their part in this disgraceful affair. You might warn both of them that they can run, but they can't hide, if that's what they're considering. I'll track them down wherever they go."

"Are you going to prosecute them?"

"Only if they fail to cooperate, which I seriously doubt. They don't deserve to get off this easily, but it's not worth making the twins testify in court. I want them to forget this ever happened."

"I never dreamed they'd be in any danger," Rosamund said with what sounded like real remorse.

"That's why they're better off with me. I hope you realize that now, but just in case your guilt wears off in time and you consider trying something like this again, don't even think about it! I won't hesitate to use the sworn statements from Nigel and Jean."

"It wasn't really my fault. Bootsie talked me into it." Now that any personal danger was past, Rosamund felt safe in justifying herself. "She said Melanie would be a bad influence on the children, and I owed it to them to ask for full custody."

"Did she also tell you to try for their estate while you were at it?" David asked dryly.

"I'm not a wealthy woman," Rosamund answered cautiously. "You know that. I was afraid if you controlled their money you'd mete it out to me in dribs and drabs to force me to give the children back to you. It was really for their sake that I wanted it."

"Your altruism overwhelms me, Rosamund. Fortunately you no longer have to concern yourself with their welfare. We're agreed on that, are we not?" he asked with steel in his voice.

"Yes." She sighed. "Will you allow me to see them?"

"In time. Let me cool off first. I'm not feeling terribly friendly toward you at the moment."

"I know I haven't been a very good grandmother," she said quietly. "And I can't even promise to change, because I probably wouldn't. But I do love those children."

"I'm sure she does," Melanie said after David had concluded the conversation and repeated Rosamund's statement. "In her own way."

"That's not my idea of love."

She looked at him with a little smile. "Would you like to show me your version? Or do you still have something else on your mind?"

"Only you, my darling." He took her hand and led her to the door.

They walked up the stairs silently, gazing into each other's eyes. No words were necessary.

When they were inside Melanie's room, David drew her into his arms and kissed her tenderly. "I never could have gotten through this day without you. I need you so." His voice was filled with emotion.

She smoothed away the harsh lines in his face. "I'll always be here for you, my love."

He wrapped his arms more tightly around her. "Promise?"

"Except for a quick trip home to pack up my things. You can get along without me for a few days." She smiled.

"I can't do without you for even one night." He molded her hips to his and explored her ear with the tip of his tongue.

Melanie moved against him erotically, glorying in the way his body sprang to life. "Then I guess you'll just have to come along."

"Shall we go before the wedding or afterward?"

She drew back to look at him uncertainly. "Do you mean it? Would you really go with me?"

"I have to make sure you come back, don't I?" he teased.

"You needn't worry about that."

He looked disappointed. "Don't you want me to come with you?"

"Are you joking?" Melanie laughed delightedly. "I can't wait to introduce you to all my friends. How many people bring home a souvenir like you from their summer vacation?"

* * * * *

COMING NEXT MONTH

MILLION DOLLAR SWEEPSTAKES (III)

No purchase necessary. To enter, follow the directions published. Method of entry may vary. For eligibility, entries must be received no later than March 31, 1996. No liability is assumed for printing errors, lost, late or misdirected entries. Odds of winning are determined by the number of eligible entries distributed and received. Prizewinners will be determined no later than June 30, 1996.

Sweepstakes open to residents of the U.S. (except Puerto Rico), Canada, Europe and Taiwan who are 18 years of age or older. All applicable laws and regulations apply. Sweepstakes offer void wherever prohibited by law. Values of all prizes are in U.S. currency. This sweepstakes is presented by Torstar Corp., its subsidiaries and affiliates, in conjunction with book, merchandise and/or product offerings. For a copy of the Official Rules send a self-addressed, stamped envelope (WA residents need not affix return postage) to: MILLION DOLLAR SWEEPSTAKES (III) Rules, P.O. Box 4573, Blair, NE 68009, USA.

EXTRA BONUS PRIZE DRAWING

No purchase necessary. The Extra Bonus Prize will be awarded in a random drawing to be conducted no later than 5/30/96 from among all entries received. To qualify, entries must be received by 3/31/96 and comply with published directions. Drawing open to residents of the U.S. (except Puerto Rico), Canada, Europe and Taiwan who are 18 years of age or older. All applicable laws and regulations apply; offer void wherever prohibited by law. Odds of winning are dependent upon number of eligibile entries received. Prize is valued in U.S. currency. The offer is presented by Torstar Corp., its subsidiaries and affiliates in conjunction with book, merchandise and/or product offering. For a copy of the Official Rules governing this sweepstakes, send a self-addressed, stamped envelope (WA residents need not affix return postage) to: Extra Bonus Prize Drawing Rules, P.O. Box 4590, Blair, NE 68009, USA.

SWP-S895

Tall, dark and...dangerous...

Strangers in the Night

Just in time for the exciting Halloween season,
Silhouette brings you three spooky love stories in this
fabulous collection. You will love these original stories
that combine sensual romance with just a taste of
danger. Brought to you by these fabulous authors:

Anne Stuart

Chelsea Quinn Yarbro

Maggie Shayne

Available in October at a store near you.

Only from 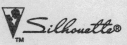 Silhouette®

—where passion lives.

SHAD95